BETWEEN THE OCEAN AND THE STARS

BETWEEN THE OCEAN AND THE STARS

A NOVEL

M.M. COCHRAN

IngramElliott

Published by IngramElliott, Inc.
www.ingramelliott.com
9815-J Sam Furr Road, Suite 271, Huntersville NC 28078

Book formatting by Creative Publishing Book Design
Cover design by H.O. Charles
Editing by Abbie Payne
Editing by F. Barnes

ISBN Hardcover: 978-1-952961-12-0
ISBN Paperback: 978-1-952961-13-7
ISBN E-Book: 978-1-952961-14-4

Library of Congress Control Number: 2022945623

Subjects: Fiction—General. Young Adult Fiction—General. Young Adult Fiction—Coming of Age. Young Adult Fiction—Romance/Contemporary.

Published in the United States of America.
First Edition: 2022, First International Edition: 2022

For Mom and Dad, who keep me afloat.

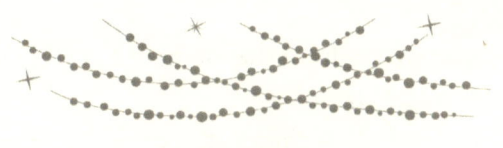

CHAPTER 1

There are twenty-six public entrances to the beaches of Ophelia Island. Numbers one through five are quiet. For families. Children.

Farther up the island, the beaches grow busier with partiers. College students. Loud music. Shorter shorts and tighter bikini tops.

But number seventeen is the boardwalk least traveled. It's a narrow entrance just off the bumpy road, canopied by draping palm branches. Past it, entrance twenty is the busiest because of the cabana in the dunes, making seventeen a number often skimmed over.

Number twenty-six has its famous sunsets, number twenty has its cabana club, and fifteen has its long, stretched-out tide.

Nine has its umbrellas and picnics.

Five has its families and sunbathing.

But seventeen—seventeen changed for me. Even though that isn't where *it* happened, that's where it felt like *it* happened. That's where I started to drown.

Because she drowns me every day, just a little.

She drowns me in her presence and in her absence, because with or without her—discovered or hidden—the weight of her secrets, of *her,* pulls me to the bottom of what feels like a hopeless swamp, where I hold my breath and wait to be untied.

She didn't look like she needed me. She didn't act like she needed me. But we all want something we can't have at least once in our lives, and she was my *something.*

She was my *something* from the moment I saw her yelling on the beach in the burning May sun.

It was a combination of things that compelled me—maybe the newness of the move, my desperate attempt to fall in love with *something* on Ophelia Island, or the desire to find somewhere to stay, someone to save.

She never needed me, but I was pretty sure I needed her.

In every moment I spent with her, forever without her seemed unimaginable, at least until the brute force of her secrets struck me, and I realized that things this good don't always last. Summer love never makes it to fall. Shooting stars rarely reach the ocean.

***

Wearing a pair of stark-white shorts and a hot-pink tank top, she stood her ground in the face of a boy who topped her by no less than a foot.

I froze, watching her. She was shouting, but I couldn't quite hear what she was saying. Her exasperated expression and swinging arms made me think it was some sort of a breakup argument, but how would I know? My perspective on the subject was limited. I'd never even had a girlfriend, much less broken up with one. My only former love interest was Jennifer Corrine, but she was from elementary school, which didn't count, and then again with her in sixth grade, which also didn't count.

Their voices quieted, merging into the flood of other noises around me on the busy beach, and I still couldn't distinguish her words from the rest of the cacophony. She stomped away, sand spraying in all directions under her heavy steps. I barely noticed as the boy stalked away right in front of me, heading straight for the ocean.

The girl ducked into a cabana-style restaurant, and its beachfront appeal was thanks to massive wooden decking that led the way to a shady, half-indoor escape from the sun.

The girl walked a few steps from the beach and onto the deck, weaving her way through the crowd until she disappeared from my sight. Without a second thought, I followed her, ambling through the mass of people, music, and salty air, on my way to the cabana.

The bar appeared hidden in the back, barely noticeable behind all the occupied tables scattered throughout the shaded deck. Dry, wooden boards beneath my bare feet were dusty with sand, so I slipped on the flip-flops I was carrying, hesitating just for a moment before I entered and scanned the sunburned faces around me. The dense smoke from a charcoal grill somewhere behind the bar choked me up, but I ignored it and plowed through.

I found her, sitting at the bar with her back to me. Her hot-pink tank top jumped out at me first, tucked into the waistband of her high-rise shorts. Right away, I noticed her hair, dirty blonde and a mess of big, fat curls that looped midway down her back. I could tell she wasn't old enough to drink, so what was she doing at the bar?

I weaved through the tables, feeding a starved part of me that needed to speak with her, and took a seat on the empty stool next to her, my foot shaking over the floor. She sipped on a Coke.

I put my elbows on the counter, then removed them, and tried laying my hands in my lap.

This doesn't have to be so awkward, Sam.

In the past, I would run in the opposite direction of a pretty girl, hide behind a trash can like I did in high school, or watch from behind the safety of my locker door.

But, under my skin, something awakened.

New place, new people, new Sam.

I glanced over, desperate to think of something clever to say. The bartender—a guy with a man bun and both arms sleeved with tattoos—asked me for my order, though I was too nervous to admit that I didn't want anything. He got me a root beer anyway. Before I could lose my nerve, the words pushed their way out of my mouth. "Been in the water today?"

Her skin was shiny, bronzed by the sun, and salty-dry from the ocean. A bubble of peace surrounded her, nothing like the image I formed of her on the beach.

Once I asked the question, I noticed the ends of her hair were wet. My idiocy made me flush a little, and I hoped she wasn't just another vacationer, on the island only for the rest of the week.

I thought she would ignore me, like the girls back home always did, take a sip of her drink, and pretend she hadn't heard me.

To my surprise, she answered, making no attempt to look at me, "Yeah. It's all right." She sipped on her Coke. Her voice was raspy, but she made it sound smooth, and I clung to the way she let each word drip into the next.

An automatic sigh of relief seeped through my lips. "I was just wondering. I haven't been in yet."

I took a small swig of my root beer, hoping the conversation would start again. What else could I say, though? If she asked for my name, I could introduce myself and ask for hers, but not even New Ophelia Sam would be brave enough to ask for hers first. Instead, I tried to determine whether she was a tourist or resident. "Having a good week?"

"Been okay."

Good effort, Sam.

"So, I couldn't help but notice you were kind of, you know, upset out there." I turned my face the other way, embarrassed to admit that I had seen her to begin with.

"You followed me?" Her disapproval was apparent and shrill, though she almost sounded pleased. She looked at me, a deer in headlights.

Any response would end up making me look like an imbecile. Should I have jumped out of the way of her question? Avoided the soon-to-be-bloody mess? Just stood there in shock and let it happen?

Even without makeup, her green eyes were bright, her irises circled with a brown ring. They stared straight into mine.

"No, no." I searched for something to say. "I came for a drink, but I just saw you were kind of mad or something, and I saw all the tables were full, and—"

"I'm fine, if that's what you're wondering." She stared straight ahead, fixated on the bottles that lined the glass shelves.

"Oh, that's good."

She dug in her pocket and slapped a few ones down beside her drink.

"If he comes back around, just tell him to keep the change." Then she turned and walked away. Her hair swung with every step.

In that moment, I was sure of two things: that I was the reason she left and that I would never see her again.

With no desire to finish my drink, I paid the tattooed bartender and made my way back to the beach, scanning for her hot-pink tank top through the crowd. But she was nowhere to be seen.

***

On my short walk across the island back home, I tried to figure out where I stood as the new guy. Seven days at the beach and you're a vacationer. Day eight and you're a resident.

Ophelia was small and easy to navigate. In my three days on the island, I had already noticed that few people drove their cars at all, and most preferred the ease of biking or walking to get from place to place.

I'd been in Florida for just one weekend, and I already craved the peace of West Virginia, the pine trees, and the real, paved streets made for actual cars.

Back home, I had friends, a job that I loved at the bike shop, and fresh mountain air that didn't make my skin feel like it was melting off my body. My parents said it would be fun to start over in a new town, since I'd just graduated high school. Dad was a graphic designer, so he could do his job from anywhere, which meant he could live anywhere, and he chose Ophelia. An island. Warm, sunny days. Deep-sea fishing with the possibility of wrestling alligators. Months later, the house was sold, and the car was full of our suitcases.

Fay University, just over the bridge on the mainland, accepted me for the upcoming fall semester, but I was still trying to accept the idea of attending Fay; the thought of staying in Florida for the next four years didn't thrill me. In fact, the dread was inescapable. I'd left a lot behind. There was the bike shop. There was my old high school, which I was leaving for good anyway. But there were also all those corners of town I knew so well that I might never see again.

When we packed up the car and were ready to start our eleven-hour drive to Ophelia, I stood outside the '93 Ford Bronco with my pillow under my arm. Then, I patted the mailbox, tucked my thumbs under my backpack straps, and blew a sigh down our driveway. The realtor's sign in the yard said "sold," a big red symbol that there was no going back.

That was when my dad honked the horn and waved me into the car.

I didn't even have a phone to text my friends on for the ride down to Florida. My iPhone was crushed by the leg of our sofa when Dad and I were lugging furniture through the garage. Perfect timing.

I still had my bike from West Virginia, which I hadn't ridden since middle school. I had tried to save up for a nicer one but never got around to buying anything. My friends made fun of me for working at a bicycle shop for six years, for living and breathing bikes, for being able to take one apart and put it back together blindfolded, but mostly for not touching the pedals of my own since I was fourteen years old. I suppose I was so busy with other people's hobbies that I neglected my own.

Our new house sat under three-hundred-year-old oak trees, draped with moss that hung down from their branches. A moving truck was still parked at the end of the long, dirt driveway that led right to the front of our white Cape Cod.

Mom and Dad walked in and out, stacking boxes on the porch. They saw me and waved, and I managed to throw a hand up at them before they ducked back into the house with another load of boxes.

Three dormers projected from the second level, yet I still didn't know which one my room was behind. Is it even considered a bedroom if the bed frame hasn't been put together yet?

I helped unload the U-Haul alongside Mom and Dad, then sneaked away to the garage, and tucked into a corner where I spotted my grimy, red bike. I ran my finger across its black seat, dismayed to see the streak of dust it cleared away. How did I let him get this dirty?

"Looks like you and I are going to get reacquainted," I said to him.

I took my time giving him a rinse because the hours were slow to drag by, made slower by the drain of the white-hot heat. Everything was white, flat. My bedroom walls were white, the ceiling fan was white, and the heat was white. Even out the window, past the massive, green trees, the sky was bleached white.

I sat in the wide, white windowsill and stared across the driveway, my mind drifting back to the cabana, to *her*. The girl.

If only I could have tagged behind her on her way out, I might have at least seen which direction she went and whether she was okay. It wasn't like she was crying. She was only mad, but I couldn't steer away from my curiosity about her situation. She'd made a fast departure, probably thinking I was just another tourist trying to hit on her.

At the round dinner table, Dad twirled his noodles on his fork in five spins, like always. "Did you explore the island today?"

"Yeah, it's nice." But I'd only walked the beach and then left after I met the girl. "The beach was pretty busy."

"I bet it was," he said. "I heard that it's even busier in March and April when all the students head here for spring break." He slurped in a noodle, leaving a ring of tomato sauce on his lips.

"I can't imagine the beach being more crowded than it was today." I waited for him to wipe the sauce away before I continued. "I came across a sort of restaurant in the dunes today."

"Really?" Mom said. "On the beach? We should definitely go there sometime. And, Sam, if you want to, after dinner, you can go out and explore again. I think your dad and I are just going to unpack some things for upstairs."

The sun would be setting soon, so it wouldn't be as hot out there, and I'd have my bike, so I could go farther than I had walked earlier.

"I'll do that."

"Great. I'm glad to hear you're starting to enjoy yourself here." Mom leaned back in her chair and stretched out her arms; she only did that when she was about to say something.

"It's like we're on a summer vacation that'll never end," she said.

The thing was, after our summer beach trips, which we typically took in North Carolina, I was always happy to go home. My job was waiting for my return, and my neighborhood friends always had a basketball ready as soon as I got back. We couldn't shoot to save our lives, but that was home and so was looking out my window and seeing a pine tree instead of a mossy oak.

I glanced past Dad's head and looked to the dirt driveway, thinking I'd seen a flash of pink shirt and blonde curls. It was only Mom's hanging flowers that had blown back into view.

Ophelia had nothing to offer me.

CHAPTER 2

After dinner, I hopped on my bike for the first time in years. Turned out everyone was correct—you don't forget how to ride. I wiped off the last bit of dust and grime from the tires and adjusted the seat because I'd grown a foot since the last time I'd been on it. Then I took a few minutes to tighten my brakes and grease the chains.

Working on my bicycle satisfied me in a way that riding it didn't. The familiar grittiness of bumpy, black lubricant on my fingertips reminded me of home and the redundancy of my day job at the shop. A repetitiveness of routine that I wouldn't have again until I started college in a couple months.

I wiped the grease from my hands onto my shorts and pedaled toward Main Street, forcing myself to escape the fact that everything from home was slipping away from me.

Was it possible to be an eighteen-year-old who's headed toward college and still thinks of a new place as home? I was too old, too grown up to believe such a fantasy.

Downtown had a general store, clothing shops filled with T-shirts and beach supplies, an ice cream parlor, and a few small restaurants.

No bike shops.

Down the sidewalk, the red, shiny booths inside Joe's Pancakes caught my attention. Downtown Ophelia Island had all but closed shop for the evening, but there, at Joe's, I could almost hear the voices and laughter of people inside bouncing off the diner's shiny silver walls.

I looked back to the sidewalk and skidded to a quick stop with a single, hard squeeze of my hand brakes. A dark-headed boy on a skateboard wobbled past me and flew off his board while I made a mental note to loosen my brakes when I got back home.

The boy cursed as my bike screeched to an abrupt stop, so I dropped my bike and jogged to the lanky Asian lying in the patch of grass between me and the road.

"Hey, excuse me. You okay?"

Blades of grass clung to his gray shirt, and streaks of brown mud were caked across it. "Pay freaking attention next time, would you? God, you know how close I could've come to falling in the road?"

"Sorry. I wasn't looking. Sorry," I said again. "At least you'd probably only get run over by a golf cart instead of a car."

He scoffed at me and brushed off his knees. "Lucky me, then. Hey, grab my board."

Without a word, I walked to his skateboard and picked it up. When I turned around, he was pushing himself up, brushing dirt from his T-shirt and adjusting his black ball cap.

I handed the board back to him. "Are you okay? Really, I'm sorry about that. I wasn't paying attention."

"It's cool. Just watch it next time." He snatched the board from me. "And sorry for cursing. I shouldn't do that in front of people I don't know."

"You're fine."

"I was on a thirty-two-day streak. I'm trying to stop."

"Best of luck."

He balanced his weight on one leg, picking at the butt of his jeans. "My mom said if I don't stop, I might go straight to hell."

"I don't think you'll go straight to hell if you curse."

"Hopefully not. I heard it's pretty d—" he hesitated. "Pretty dang hot down there."

"Yeah, I guess so. Wouldn't know. I've never been." My poor attempt at easing the awkward moment didn't impress him.

"What's your name?" His brow furrowed, and I knew he was thinking he hadn't seen me around before and assumed I was just a visitor.

"Sam. And I just moved here a few days ago, so I'm not a tourist." My irritation was undeniable, even to me, but at least I was established as a resident now.

"Logan. Sorry. I just get pissed when I fall." His voice softened, and he smiled a little as I stood there trying to decide whether I'd just ruined any chance at a friendship.

"Don't be sorry, it's fine. The whole thing was my fault anyway." I picked up my bike, and Logan readjusted his ball cap.

Following me down the sidewalk, he said, "Where do you live?"

"Just down the road past Main Street."

"The house with the long driveway? About time that thing sold."

"Yep, that's the house. Do you live here?"

"Born and raised. Some people think it's crappy, so I hope you don't hate it."

I started to take note that he was being extra careful to replace the curse words he would rather be using. "Oh, yeah, it's good so far. Hot."

"It's summer. Not going to be getting any cooler, man."

My mood tightened with a cynical grip. "That's just great."

Logan dropped his board to the ground, and, in a single fluid motion, landed one foot on top of it. "Well, I guess I'll see you around. Welcome to Ophelia."

"Yeah," I muttered as he rode off. "Welcome to Ophelia."

By twilight, I had found my way to a back road and discovered that it led to a narrow concrete path through the woods. The trees thinned and shortened, revealing something white hidden behind them. I followed the path to get a better look.

In the clearing, it eased onto a dirt road that branched out to a driveway. Judging from the untouched dirt and upright weeds, this wasn't a road often traveled by cars or feet.

I veered onto the driveway, then came to an immediate stop. Just ahead, someone was walking toward the house. He was yards beyond me and had his back to me, too far away to notice me slamming on my brakes.

I wheeled my bike closer, inching forward one click of my gears at a time, and looked more closely.

He was a *she.*

I recognized her right away. Her blonde curls, her sun-kissed skin, her toned legs—it all came flooding right back. My charcoaled memory of her came simmering to the surface.

I jumped off my bike and pushed it alongside me, shadowing her with slow and silent footsteps. The bike clicked as the wheels turned. I stopped every few seconds to make sure I wasn't heard.

She was still wearing those white jean shorts that accentuated her tan, but her pink tank top was covered by a lightweight jacket. I wondered whether she was one of those girls who got cold often, even when it was eighty degrees outside. Her fists hid in her jacket pockets, and she kept flipping her hair over her shoulder, making her seem younger and more vulnerable than she had on the beach. The charm of that small action surprised me.

I was finally close enough to the house to see a green lawn with no trees and a rusting old flagpole with an American flag that sagged in the stagnant heat. The two-level white house was similar to mine, but its front porch looked like it had been dragged right out of the 1800s. In the distance, I could see a shingled roof poking through trees, but it was too tall, too high up to be part of the roof of the main house, looming among the oaks.

It was a lighthouse.

The girl crept across the lawn and made her way to the porch. This eccentric home, this lighthouse—was it livable?

When she stepped up to the front porch, I paused and backed against a tree, pulling my bike with me. Hiding together, I felt a dorky bond between my bike and me, something I hadn't experienced since childhood. Then I determined my bike would need a proper name.

Ole Red.

He deserved that for being ignored for all those years.

The girl stood on the porch for a moment, hesitating at the front door, and I wasn't sure whether she was going to ring the doorbell or walk right in. Instead of knocking or ringing the bell, she stalked past the heavy, paneled door to the window next to it, pushing it halfway up its wooden frame. She lifted one leg in first, then ducked her head through, continuing with her other leg, and then she was gone. I couldn't tell whether she had closed the window behind her, so I stayed where I was, watching for movement in any of the other windows. No curtains blew, no light came on, and nothing seemed to shift inside.

Ole Red and I started walking toward the house again, a tedious task of trying to be quiet and, of course, failing because I never did anything as planned. I kicked Red's pedal by accident, and the chain spun in three loud circles around the gears.

"You're so embarrassing," I said to him.

At the end of the drive, I leaned him against a tree and told him I'd be back soon.

I dove across the yard and up the front porch steps, my mind racing with all the possibilities of who else might be behind the door, so I put my ear against the weathered wood, hoping to hear something. Anything. I almost knocked but chose not to because she hadn't. Maybe no one was home. Except she was there. If she were just a vacationer, there was no way she'd know where this place was, let alone how to get inside, and she definitely wouldn't be coming here alone.

I planned out my excuse for getting caught here, coming up with the automatic and believable explanation that I was just another lost tourist, but I'd never remember even a simple cover story like that if it came down to it.

Wooden rocking chairs flanked the front windows, though they should have been tranquil in the windless humidity. Beside them, an old chest with a broken lock sat against the wall, and, above me, the paint on the splintering ceiling was peeling away. Some of the boards hung down, held in place by a single nail. To my right, the window the girl had climbed through was still open. I stalled. I should've just left and stopped worrying about the fact that I was trespassing and the consequences that would surely come if I got caught. But where would I go if I turned back? Back home to my parents?

I looked at Red down in the driveway and could practically see him mouthing the words: *You're still just as uncool now as you were when I met you.*

Enough was enough—I propelled myself through the window.

When my eyes acclimated to the dark room, I found myself standing in the living space of some sort of vintage lighthouse. In front of me, a dusty stone fireplace was crammed into the faded wall, and a narrow wooden staircase led to the second level. An antique sofa sat in the shadow of a wingback chair that would have been pretty if it were cleaned, and, above, a small but ornate chandelier hung from the ceiling.

I turned to the empty dining room. Damp air washed over my skin and up my nose, stale from what smelled like decades of unnoticed water damage. There had been no life under this roof for a long time.

Motionless, I waited for some kind of a sound. Everything was still. Noiseless.

Afraid the floors might squeak, I tiptoed into the dining room. An old china cabinet stood against the wall, filled with antique blue dishes coated in an extra layer of gray dust. The forgotten valuables and elegant décor were once the shining evidence of a wealthy family.

I continued past the china cabinet and sneaked through the maze of doorframes, hallways, and scattered, unkept furniture.

And there she was.

I stopped in my tracks. Her back was to me, her face pressed against the foggy glass windowpane, gazing out over the back lawn that was littered with dead palm tree branches.

Seeing her from this angle, I realized just how much of her I'd missed earlier this morning. Her hair was tied back and swept away from her neck, revealing her distinct square jawline. Faint light from the sunset shone through the window, giving her skin a golden glow.

I struggled to exhale, fearing she might hear it, but I had to make myself known.

"This a habit of yours?"

She swung around and glared at me in the doorway. I took an awkward step back. Startled, she recovered fast, drawing herself up straight and transforming once again into the self-assured girl from the beach.

Her eyes held a sense of wonder that didn't appear to belong here, not on an island like Ophelia, but she didn't seem like a summer tourist either. Something raced through her mind—I could see it happening right in front of me—and whatever it was, she was miles away from this island.

"You mean breaking into lighthouses?" she said. Her tone was light, assuring me that she recognized me from this morning at the beach, but her voice had changed into something different than before, less stressed somehow, less solid.

It opened a rift of fear inside me. As I spoke, she stepped closer to me, one easy foot in front of the other.

"Uh...yeah." The way she moved reminded me of a cat. A tiger with lion hair. "What are you doing here?"

The way she carried herself was effortless and polished. She was like an ocean wave, rolling in and sweeping over me, and I knew in an instant that I had no choice: She would be dragging me back out to sea with her.

"I could ask you the same thing," she said.

Without warning, she escaped through another doorway. She gave a sly, little hum, convincing me to follow. I suspected there was some sort of game she wanted me to play. Catching up with her was my first move as her opponent.

"It's just that I'm new here, and—"

"Yeah, I can tell," she interrupted from the living room.

At least I was positive she wasn't a tourist. I found my way to where she was sliding her thumb across the arm of the wingback chair.

She was far more conversational all of a sudden, delighting me that I'd captured her attention.

"How long are you staying here?" she said.

"I'm not on vacation. I just moved here a few days ago."

"Oh? You'll love it." False. Her expression changed, and her sense of wonder filed back into the room. She wanted to be somewhere else, I assumed. Maybe that was why she was in this lighthouse.

"So you live here too?" I said.

"Sure do."

Something jumped behind my ribs, and I shifted to act like it didn't happen.

"Well, I was out exploring and—" I stopped. *And what? And I followed you here? Change the subject. Fast. Change it now.* "Is this okay?" I asked. "Is it okay for us to be in here?"

I motioned to the cobwebbed chandelier, indicating the abandoned appearance of this lighthouse. For my whole life—childhood, teenage years—I was a good person. A good son. Never a criminal who thought of breaking and entering. The entire situation set my stomach to concrete.

She tilted her head at me, her hair fanning out. Her green eyes hadn't been as colorful, as bright, at the cabana. "It's not illegal unless you get caught."

Her mischievous grin kept making me ask the same question over and over: *Who are you?*

"Have you ever gotten in trouble doing this?" I said.

"Breaking in or doing something illegal?"

My silence told her I would take either answer.

A snuffle of laughter came from her pink lips. "I didn't technically break in. The window is always unlocked. It just needs a little elbow grease."

I nodded. "Come here a lot?"

She sauntered around the room, touching pieces of furniture, contemplating something. "Sort of. It's my thinking spot."

What could she think about in this place? She faced me again, but I couldn't understand her dialogue, couldn't decipher any meaning behind it.

"So, are you going to make a habit of following me?"

My embarrassment ruined any chance at flirting with her, but I tried anyway.

"Not if you keep leading me into houses you've broken into."

Gliding around the corner again, she moved out of my sight once more. "You never have to come as far as I do."

"It's okay," I said, following. "I don't mind the extra mile."

We were in the hallway now, facing each other as she walked backward, dragging her fingertips against the wallpaper.

"Are you sure? I get pretty close to the edge sometimes."

It was quiet for a moment, but she kept moving, and I kept moving with her.

"I'm sorry for being rude to you today," she said. "I was a jerk."

"No, you weren't." We paused. "Was everything okay? You seemed upset about something."

She didn't answer.

"Was he your boyfriend?" I regretted asking her the second it came out of my mouth.

"I'm fine. And yeah. He's still my boyfriend." Her shame bent her body, an embarrassment I knew all too well.

"Oh—oh really?"

"Sure. He does this a lot. Starts arguments with me."

"Why do you stay with him, then?" Before I had the chance to continue, she answered with a defiant shrug.

The sun had set, and the hallway darkened, erasing the shadows that had previously puddled on the floor.

"Does the light ever come on? In the lighthouse, I mean." I pointed up.

"No. Hasn't been lit in decades. No one ever comes here, if you haven't noticed. It used to be Ophelia's lighthouse, but the keeper and his family left when Jacob's Point next door built a taller one, so this one just sits here."

"How do you get up there?"

She turned around and beckoned for me to follow, as if I needed beckoning. We walked to the end of the hall and into a room on the right. A table in the center of the room held a weathered checkerboard. Some lounge chairs surrounded it and, underneath, was a braided rug. The room must have previously been some sort of small sitting area, some cigar-smoking lounge where the men got drunk and the women came to restock their liquor. Two windows framed a front yard that smoldered with dusky light. I should've been getting home, but the girl's presence kept drawing me closer.

I wanted to know more.

Behind her, a spiral staircase twisted upward. "This is how you get up there." She pointed. "Right here."

Stairs twirled all the way up to a platform, and I took the first step.

"Have you ever been up there?"

"Lots of times," she said.

I stepped back, retreating. "Is it high enough? I mean, how did the boats see the light from here? Are we close to the ocean?"

"We aren't that close, but you can still see the water. There used to be fewer trees between here and the ocean, so they could probably see it better back then."

Just as I had made the decision that I needed to get out of here, a startling knock came from out of nowhere. The girl shrank with fear, but I tried to keep my cool in front of her.

"What—" I started.

"Shush." She put a finger up to silence me and rushed to the window, pushing away the curtain.

I tried to see outside from where I stood, and I caught a glimpse of the rear end of a car. A police car. My palms moistened with sweat, and nausea rolled through my stomach in waves.

"What now?" I said.

He knocked again, louder this time. With a hefty volume of authority, he said, "Come on out. I know you're in there."

"It's okay, just—" she whispered, and then a clatter interrupted from the living room. The heavy front door, perhaps? A deep grunt made its way back to us, the unmistakable sound of a man's large body folding through the open window.

She passed me. "Come with me."

I trailed behind her, letting her take the lead. Whether she was planning to hide or try to avoid getting caught, I wasn't sure, but in my panicked state, the only thing I could do was trust her. Just as we stepped into the dark hallway, she stopped.

A bald officer wearing a big belt to support his round midsection stood at the end of the hall.

He could fit through the window? I thought. I bumped into the girl and staggered back a few steps.

The officer walked toward us, his shoes smacking against the thin floor. My head swam in a bottomless pool of sickness, and a line of sweat began to bead across my hairline.

He blew a flat, unamused sigh. "Mind telling me what you're doing in here?"

I kept quiet so she could answer for both of us.

"I was out for a walk and came across this place."

"Been here before?"

She put her hand on the wall, an artificial act of curiosity. "No, but this lighthouse was just so interesting—"

"Right, yeah. That's enough." He looped his fingers around his belt. "You're both coming with me."

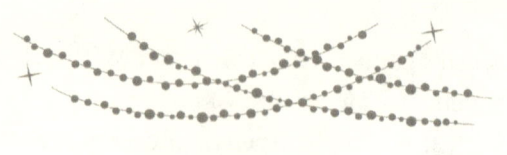

Chapter 3

He didn't cuff us or read us our rights like I expected when he forced us both into the back seat of his squad car.

I buckled my seatbelt. The girl didn't bother. She seemed to be managing the situation well, her poise remaining unchanged, while I couldn't stop myself from shaking. Of course, I was shaking. I put my elbow up on the door and rested my head on my knuckles. Third day on the island, and I was already in the back of a cop car. *This isn't who I am,* I kept reminding myself. *I'm a good person.*

My parents. Would I have to call them from jail? Whatever was in the pit of my stomach began to creep into my throat, and the back of my tongue sizzled with the taste of acid. I wiped my hands on my white T-shirt and tried to focus as the locked doors of the police cruiser started to feel like they were closing in on me.

The girl leaned forward behind the officer's headrest to speak to him while he backed his car out of the yard.

"Okay, so was it considered breaking in if the window was already open?" Her sarcasm made me angry. She was making me look bad.

He watched her through his rearview mirror. "Did you climb through the window?"

"Practically walked right into the charming home."

"Is it either of your homes?" He glanced at me.

She said, "No," and I shook my head.

"Then it was breaking in. You were also trespassing."

20

"Oh, please," she said, "I'm sure people come here all the time."

"Well, I finally caught two of them."

She sat back in her seat and flipped her curls over her shoulder and tucked her hands down in her jacket pockets again. Still, she seemed too carefree.

We passed Ole Red when we entered the dirt driveway.

For the first time, the cop spoke directly to me. "That your bike, son?"

Thinking he might slow down and let me go, I unbuckled my seatbelt and prepared to get out of the cruiser. "Yes, sir, it is."

"I'll get it back to you; don't worry about it."

He kept going, and I watched Red grow smaller through the back window.

A moment of prickly silence ensued, and then the girl leaned forward again.

"How about you let us go, get us out of your hair, and we'll swear we won't come back here?"

The cop rubbed his bald head.

Rage burned up my neck. "Negotiating with a cop? Seriously?" I said.

She licked her lower lip, amused by my frustration, and settled back in her seat.

"Hey, Sweaty, what's your name, anyway?"

I looked straight out the windshield so she wouldn't see how angry I was.

"I'm Sam."

But I couldn't help myself from looking her way to see how she would respond.

"I'm Georgia."

Her closed-lipped smile made me want to pry open her mouth to see what secrets she kept sealed behind it. See what might come heaving out. She was just so—*what, exactly*? I hated that I was wasting my time trying to figure her out. But why was she wondrous? Loud and quiet at the same time?

The cop found us in his rearview again. "You two don't know each other?"

Georgia let out a "Hmm," eyeing me up and down. "We've never formally met."

She was loud in her actions, in her speech, but calming somehow too. I wiped my arm over my forehead, which did nothing to dry my sweat, so I tried running my fingers through my brown hair instead.

My nerves didn't ease until we were back in town at the police department. It was after nine thirty at night when the officer led us into his office, asking us to take a seat. He interrogated us about why we were at the lighthouse, where we lived, and just about everything in between before he concluded he would let us off with a warning. I figured he had brought us in just for show, to scare some sense into us.

"If I find you there again, we're going to have some problems. You won't get off this easy next time. You understand?"

Georgia said, "Yes," and I added, "Sir."

He handed me the phone on his desk and told us each to call someone to pick us up from the station.

"You're both adults, but at this time of night, I'd rather you call someone to get you."

I think he must have wanted us to feel ashamed in front of our parents, which I did when I had to explain over the phone what had happened.

"You're where?" Mom said in a tone that she only used on Dad when he forgot an important ingredient at the grocery store.

"I'm fine," I said. "I just need you to come and get me. The policeman won't let me walk home, but it's not as bad as it sounds."

"It sounds like you snuck into a house?"

"Yeah, an old, abandoned lighthouse. No one lives there, and the window was already open, so I just went in. It's actually really cool."

"Your dad will be there in a minute."

Georgia and I waited in the sticky metal chairs in the lobby, my foot still shaking.

She seemed to melt into her chair, the way wax melts around a candle stick. She'd burn me if I touched her, I thought, at least for just a moment, until I got used to the heat.

"You've never been in a police department, have you?" she said.

"Have you?"

"To post bail for my mom once or twice. Unwind a little bit. It's not a big deal, Sweaty. He let us off with a warning."

In my peripheral vision, I could see she was looking straight at me. I took a breath, then a deep exhale as I turned to return her stare. She raised her eyebrow, put her head back until it rested against the wall, and closed her eyes, possessing all the ease I would never be able to muster. Her hands locked over the top button of her shorts, and I could barely make out the remnants of a purple and yellow bruise that wrapped around her wrist; a perfectly round bracelet of healing tissue. She noticed me staring and yanked down the sleeves of her jacket, but that didn't stop me from looking.

Back in West Virginia, I had never met anyone this strange. For that matter, I'd never even seen anyone like her, skin so tan, hair so big with her bouncing sandy curls, and a fearless curiosity.

The bell on the front door jingled and interrupted my thoughts, tearing my gaze from her. Standing in the doorway, the tall, muscular boy from the beach loomed over the lobby. His buzz cut was military-style, but his posture said otherwise. He wore a neon-orange shirt, too bright for my tired pupils, and stalked right past me, blowing a trail of cool wind behind him as he went. She perked up in his shadow, making me jolt upright too.

His oppressive size was like a boulder looming over her—massive, able to crush anything he rolled over.

"You ready?"

Georgia stood and walked right in front of me without saying goodbye or even looking at me. I moved my feet back so neither of them would trip, and the boyfriend scowled down at me after she'd passed. Then, he followed her to the door.

"Who's that guy?" He jerked his thumb in my direction, and I cowered lower in my seat. His question was deep and unforgiving.

Ding! The bell rang again on the door when Georgia pushed through it.

"No one." She turned around and gave me the slightest half wave. Her boyfriend didn't even notice.

Two minutes later, my dad walked in, keys in his hand. I stood, not knowing what to expect. We were the same height these days, but the fluffy hair I inherited from him made me appear an inch taller.

"What happened, son?" he said. Under the fluorescent lights, his gray hairs seemed more prominent.

"Wrong place, wrong time."

"Do I need to talk to anyone? Get anything straightened out?"

"No, everything is fine. Let's just get home."

***

There wasn't much of an argument other than a short lecture about how the island wasn't our small town in West Virginia, and I needed to be aware that I was in a new place with people who might be less forgiving of wandering into interesting old houses. I explained to my parents everything that had happened, that I was riding my bike, came upon the old lighthouse, and chose to go inside moments before the cop found me.

They were irritated but dropped the conversation once I apologized. I chalked up their forgiveness to being preoccupied with the move and the house, and I failed to mention anything about Georgia, glad that she had left the department first. Maybe I didn't tell my parents about her because I didn't want them to think that I could be that easily influenced by a girl I didn't even know, let alone a girl like Georgia. Or maybe she was just the kind of person who was born to be a mystery.

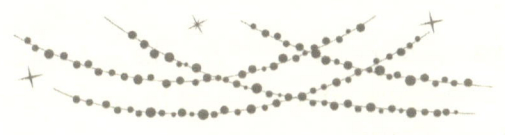

CHAPTER 4

I didn't see Georgia anywhere on the island for almost a week after our night at the police station.

As promised, the morning after I got back from the PD, the same bald cop who took us there brought me my bike. I was already outside when he drove up, and I jumped at the sight of his squad car. The cop detached Ole Red from the back of his car and walked him to the base of the porch steps.

"Good morning," he said.

"Morning. Thanks for bringing my bike." I stood and looked down, nearly unable to show my face.

"No problem." He set Red against the railing, and I met him down there.

"Sorry about last night. I didn't mean any harm." I stuffed my hands in my pockets.

"You're new here—I'll give you a break. There was no harm done." He had just woken up, and I could tell he was still tired. Perhaps I would be his morning coffee talk.

Hey, Doug, how's your morning been?

Oh, you know, scared some teenager first thing. Had to give him his bike back.

D'he steal it or somethin'?

Nah, caught him trespassing last night with it. Nothin' new. Say, how's the wife?

25

"Thank you so much," I said. Again, he said it was no problem, and he drove away, brown dust clouding the air in his wake.

I washed my bike with some soap and a rag and shined him until I was satisfied. Then, I sprayed the tires with tire shine, and by the time I was through, Ole Red had brand-new style.

Red and I explored daily, heading out on expeditions around the island, but I didn't run into Georgia again. My irritation with her still stung, and I couldn't stop thinking about how she acted that night, her defiant sass making it worse, but there was still a part of me that wanted to talk to her again about the lighthouse, her boyfriend, *her.* Everywhere I went, I looked for her, and I let myself believe it was because I was desperate to be interested in something on this island. Anything to take my mind off missing home. And she certainly did just that.

I spent the rest of the week putting the house together, including lots of hanging and lifting. My bed was sleepable again. All the things from my room back in West Virginia were in place, and my new room started to feel like my old one. The guitar I never learned to play leaned against the wall, already starting to gather dust, and my cheesy posters were rolled up in the corner, where they were destined to stay.

Mom grabbed us some take-out pizza to celebrate the completion of our unpacking, and it occurred to all of us that a meal like that called for dessert. I offered to make the trip to Piggly Wiggly, the local grocery store, only because it was clear across the island and I wanted some silence to reflect on Georgia and why, after a week, she was still on my mind.

Mom and Dad requested rocky road ice cream, so I set off for the store, taking the Bronco because it was too far and already too dark to ride Ole Red. I drove down Main Street and passed Joe's Pancakes on my way, deciding I'd give their breakfast a shot tomorrow.

By the time I arrived at Piggly Wiggly, there was only one cashier and one bagger working because the store was closing in thirty minutes, early, just like everywhere else on Ophelia. When it was my turn to check out, I came face-to-face with Logan, the cussing skater.

He laughed and uttered a curse word when he saw me walk to his register. His hands flew up and covered his mouth as he tried to recover.

"Dang it. I'm sorry. Crap." His hair had been combed back into a less disheveled style than the last time I had seen him.

I aimed my smile downward, trying to hide my laugh. "Don't worry about it."

He made a joke about hitting people with my bike that I pretended to find funny. We laughed it off, and he shouted, "Bye, Sam!" as I walked out of the sliding doors to leave.

Two light poles in the parking lot flickered on at the same time, casting an ominous white flash over the Bronco. On my walk back to it, I noticed a red piece of junk that had pulled in a few spaces away from me while I was inside, just outside of the light beam.

I unlocked my car and put the bags in the back seat, but a squeaking noise came from the red car, so I turned and found two people making out in the back seat.

Ignore it.

Getting in the Bronco and putting the key in the ignition, I recalled the bright-orange shirt the boy was wearing from that night at the police department.

Georgia and her boyfriend were just feet away from me.

But in a grocery store parking lot? Why? This place was dark, almost deserted. But still.

Then I caught a glimpse of her hair, her brunette mane, and then her pale neck as he kissed his way up to her ear.

I said to myself, "Oh, my gosh. Oh, my gosh. Don't look. Just look away."

He was wearing only his underwear, and the girl still had on her bra and her shorts.

Those weren't Georgia's glorious blonde curls or tan skin or busty chest.

He wouldn't, I thought. *Would he?*

Don't look, Sam. Don't be weird. I shouldn't have, but I couldn't help myself.

Still in park, I glanced out my window, pushing myself up and trying to get another vantage point, telling myself that they would be too busy to notice me. Almost as if she could sense me, the girl froze, shifting her weight under the body of Georgia's boyfriend, and locked her eyes on me. Her face was slim, her eyes small, her hair, dark and thin.

I panicked, but before I could move, the boy had his window rolled down and was yelling at me.

"Get out of here," I said to myself. "Get out of here, get out of here. Don't panic."

In no time, I had the car in drive and was speeding to the safety of the highway, leaving the guy, the maybe, maybe-not boyfriend of Georgia, in my rearview mirror.

All I could see were his arms up in the air as he shot me the middle finger, yelling something I couldn't hear.

My pulse didn't calm down until Piggly Wiggly was out of sight. Did he recognize me from the police department? He absolutely got a look at me at least once that night, even it wasn't for long. I couldn't tell whether he had recognized me, and I comforted myself with the explanation that he'd had almost no chance to see me before I skated out of there.

To get my mind out of that parking lot, I flipped on the radio and was met with the sounds of a familiar David Bowie song, so I kept the volume turned down low.

Maybe Georgia had broken up with him. They'd have to be split up, or he wouldn't have been with another girl. *Right?* That had to be it.

I hated the way I said her name light as a feather inside my head. We weren't friends. No, we were merely criminals, strangers who took a ride to the police department together, who shared a brief conversation in a lighthouse. She didn't even tell me goodbye. On the other hand, if she and her boyfriend were still together, I cared at least enough about her to worry. That was the least I could do. That was the least anybody could do.

What would she think about him doing that? Would she even care? Did she even know?

At the lighthouse, she seemed a bit resistant toward the idea of him. She had seemed indifferent about their argument earlier that day too. Was that all just an act?

Was anything about this girl real?

Either way, I felt sorry for her. That jerk was either cheating on her or he'd gotten over her way too fast.

When I arrived home, the house was all lit up.

"We throwing a party?" I said. My parents were happy here, much happier than I was, and I felt awkward sometimes living with parents who were still so madly in love, but I always convinced myself that I was lucky to have them. I was happy for them. Happy that someone got to be happy.

Mom bounced on her toes. "We're staying up all night to watch movies."

"So that's why all the lights are on," I said.

"You're staying awake too."

"No, no, I'm going to try out the diner tomorrow for an early breakfast." They were standing in the kitchen where I handed them the carton of rocky road. "I believe you requested this."

Dad ignored me and said, "Joe's Diner?"

"Joe's Pancakes. You guys should join me."

"Sorry, hon," Mom said. "Tomorrow morning I'm going shopping off the island for a coffee table and a few lamps, but I'd love to next time."

"I'll go, son," Dad said. "If I'm awake, of course." Then he tickled Mom, and I looked away, ignoring their affection.

I did stay up to watch a couple of movies with them, each of them beach themed. First up was *Jaws*, followed by some other old movie I didn't care for, so at two in the morning, I headed off to bed.

The ceiling fan spun above me, making spirals and curls that I dreamed about.

I woke up several hours later in the still dark. The light just beginning to pierce the horizon fooled my sleepy brain into seeing deep shades of hot-pink sky, yellow streaks of clouds, and the tip of a hypnotizing green sun.

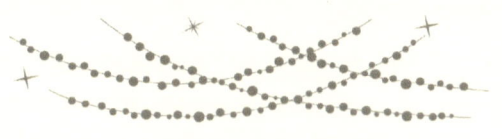

CHAPTER 5

Expecting my parents to still be awake, I was surprised to find them curled together under a blanket in front of the television, another beach movie playing in the background. I left a note for my dad by the coffee maker because that was always the first place he went when he woke up.

> Took my bike to Joe's Pancakes. Don't rush. Just gonna relax with a cup of coffee. See ya there.
> — Sam

I left Ole Red against the wall at the diner because the bike rack was already full of beautiful, shined-up ten-speeds. I told him to be good while I was gone and thought that maybe I should have gotten Red a silver bell, spruced him up a little more.

Inside, the floors were checkered with black-and-white tiles, and the walls mirrored the reflection of silver aluminum from floor to ceiling. A vintage soda-shop bar ran along the length of the seating area; meanwhile, an Elvis Presley song played from the old-fashioned jukebox as the hostess led me to a red-and-white booth and handed me a single menu.

An older, dark-skinned lady stopped by my table after a few minutes and adjusted the blue skirt of her waitress uniform, smoothing down a white apron that was a bit too tight for her big waist.

"Welcome to Joe's. What can I startcha off with?"

"I'll just take coffee right now."

31

"All right," she said, her accent deep and southern.

She hobbled away, and I listened to the sounds of the noisy diner. Over the crowd, I could even hear the voices from the kitchen, people working to prepare breakfast. Out the window to my left, I had a clear view of the exact spot on the sidewalk where I almost ran over Logan as he rolled by on his skateboard.

Dew clung to the windowpane, and the day's first rays of sun highlighted Main Street. Even the ocean waves seemed to be more energized and louder before noon, I remembered from this week's morning walks.

My mind drifted to Georgia. Without realizing it, I scanned the tables of the diner, looking for her. Each time I thought about that night at the lighthouse, I looked for her. But it was wrong for me to look. I had met her only twice, and that was days ago. Ophelia, though, was much less interesting if I stopped searching. Could it have been that she made me like this island? Made me like an adventure? Risk? Not that I enjoyed the ride to the police department.

Ugh, I was weak. Childish, too, for chasing the hope of feeling those things again.

As if my thoughts had willed her to appear, she was there, emerging from my memory and rounding the corner next to my table with her head down, scribbling on an order pad.

Her blue uniform hugged her curves, cinched by the ties of her apron, and her wild blonde curls were tamed by a ponytail, which was a whole new look for her, and my attention lingered longer than was appropriate. With her hair tied away from her face, her features became more defined, sharper, each eye and ear and lip smooth and sure of its place.

She caught me staring and smirked as she came to an easy stop at the end of my table.

Puppy dog eyes. Big and droopy.

The simplicity of her allure gave me a flashback of our time at the lighthouse, how she was so relaxed.

"Hey," she said.

She adjusted her apron, expecting something in return other than my uncomfortable shifting and habitual fingernail picking. I felt like an apology was in order for the lighthouse night, but I had no reason to say sorry. If anything, she owed me one.

"Hey, how are you?" I said finally.

Georgia stood still next to my table, seeming abruptly small and quiet compared to the bustling waitstaff around her. She was less intimidating now, standing here before me, than she had been in my mind this past week.

"I'm all right." She folded a loose curl behind her ear. "Been here before?"

The way she talked was so effortless, each word falling right off her tongue and spilling into a serenade.

"No. No, I never have." I was talking too fast.

"Eating alone?"

"Well, my dad is supposed to be meeting me here at some point. He's still sleeping."

Curiosity about her family sailed into my mind, and though I wanted to bombard her with questions—*Who are you? Where do you come from? What is your story, Georgia?*—I said nothing.

"Ah," she said. She glanced around the diner, searching for something to say, and when her focus came back to rest on me, she shrugged. "Well, Joe makes some pretty good pancakes."

"I'll be sure to try them."

I gaped downward, unable to meet her gaze, but could still feel hers bearing down on me.

Bedroom eyes. I knew there was a name for it.

I offered her the seat in front of me, and she paused, biting her lip. She looked back at the kitchen, measuring her options, and with a slight shake of her head, she accepted my offer. Her hands lay across the table in a white-knuckle embrace.

"On your bike again today?" she said.

I wiggled my hands free from under the table and pushed down the wrinkles on my shirt. "Yeah, yeah, I am."

"You got a car?"

"No, but I borrow my parents' car when I need it. For now, I'm fine with my bike. Ophelia is pretty small, and I love riding."

"I hope your bike is okay with you leaving it parked outside while you eat your breakfast. He could get lonely out there."

The playful grin she gave me faded the awkwardness, but her personification of Ole Red made me laugh. I thought I was the only one who did that.

"He'll be fine. It'll give him the opportunity to make friends."

She pulled her order pad from her apron and held it to her chest.

"Hey, I'm—I'm sorry about the other night." Again, I couldn't read her, but I sensed she was feeling something deeper than an apology.

"It's not your fault."

I recalled the way her boyfriend's stare had unsettled me, and the disgust I had felt when I recognized his bright-orange shirt in the Piggly Wiggly parking lot. I wondered if she knew about him hooking up with other girls, a thought that made me itch with discontentment. The vision of him in the back seat of his car with someone else was etched into the insides of my eyelids. Georgia didn't deserve to be treated that way, even if they had already broken up. Who would ever deserve that? The entire thing, the whole scene, still bothered me. I could see it, could taste it souring, and I wanted to spit it out.

I seared with a sudden fever. Beads of sweat began to pool in the bend of my arm, and my hands became clammy, so I brushed them over the cool cotton of my shorts.

She tilted her head toward me. "So where did you come from?"

"What?"

"Where are you from?" she asked again.

"Oh. I'm from West Virginia, right on the border of Ohio."

"Why are you here?" All that translated through her tired voice was: *You could be somewhere so much better.* But where exactly did she want to be?

Our conversation was cut short by my waitress as she set down my cup of black coffee.

"Will that be all?" She raised a brow at Georgia and crossed her arms.

"For now. Thanks."

She towered over Georgia, who simply looked away.

"Sittin' on the job," she mumbled just loud enough for us to hear. Heaving a heavy sigh, she walked away.

I leaned over the table and whispered, "Is she always that grumpy?"

Georgia joined me halfway. "Always. Don't worry about her. She loves everyone, just doesn't show it at first."

"Are you going to get in trouble for talking to me?" I hoped not. Georgia might've needed this job more than she was letting on, which I kind of thought was the truth.

"I'll be fine for now." She fell back in the booth again. "So why are you here?"

"My dad works remotely, so he wanted to move someplace tropical, and we left after my graduation."

"Oh, so you just left high school?" She smiled, her assured exterior returning. Pure humiliation bit away at my dignity. I couldn't be that much younger than she was. *Could I?*

I reached for my coffee.

"Yeah, just a few weeks ago. What about you?"

She chuckled. "I graduated last year." Then she sighed up at the ceiling. "Been here ever since."

Why here? I wondered. *Why hasn't she gone to college?* Questions wandered around in random spurts, questions about who she was and what her life was like.

"Where are you from?" I said.

"Here. Ophelia." Then she backtracked. "Well, actually, I was born in Mississippi. Then my mom and I lived in Alabama for a while, but when she got pregnant with my little brother, we came here to little Ophelia, and I've been stuck here ever since."

"How old were you when you came here?"

"Twelve. Feels like I've lived here forever, though. My brother is seven now."

New questions took shape in my mind, wanting answers. Her past sounded displeasing to her in some way, and somewhere along her way to Ophelia, I suspected she'd lost her father.

"What's your brother's name?"

"Jeffery," she said. "He's great. Love him to death."

"What about your dad?" I didn't mean to come off as so bold, but I told myself, *New home equals new Sam.* I'd never be able to disguise my fear with bravery, though.

She shrugged again, dismissing my obvious overstep. "I don't know him. As far as I know, he was just some bartender from Mississippi."

My pity must have shown on my face because she grinned to reassure me.

"But I don't care. I don't need him, never have. He doesn't matter to me." She picked at the curl behind her ear. "Are you going to college here?"

"Yeah, I'm going to Fay University."

"Okay, nice. So you're staying close. Staying in Fay County."

"Are you planning on, you know, doing something else?" I stammered, embarrassed. There really was no good way to phrase that kind of question. How do you ask someone you barely know what their life plan is?

Her expression clouded and moved far away again despite her looking straight into me. "Maybe. Maybe not. I want to leave the island. Go up north."

"Why?" I said. "When?"

"I'm not sure. It's just too confining living on an island like Ophelia. I want to get away, live my life." Plopping her chin into the palm of her hand, she daydreamed out the window.

I wanted to ask her what Ophelia was like for her, what made her feel like she couldn't escape, but her raspy voice interrupted my thoughts.

"What do you want to do? Besides college?" she said.

"Maybe something with computers like my dad." But I'd never spent much time considering what I would do after college. My only focus had been getting to college, and, now that it was happening, the rest of my life was spread out before me, and I had no idea what it was supposed to look like. "I don't know about a major or anything. I'm just gonna go." *Just go?* I must have sounded like an idiot to her. "Maybe I'll open a bike shop around here," I added.

She giggled, a hysterical gush of lovely, feminine laughter. I wasn't trying to be funny, but I laughed along with her anyway.

"Think you might get tired of that?" she said.

"I don't know. The Wright brothers owned a bike-repair shop and then they built an airplane, so anything's possible, I guess."

"Oh, really?" she asked. "Then, maybe you'll become a pilot."

"That seems pretty cool."

"Perhaps you could build something cooler than an airplane."

"Like a bike."

She laughed. "Riding's that much fun, huh?"

"It's just that, back at home, I used to work at a bike place. I think it's the only thing I'm good at."

"Good at bicycles?"

"I guess so."

My lack of skill, shining front and center, never ceased to shame me.

"Well, I'm only good at waitressing," she said, but I was certain waitressing wasn't the only thing she was good at. Before I could express my thoughts about her potential, someone shouted her name from the kitchen.

"Georgia, get back to work."

He must have been her boss, since he wasn't wearing a blue button-down shirt or chef's hat. Snapping his fingers, he wiped his forehead with a white handkerchief and turned to go back through the kitchen door before she could respond.

Georgia jumped up from the booth and pressed down her apron, the collar of her uniform slipping beneath her clavicle. "Well, I have to go. I'll come back around, though. Bye, Sam."

She spun on her heels, and her shirt caught in her breeze, revealing a fading blemish on the base of her collarbone. Opaque shades of purples and reds made a perfect thumbprint shape, a perfect hickey. Annoyance rippled through me.

She didn't look back while she walked toward her section, but perhaps she realized the hickey was on display because she pulled at her collar, nudging it upward to cover the mark. Her boss met her at a table and began a discussion to which Georgia had no reaction.

I couldn't decide if it was anger or condolence that made me want to reach out, drag her back to me, and tell her what I saw last night in the Piggly Wiggly parking lot. Guess that breakup never happened.

Worried that she would catch me still staring at her, I looked out the window and sipped my coffee, lost in a guessing game of who was thinking about whom.

Her boss released her from his lecture, then she sliced through the tables again with a cunning smile aimed right at me. I pretended to not notice.

"Hey," she whispered under her breath as she passed. She angled herself toward the front of the diner and scribbled on her pad to fool anyone who thought she was wasting her time again.

She leaned closer, and the seductive roll of her shoulders had me hooked.

"I know the guy who owns the cabana where we met."

All I pictured was my horrible endeavor to find out whether she was a tourist or a local. I nodded.

"He's throwing a party there tonight. Late. It should be fun, if you're into that sort of thing."

Sounded like she was challenging me.

Partying wasn't my sort of thing, but I wouldn't turn down this invitation—if it was one—to see her again. Also, it was the summer before college. Why not go check out a party on the beach? *Lighten up, Sam.* But my experience with parties was nonexistent. In fact, for the majority of my entire teenage life, I had never even been invited to a party.

I started to form a response but then my dad appeared, wearing a yellow fisherman's hat.

"Dad, hi. This is Georgia. Georgia, this is my dad."

Georgia dropped the pad and pen into her apron pocket and took Dad's offer to shake hands.

"Good morning, Sam's dad."

His crooked smile only highlighted his confusion. I hoped he didn't spot the hickey on her chest.

"Oh, call me Gene."

"Well, I have to get back to work. It was nice to meet you, Gene," she said to Dad. "See you later, Sam." She pulled the pad from her apron and gave me a quick wink as she walked away.

"Wow, she sure is pretty. Who is she?" Dad adjusted his fisherman's hat that I was certain he picked up at an Ophelia gas station.

"Just a friend I met the other day. Is that new?"

"She's quite lovely, son," he said, taking his hat off and then putting it back on to get it comfortable.

"Yeah, but your hat. I mean, it's...it's interesting."

"I picked it up a few days ago. Don't you like it?" He fumbled with the edges of it, twisting it around. He was in love with it already.

"Definitely," I said.

"That girl is pretty. Is she the reason you've been spending so much time away from the house this week?"

I lifted my mug and took a sip of coffee.

"Well, is she, son?"

"Some. A little." I took another sip and opened the menu. "Where exactly did you get that hat?"

"Some knick-knack store where all the tourists go." He kicked my foot under the table and smiled. "Where'd you meet her?"

I spotted our waitress heading toward the booth and flagged her down, shutting Dad up. She pulled a crumpled paper menu out of her apron and handed it to my dad. I wanted to tell him that I had met Georgia in the lighthouse a few nights ago, but there was no need to make her look bad.

"Around the island," I said. "She's nice." Even though she wasn't at first.

Dad asked for a large orange juice to go with his coffee, and once the waitress was out of earshot, he pressed me for more.

"You going to see her later? She made it sound like you guys had some sort of plans."

I picked up my menu and pretended to study it, hiding my face behind it.

"Maybe tonight on the beach. I might meet her at the cabana. Some of her friends are going to get together later tonight. She thought I might like to go."

I kept my eyes steady on the menu but could still see him trying to read me for more. There was nothing more I could say about it. Something about Georgia made words inadequate in describing her.

And I certainly wouldn't try to do so.

CHAPTER 6

"Sam introduced me to a very pretty girl today," Dad said when we arrived home from the diner. Mom had already returned from the mainland with a new glass coffee table that she'd placed right in front of our well-worn leather sofa.

Ugh. I had no idea he had even been thinking about Georgia since he had dropped all the prying at the diner. Mom's face lit up.

"Oh, who is she?"

"You guys, it's really nothing. I just met her a few days ago," I said. I started to make my way up the stairs to escape their budding interrogation.

My parents exchanged a pointed glance, trying to gauge my reaction before they continued. It was one of their weird parental moments in which they could tell what the other was thinking, like the time prom was just around the corner and they knew I was too scared to ask a girl to go with me.

Dad finally broke through their excitement to say, "They're seeing each other later."

Mom clapped.

"Is that so? Where are you two going? Maybe I should meet her."

"No, no, no, I'm not doing this." I moved up a couple of steps, but their meddling dragged me back down. "She invited me to meet her on the beach tonight because some of her friends are getting together to hang out. It's no big deal, really."

"Are you going to go?" Mom said.

"Of course, he's going to go," Dad said before I could respond. "He'd be a fool not to."

The voice in the back of my mind screamed at me that he was right.

"Yes, I'm probably going. I might be home late, though, so don't wait up."

"Remember, you're still new here," Mom said, "and I don't want you to stay out too late."

"Wouldn't dream of it."

"Sammie—"

"Yes, Mom? What?"

"I was just going to ask if you liked the coffee table."

***

For the next few hours, I debated whether I should take Georgia up on her invitation, even though, as Dad said, I'd be a fool not to. I wouldn't quite blend with Ophelia's locals, especially not jumping into a party alone. I needed to do something with my outdated, non-faded hairstyle, and I needed to figure out what to wear with my new Rainbow sandals. What *would* I wear, actually? A pair of swim trunks and a crisp white T-shirt? I had no idea if that choice was appropriate or practical, but either way, that's what I settled on.

Now or never, I kept reminding myself all afternoon.

The desolate beach was blackened by nightfall as I walked alone toward the cabana, starting at beach entrance number fifteen. Moonlight reflected in the thin waves that stretched up to my feet, giving me enough light that I didn't have to use the tiny flashlight my dad had given me for the walk.

The ocean sounded tired at night, serene and gentle.

I'm glad one of us is calm.

Following the shore, I crossed my arms and realized that made me appear more nervous than I truly felt, so I unfolded them. That was even worse. Letting them hang looked even weirder, especially considering they were lanky, skinny, and long, so I pulled them together again. Nobody from the party could see me. All of Ophelia's teenagers were gathered around the orange-and-yellow gleam of a huge bonfire burning on the beach near the cabana.

I could already hear the beat of someone's music blaring from a portable speaker and could see the sparkle of cascading light from what seemed like hundreds of camera flashes bouncing off the dunes in the distance.

When I was close enough to scale just how many people were there, I slowed to a stop, my nerves pinching at me to stay put and just watch from a distance.

It's still not too late to turn around. No one had seen me yet, and, even if they had, they wouldn't have known me or why I was there. Georgia wouldn't miss me. But the thought of seeing her pushed me closer, pulled me forward.

I proceeded to the party, past the bonfire and up the weathered wooden staircase, convinced that every teenager on Ophelia was here. All the tables from the covered deck had been removed, creating space for a makeshift dance floor where a sea of bodies danced against one another, beer splashing from cups and slopping down around my ankles.

Pink, green, and blue strobe lights flashed, illuminating me for a split second and then spinning away.

Almost every guy here wore a pair of swim trunks, and every girl seemed to be dressed in cutoff denim shorts and a bikini top.

One point earned for amateur Sam; I blended better than I expected.

Everybody held some sort of drink—brown beer bottles held by their glass necks, pink drinks with paper umbrellas, or flimsy red solo cups.

I said to myself, "I am way out of my element," only because no one could hear me over the music.

I stood at the railing with my back to the dance floor, scanning the faces on the beach below me, searching for the bounce of Georgia's blonde curls. Even from above, I couldn't tell one person from another.

But I held my resolve. If she were here, I would find her. How could I miss her?

Plowing through the party dampened my shirt with everyone's sweat and alcohol. The bump of some girl left me with warm, sticky liquid splashing down my calf. She laughed, rubbing her hand down my arm and slurring, "Oh, my gosh, I'm—" She bent over in silent laughter, spilling more beer from her cup.

I lifted her hand off me. "Drunk?"

Then another girl took her by the wrist and dragged her away.

While I shook her spilled beer off my leg, I was knocked off balance by what felt like a bony elbow digging right into my back. I whipped my head up, ready to give my own shove, when I recognized Logan. His black hair shined with some type of styling grease, too thick to be natural oil. Despite his hair, Logan's party style was similar to my own, though he definitely pulled off the island vibe better than I did.

He patted me on the back and raised his red solo cup in some sort of salute.

"Hey, Sam. Glad to see you here tonight. Biggest bonfire of the season so far. It's freaking amazing."

I sighed, relieved to see someone I kind of knew. The music was too loud to determine whether Logan had actually said the alternative word to "freaking," so I gave him the benefit of the doubt.

"Yeah, I'm glad I came to check it out. Hey, this is random, but do you know a girl named Georgia?" I had to yell so he could hear me over the music. "I'm supposed to meet her here."

He leaned down a little closer, his long hair brushing over my ear, leaving a streak of greasy oil where it touched.

"What?" The smell of beer permeated his dense breath, forming a swampy odor around my nose.

"Do you know a girl named Georgia? Curly blonde hair?"

"Georgia? Oh, yeah, I know her." He stepped back and pointed down the beach near the bonfire. "Check down there. I think I saw her."

I turned and appraised the beach one more time, searching the groups more carefully for Georgia's wild mane.

Taking the sandy stairs two at a time, I thanked Logan over my shoulder. "See you around."

"No problem," he said, going back to his dancing.

I pushed my way down the beach and into the swarm of dancers in the dunes.

She was close, I could sense it.

A passing green light blinded me, and I tripped, losing my sense of direction in a fog of sand. Maneuvering through the crowd disoriented me, so I paused for a second and found myself in the center of the party.

Thick clouds of sand swirled with smoke from the fire. Dancing girls in bikinis raised their glasses in the air, and bright lights all around me flashed different colors, but I didn't see the only thing I was looking for.

Then someone shoved me from behind, and I found Georgia looking up at me. She'd found *me.*

Her navy-blue bikini top was tied into a bow around her neck, and the tiny, metallic silver stars on the material shimmered in the light of the bonfire. Hugging her perfect curves, her shorts showed off her tanned legs, but I didn't gawk.

Georgia's bare feet were caked with sand, so I felt lame for still having on my flip-flops.

Most people had to shout to be heard over the music, but she spoke under it, somehow beneath its surface, ignoring the noise from the party around her and making the music her own.

"I didn't expect to see you tonight."

"You're the one who invited me." Unable to ignore the loud music and meet her underneath it, I remained above.

"You really don't seem like the partying kind, Sam." She looked me up and down, observing my red swim trunks and plain white T-shirt, smirking the whole time. The way she said my name gave me a burst of anticipation that spread all the way up from my stomach.

Something about Georgia made me want to open up to her, tell her everything about myself just so she'd feel comfortable enough to do the same and confess some details about her boyfriend, what kind of relationship she was in. Where was he, anyway?

I took a step closer and lied, "I'm the hardest partier you'll ever meet."

She shifted to the music, and the bruising on her chest caught my eye again. It was difficult to focus for all the movement going on around us, but, this close, I could tell that it wasn't what I'd assumed at all. The marks were long and narrow, stretching from her collarbone to her shoulder, and the color wasn't a dirty reddish brown a hickey would have been, but blue and fading into purple at the edges. I started to wonder who did that to her but didn't allow myself to make any assumptions. She'd probably just fallen, bumped into something at the diner.

She bit her bottom lip, studying me, tempting me with some wild thrill.

"Then come dance with me," she said.

I couldn't tear my eyes away from her chest quickly enough, and she caught me staring at the bruise. Rather than call me out, she began dancing. The way her body moved made me think she liked me looking. That maybe she liked *me*. I made a vow to myself never to come across as the kind of boy who was interested only in her appearance. Whatever her boyfriend was, I wanted to be the opposite.

Georgia reached out her hand, an invitation for me to take it, so I did. Her fingers clasped with mine, and she spun herself around me, eyes closed. Dancing was not something I had ever done, mostly because I spent high school as a wallflower.

But Georgia extracted it from me. I swayed with blocky movements, but she didn't seem to notice. The soft sway of her body that close to mine mesmerized me. Though her dancing was on the risqué side, she did it with such elegant waves of her limbs, pressing in and bending away. At last, she grabbed my arms and drew me to her, closer than I expected, but it was exactly what I wanted. She wrapped herself around me, laying her head in the crook of my shoulder, and let go of my hands.

My eyes closed, and I allowed myself to hold her a little tighter. When I opened them again, all I could see was Georgia's hair, tucked in a perfect fit beneath my chin. The pink, purple, and green hues from the strobe lights still flashed all around us from up on the deck, but they didn't seem so blinding anymore, and the music wasn't deafening anymore, and she and I couldn't have been closer.

In fact, the music wasn't loud enough, and the lights weren't going to be bright enough until they outshined the stars.

I had made it to her place beneath the music.

And then, just as suddenly as she had appeared, she vanished, and I was above the music again. I had gone from having her in my arms to losing her in just a few seconds, left with a furious determination to find her. People closed in around me, and I became out of place once more. Alone. Helpless. She would never have been able to hear me, but I yelled for her anyway, spinning around and calling for her.

In that moment, a noise—just a soft echo above the music—made it to my ears. It sounded like—like my name?

I whipped around, searching the circle around me until I spotted her near the waves, being pulled through the party and away from the bonfire by some other boy who wasn't her boyfriend. Looking right at me, her lips said *Sam,* but the music drowned out the rest.

"What?" It was a desperate plea she would never hear.

She shouted again, but her words lost all structure through the loud bass. "The lighthouse," she mouthed. "Tonight."

The next thing I knew, she was gone, vanished again into the party, enveloped by the lights, the people, then the dark.

The lighthouse, I thought. *Tonight.*

Chapter 7

I had no clue what time she meant when she said "tonight," but I didn't care and left the party right away. I would wait for her as long as it took, so I jogged straight to the lighthouse. If I hadn't left Ole Red at home, I could've gotten there quicker, but I hadn't wanted to leave him outside the party where he could've been stolen. Maybe I should've gotten a motorcycle and named him Big Red, but even that couldn't have gotten me there fast enough.

The thought of breaking into the lighthouse again made my skin crawl. Memories of the ride I took in the police car sped back with a vengeance. What if we got caught again? Then, like the officer had warned us both, it would be a problem. What if, by some chance, he drove by on his nightly patrol while I was climbing through the window? What if they'd installed security cameras? It would be too dark to see me, and they probably wouldn't even know who I was. But what if they snuck in behind me? I didn't want to have to ride back to the police department. Especially without Georgia. But I decided the risk was worth it.

I arrived at the lighthouse in the pitch-black night, and, despite my tired legs, I was pumped full of energy.

At the base of the front porch stairs, I stopped. The last time I was here, the lighthouse didn't seem so tall and towering, so a part of the night woods. Tonight, though, it was a creaking, old structure where no one had lived in years; it was the place where I'd gotten myself in big trouble.

Don't go in, Sam. This is not who you are.

But I ignored my subconscious and tiptoed up the stairs, feeling my way past the heavy front door to the window and waiting to hear the sounds of movement in the darkness inside the house or even behind me.

Silence.

Hoping the window would still be unlocked, I pushed. It squeaked as it slid up its tracks, resistant at first, before it finally cracked open enough for me to fit through. I didn't step inside. But I didn't want to risk being seen out on the porch either. If I waited for Georgia, she could be the one to break in; I would merely be her accomplice. On the other hand, she would think I was a coward if she found me waiting outside the open lighthouse window.

Is it considered breaking in if you don't actually go inside?

"Just kill me now," I mumbled and scuttled through the window.

Inside, any possible light was blocked by the damaged walls. I stood, feeling my way up the window trim to align myself. I couldn't tell up from down, couldn't decipher what, if anything, was waiting there in darkness.

Georgia could have chosen anywhere to be her thinking spot. She could have chosen to meet me anywhere else too. Anywhere but here.

When my eyes finally adjusted to the dark, I took a wary seat on the dusty wingback chair in the living room. My senses tingled on high alert, waiting for a sign that she was here. I sat motionless, listening for her, for someone else, for any noise whatsoever. In the still darkness, my imagination ran a hundred miles per hour, plotting how I could escape the authority of Ophelia police when they discovered me here. It was Friday night, and there was a huge party on the beach, so an officer might assume some teenager would wander over to the lighthouse and come check it out.

I tried to reason with myself. Maybe with all that was happening on the beach, the police would assume no one would come to an abandoned lighthouse.

Sitting on the edge of my seat, my muscles tightened too much to move, my jaw grinding in strict circles. I should have just waited for her by the cabana. I should have just asked her why she wanted to come to the lighthouse in the first place.

The deafening silence emphasized the noises from the woods, the cicadas and rustling leaves. I had no idea how long I waited to hear something—a creak in the floor, steps up to the front porch, a car in the driveway—but nothing came down the drive. Surrounded by the quiet lighthouse, every pump of blood coursing through my veins was magnified in my ears, becoming a freight train barreling through my brain. My mind played tricks on me, telling me I heard her and then letting me down every time she didn't leap through the window.

I must have been close to dozing off when her flat footsteps started pattering across the front lawn. They were light and quick, too light, I thought, to be the police officer, and although I assumed it was Georgia, I didn't move, didn't want to fracture the quiet placidity of the room.

And then, nothing. The footsteps stopped. I turned toward the porch, questioning whether I heard anything at all, seeing nothing and nobody.

Maybe it was some sort of animal.

Then the outline of a leg thumped down on the dirty wood floor, landing just a few feet from where I had tucked myself into the safety of the wingback chair. In the dark, Georgia's vague frame curled over into a ball as she launched herself through the open window.

She stood, brushing the dust from her bare legs, making the slightest swooshing sound. Every delicate move she made was feather-like, trying to be quiet, floating on a graceful gust down to the floor.

She took a step in my direction. "Sam?"

"Georgia." Standing, I reached for her shoulder, having her turn to me.

She flinched and swiveled around, but neither of us could see the other's face until we were inches apart. When she finally saw me, I could feel her body relax, the tension in her arms falling away.

"You came. I wasn't sure you'd heard me." She stumbled on her unsteady feet, her voice soggy with alcohol. Mumbling something incoherent, she stumbled again and caught herself on the antique bookshelf before regaining her balance.

"Whoa, are you okay?" I grabbed her other arm to steady her, feeling how close we were to each other, and then I felt ridiculous for touching her for so long and realizing that she'd put on a tank top over her bikini.

She rested her head on her forearm, which was still braced against the smooth wood of the shelf. Closing the distance between us, she took a clumsy step toward me.

"I'm fine, I'm fine." She exhaled.

In the pitch-black shadows, her entire face remained invisible. There was not a shred of light shining through to the spot where we were standing. Not even her hair had a halo of light surrounding it.

"What's up, Georgia? Why'd you want to come here?"

She stumbled to the sofa and slumped down. As she passed me, I caught a whiff of whatever alcohol she had been drinking. She didn't answer.

"Georgia?"

"Thank you," she said. "Thanks for coming."

I made my way to the sofa and sat down beside her, placing my arm around her trembling shoulders. She was close now, and I was finally able to distinguish her features, her nose, eyes, lips, all downcast.

"Are you okay, Georgia?"

Waiting for her to answer kept me bolted to my seat. What if she wasn't okay?

A glint of emotion raced over her face, and I thought she might cry.

"Yeah. Thanks, Sam, I'm fine. I just couldn't go home or to his place. Not like this."

His place? As far as I could tell, Georgia hadn't yet looked up at me.

"I understand," I said. But I didn't. I couldn't comprehend anything except that she was here, sitting next to me, with my arm around her.

Silence settled around us. Her eyes closed, and, for a moment, I wondered if she had fallen asleep there.

"This is why I can't stay, Sam." Georgia's solemn mumble slurred, and I wanted to hold her, to comfort her somehow. Instead, I gave her arm a squeeze and pulled her just a little closer. "This is why I have to go. I need to get out of here."

"Go? Georgia, where will you go?"

"Anywhere. It doesn't even matter. Somewhere north. Maybe Boston."

"Boston? That's pretty far from Ophelia," I said.

"Maybe even farther. I know I want to go north. I'm getting out of here someday. Away."

Anxious to know what she meant by that, I remembered her words from the diner when she said wanted to leave, but this badly?

"Away," she said again.

"Why do you want to leave?" I tried to be subtle, but it came out more like a demand, determined to get her answer.

"So, so many reasons."

She sighed and began spitting her answer out, words coming too fast and with an incoherent slur.

"Such a drunk, doesn't know how to raise her own kids. Can't even keep a man for more than a week." She went on, murmuring, "It's not like they love her anyway, single mother of two kids. They just get what they want from her and leave."

Georgia turned toward me, sending another hint of the alcohol scent she'd carried in with her.

She told me once more that her dad was just some bartender in Mississippi, he had no interest in being a father, and he had barely contributed to her childhood. Her statements were thick with emotion, something I hadn't noticed at the diner earlier when she was talking about her past. She must've made every attempt to mask her pain.

My thoughts were a cloud of disgust for him, for anything that could hurt an innocent girl. Her conception was an accident, just a result of some one-night stand. I had no respect for her mother or her father, neither of whom wanted her. All her life, Georgia must have felt like an outsider, knowing forever that she was thought of as a mistake.

Guilt tried to eat at me for how many times I'd been annoyed at my parents' affection for me, so I shoved it away. It wasn't important right now.

"There's no good place." Her drowsy body started to slump. "He can't keep doing this…thinks he owns me…"

"What? Georgia, who is he?"

Ideas floated around my head, but I had to listen, focus on putting her puzzle of a sentence together.

"I can hurt him too, you know."

Of course. We came full circle, back to the argument with her boyfriend on the beach. I shuddered, remembering the bruises I had seen on her wrist and chest, the purple visions that had me seeing red.

"You have to promise me you won't tell anyone. Not even him."

The pain she must have felt—the agony that had to have come with asking me, a stranger, in essence, to keep her secret—fell with a solid thump into my lap. It was mine then, her secret, whatever that might have been. I somehow doubted she would even remember the conversation the next time we ran into one another.

She craned her neck to look up at me. Somewhere in the deep shadows, our eyes stumbled upon one another's.

"Tell what? Tell them what?" Without meaning to, I leaned closer to her.

"Promise me," she whispered. "I don't want them to know."

If her boyfriend was at the party tonight, I hadn't seen him. Maybe they'd already broken up. I hoped so. But who was *them*?

The warmth of her breath spread through my T-shirt and heated my flesh. It aroused me, but the serious tone of the moment was enough to force myself to calm down.

"I feel so trapped, Sam. I can't go anywhere. Can't seem to get away."

"From who?" *Georgia, tell me,* I longed to say. Whispering her name in my thoughts brought some sort of comfort that I couldn't exactly pin, but when she said my name out loud with the perfect amount of grace and desire, I suddenly wanted to beg her to say it more.

Half asleep, she rubbed her chest where the hickey—bruise—was, and she winced.

"Promise me you won't tell anyone."

I leaned into her, urging her to stay awake, but her eyelids drooped until they were closed.

"Are you okay?" My whisper came out loud enough for her to hear but quiet enough to sneak in even closer. This time, my question had a whole new meaning.

"Promise, Sam."

"Okay," I said, though I wanted to hear so much more. "I promise."

"Pinky promise?" She held up her finger. Light flashed across her green eyes again.

"Pinky promise."

I wrapped my finger around hers, electrified by the touch of her skin, and held on longer than I should have, but that was the closest I'd ever come to really holding her hand and keeping it in mine, other than when we were dancing. A gut-wrenching feeling told me it could be the very last.

"Take this," she said, sitting up a little more. She pulled a ring off her thumb, a piece of jewelry I hadn't noticed earlier while we were dancing, and she handed it to me. "I want you to have this to remember our promise."

I took the band and held it up to the window, seeking light to see it better, but all it disclosed was a purple design around the entire ring.

Sliding the band down my pinky, it barely fit over my knuckle, but she wrapped her finger around mine again, as if asking for confirmation.

"Of course I'll remember," I said.

I tightened my grip when she put her head against my chest, causing me to slide my arm up the small of her back so it came to rest around her shoulders once more. I mocked myself for debating whether I should have pulled her even closer. My head kept saying, *Grow up. She's just a girl. Human, just like you.*

Georgia was drunk and didn't notice or care about my nonsense. And while I exploded with shock, she still possessed the utter sameness of herself. Everything about that truth hurt, but what could I do? I was just a placeholder for her, a place to rest, but for me, it was about figuring out where that bruise came from and who she felt she needed to get away from.

She stayed cradled into me, and I tilted my head downward, touching my cheek to the top of her curls.

"Georgia," I whispered into her ear.

No response.

"Does he hurt you?" Just the thought disturbed me, boiled inside me. Another vision of purple and red simmered into my memory—the night at the police department, when she covered the ring of bruises on her wrist with her sleeve. She had guarded it from me then, but who was I to her now? A friend? A confidant? Whatever the answer was, I believed it was because she harbored a desperate need to be rediscovered by someone as a girl who wasn't defined by her past, by Ophelia.

The bruise on her collarbone wasn't covered, so I could make out the outline of a handprint, evidence of the force of her boyfriend's strength glaring back at me from her weak body. I imagined the anger behind his actions and pictured what she must have felt when he grabbed her and thrust her to the ground.

I couldn't tell whether Georgia had fallen asleep, but she remained still for so long that I assumed she was finding peace in a dream. Her left foot twitched every now and then, and her body had become heavier, dead weight.

Trying not to disturb her, I leaned over to see her face, but her features were blurred by the dark and my exhausted eyes.

She was asleep, knocked out cold, so I raised my arm from her shoulders and placed it across her side, thinking that would make her feel safer only if she excused my accidental shakes and bumps. I swallowed with a loud gulp, hoping it wouldn't jar her awake, but I told myself that if she stirred, I would pretend to be asleep as well.

She didn't budge, so I nestled further into my seat on the sofa and nudged Georgia's head so that it rested over my heart. Closing my eyes too, I kept my protective arm over the length of her torso. With Georgia sprawled over my lap, it was easier than I expected to drift off.

CHAPTER 8

I jolted awake in the thick night.

She was gone. My arms were empty.

A breeze from the open window behind me worked its way through my hair and gave me a chill as it moved down around my neck. Then I spotted the shape of a crescent moon hanging high above the tree line.

How long have I been asleep? My parents must've been getting worried by now.

Panic slapped me right in my gut but intensified even more when Georgia bounced into my mind. How did I not feel her move?

"No, no, no," I mumbled.

She would have had to remove my arm that was draped around her waist, seeing that I was, well…holding her. I must have been completely out. At least I didn't have to pretend I was sleeping like I'd planned.

I stood up and scratched my head, listening for any sound of her, but I already knew she was long gone. There was no sign of her and nothing left behind to suggest that she was ever here.

Except her ring on my pinky finger. Like before, I held it up to the window, and this time the moon was high enough to shine light down on it.

The outer edge of it was cold, purple with tiny stars.

What had she meant earlier? What was that promise she had asked me to make?

You have to promise me you won't tell anyone. I don't want her to know.
Her mother.
I can hurt him too, you know.
Her boyfriend. The bruises.

I turned my attention from our conversation long enough to sneak out the window and begin to walk home. No one was out on Main Street, but I could still hear some music coming from the party down at the beach, so it must not have been too late. I hoped I would be able to find my way and get myself inside without being noticed by Mom and Dad because I wasn't ready to discuss the events of the night with them yet. Or ever, probably.

As the Cape Cod came into view, I saw that the front porch light was the only one on. My parents had been expecting me to come in late, so they'd already gone to bed. Otherwise, they would have had the living room lamps on.

Retrieving the spare key from its hiding spot under the metal mailbox, I unlocked the bolt and went inside.

Upstairs, my parents' door was closed, but Mom's quiet snores still sneaked out from under it and into the hall.

I crept into the safety of my room and shut the door behind me. The alarm clock on my bookshelf said 2:17, but Mom or Dad wouldn't know when I got back. If they asked tomorrow, I'd tell them twelve thirty, since they probably went to bed at eleven.

I didn't bother changing clothes but crawled into bed fully dressed in my T-shirt and swim trunks, and I didn't wake up until almost noon the next day. It was the kind of sleep that was as deep as an abyss, coupled with a groggy awakening that kept sucking me back under.

Of course she was my first thought.

On an island as boring as Ophelia, she was the only good thing to think about.

Still on my finger, her ring fit just under my knuckle, so I slid it off and laid it on my nightstand.

***

Swimming, beaching, tanning—it was a way of life on Ophelia. I wanted to be ready if an opportunity presented itself, especially if Georgia invited me, so I'd dressed in a fresh pair of swim trunks this morning and headed to the beach.

The feeling of my arm around Georgia's waist kept flooding back, and I replayed everything again and again. The glimmers of light in her eyes, the intent of our pinky promise, the ring she gave me, and, more than anything, the way she laid her head against me, allowing me to become her pillow.

An hour later, someone kicked sand all over my back, shaking me awake, though I didn't realize I'd fallen asleep under the shade of the palm tree.

The piercing white light blinded me through the green branches, so I shielded my face from the sun to find Logan standing over me.

"What's up?" he said.

"Hey." My voice crackled, and I coughed to clear the sleep out of it. "Hey."

Logan bent down. "Hungover?"

"What?" Then I remembered the party. "Oh, no. Definitely not."

He lay down a few feet away from me. "Did you ever find the girl last night? Georgia?"

I sat up a little and propped up on my elbows. "Yeah. We danced some. Do you know her?"

"Yeah, of course I know her. We went to school together forever."

"Wait, so, are you friends?"

"Not really. Just acquaintances."

"Oh." I was too indecisive to decide whether I was disappointed that he couldn't give me any information or I was happy that they weren't closer than acquaintances.

"Why?" he said.

"I don't know. We're kind of friends, but I don't really know anything about her. Do you?"

"Nothing much. I used to feel sorry for her when we were kids because she had a bad home life, and she's got this really lousy mother. Kind of slutty. You know the type. Still feel kinda bad for her."

"Sure, yeah."

"Then Georgia got with some dude a couple years ago and—"

"Some dude?" I said.

"Yeah. He's older than her by a few years and works at the gas station. I don't know a ton about him. But I do know he grew up hanging with a different crowd. All those boys went off to college, and he stayed here to work. But Georgia? Yeah, she's a real one."

I looked past the dunes, recalling that the gas station was a few streets up.

"How did you meet her?" he said. The way he asked gave me a quick sting in my side. "You're pretty new here, right?"

"Yeah. We met on the beach, and we've hung out a few times since then." It was the easiest way to explain it. If Logan had wanted to know more about who Georgia was to me, I would have had no idea how to respond.

"So do you know anything else about her boyfriend?" I said. "He's a big guy. Buzz cut. Seems like a jerk."

"Unfortunately. Ugh, he's such a freaking tool, dude." Logan shook his head, flipping his long hair back.

I sat up. "Really? How so?"

Logan shrugged. "He's just a mean guy. Like I said, I never hung with that crowd, but I can tell something's up with him. He's got to have something wrong in the head. He's, like, messed up."

"Like how? What?" I pushed.

"Like, there was this one time, I was at the gas station up the road where he works, and there was this old lady at the cash register, right? And she was complaining because she was having some trouble getting her pump to work, but he totally ignored her because he was distracted by some girl that was at the counter talking to him, and he never turned it on. And, by the way, it wasn't Georgia he was flirting with, which is kind of suspicious, but anyway. The old lady came back in the store to get him to help her, and he just said to her, 'Shut up. I told you I already fixed it. Now get out of here.' Then he told the girl that he'd like to go—well, I'm trying not to curse—but he just told her what he'd like to do to her. You get the picture."

Trapped, Georgia had told me. She was trapped.

"The girl wasn't Georgia?" I needed to hear it again.

"No. Different girl. But yeah, man, he's such a weird guy. I don't know anything about his family, but I know he lives on the island by himself. He's just a weird loner type."

"He works at the gas station?"

"Yeah, he was just there about an hour ago."

I thought about going to pay him a discreet visit, seeing for myself what this guy really looked like, acted like in public. But he would tower over me and would maybe recognize me from the police department or that night in the grocery store parking lot.

I imagined how the conversation would go.

Hey, weren't you the guy who snuck off with my girlfriend last night? Are you the creep who was watching me and my girl in my car that night? Aren't you the one who got my girlfriend in trouble at the lighthouse?

"Is he kind of—" I started, "I don't know. I feel like he's a little harsh with Georgia. Do you know if he hurts her?"

"Yeah, I wouldn't doubt it. He seems like he could be really violent if he wanted to. But, on the other hand, something tells me Georgia can handle herself."

Logan avoided my glance by messing around in the sand while I tossed his comment around in my mind.

"Hey, did you hear about the storm?" he said.

It hadn't rained once since I'd been on the island. "What storm?"

"There's some hurricane that's hitting a few islands above us. Ophelia is supposed to get some wicked storms. Not evacuation level but still pretty bad."

"When?" My parents and I had no idea how to prepare for a hurricane. We'd never even endured a tornado. "I haven't heard anything about any storms."

"Soon. I think, like, three or four days."

"Wow, thanks for telling me. Should I be worried? I'm from West Virginia, you know."

"No, just lock up your house all tight and you'll be fine. But you'll see it on the news. It's supposed to be a monster, dude."

A monster? Ophelia seemed to have a lot of monsters.

"Oh, I haven't watched a lot of TV since I've been here. I've been out trying to get my bearings on the island and stuff."

Logan jumped to his feet and wiped the sand from his bottom. "Check the weather on your phone, then. Don't wanna be sorry. But I've got to get going. Stay safe, Sam."

Jogging away, he waved goodbye before I could explain that my phone was crushed by our sofa during the move.

"I'll see you around," I called.

If Logan knew about the hurricane, then Georgia probably did too. I could only hope I'd see her before the storm ruined my chance to examine her wrists and collarbone while her bruises were still fresh.

As soon as Logan was out of sight, I hopped on Ole Red and rode across the street to the gas station. That familiar red car was parked beside the building.

The jingle of bells on the door announced my arrival, but Georgia's boyfriend didn't look up from behind the counter. I dipped down the closest aisle. His drawn-in brows and permanent frown matched the face of the angry boy from the police department.

He flipped through a magazine, turning the pages with such force that I thought I heard one rip.

I eyed him from my point of safety, tucked behind the snack aisle. Inattentive. I wasn't surprised.

The convenience store smelled of stale cigarettes, and my shoes felt sticky with the remnants of spilled soda on the tile floor.

I grabbed a bag of potato chips and walked to the counter with my head down, money already out. He tossed his magazine aside without even a glance in my direction. As he scanned my bag, I snuck a look at his nametag.

Hello, I'm Mat Corbin.

Corbin was a zombie—slow, impersonal, ugly. How could someone as lovely as Georgia ever kiss someone so rotten?

I etched his name in my brain, considering what my next step would be. Googling him? Spying on him? Asking around about him?

Mat Corbin had large hands, rough and calloused, and they were exactly the kind of hands that would hurt a woman. He spit out my total, sloppy, with obvious annoyance. I tossed him a few ones and recoiled as he returned my change.

"Thanks," I said, scooping it up and bolting away. *Thanks for what?*

I left the store and rode straight home.

The complimentary phone book, part of the welcome gift from our realtor, was already collecting dust on the coffee table. Who used a phone book anymore, anyway? What a *welcome-to-your-new-home* present. Whatever. It was the quickest way to find him because I was pretty sure my laptop wasn't charged.

I flipped the pages until I found C. *Cambridge, Clark, Corbin. Corbin,* at last. My index finger ran along the list of names. There he was. *Matthew Corbin.* His name jumped up at me from the middle of the page. *168 Shell Way, Ophelia Island, Florida.*

I scribbled his address on the back of the realtor's business card and tucked it in my pocket. His identity, his background, had to be revealed in the way he lived his life on Shell Way.

But I'd be trespassing—yet again—if I sneaked over there. So, instead, I allowed myself some time to sit on the information I had and contemplate what to do with it.

I hopped on Red and headed down to the beach. Sat there. Dug my toes in the sand. Schemed my next potential crime.

This isn't who you are, Sam, I told myself once more. *You don't go breaking into people's houses. Twice.*

I watched the crowds on the beach for Georgia, hoping she might find me here to rationalize my thoughts, though I feared if I did see her and the bruises on her body, I'd leave her to go see what secrets might be hidden on Shell Way or what Mat had over there to entice her to stay.

***

She didn't appear. After an hour passed, I left for home, and, on the way, I overheard some tourists discussing the storm. They were planning on getting off the island, cutting their vacation short to reach the safety of the mainland before it hit.

"Imagine living here and braving it," one woman said.

Yeah, imagine...

I pedaled Red quicker than he was made for, then burst through the front door just as my dad was coming through it the other way. The force of our collision nearly knocked his beloved fisherman's hat from his head.

"There's a big storm coming, and people are already making plans to get out of here. Did you guys know about this? Do we need to get prepared?"

The words rolled off my tongue too fast for my parents to comprehend right away, but, really, I just needed to know how much time I had to find Georgia once we began all the storm prepping.

"Do you think we should leave the island?" Mom said, her tone even.

"No, Logan told me it's not supposed to be that bad. But still. Did you know about this? Like, maybe we should board up the windows."

"Logan?" Mom asked.

"A new friend."

"Oh, good, you made a friend—"

I held up my hand to get back on topic. "Anyway, do any of us know how to handle a hurricane?"

"I think we're going to be okay. This must have been what that loud notification was on my phone earlier. I was hanging a picture frame and ignored it. Isn't that funny?" She and Dad laughed. "But just in case, let's watch The Weather Channel tonight to see the path the storm is taking, and we can try to get an idea about what's going on," Mom said. Like always, never in a panic.

"Where exactly is the hurricane heading?" Dad's cheekbones shifted downward, sloping with concern.

"I'm not sure. Logan said it was aimed for a direct hit a couple islands above us," I said.

"It sounds like we should be okay, but it couldn't hurt to gather a few supplies to have on standby."

Dad started counting on his fingers, making a mental list of items to gather.

Mom said, "Even if we don't need them this time, we're island residents now; we'll just get a jump on whenever we'll need them. Right, Sammie?"

She smiled.

"Yeah, right," I said. "Right."

That evening, instead of eating dinner around the dining table, we parked in front of the TV and listened for news about Hurricane Anita.

The weatherman said, "Residents of Ophelia Island and areas north of Ophelia can expect a big storm surge and a high potential for some flooding. For the duration of the storm, which is expected to make landfall in the next twenty-four hours, it's recommended that residents limit their activity to only things that are absolutely necessary. It's advised to bring all pets inside due to heavy winds, flooding, and the potential for lightning. Residents of Jacob's Point are in the direct path of this storm, so evacuation is recommended. Though this storm won't be as severe as others we've seen in the past, it is still considered dangerous and will cause damage. Island communities south of Jacob's should expect the storm to linger, with additional bands of rain to follow. We are tracking Hurricane Anita very closely, and we'll alert you with any updates if things change."

Just thinking about riding out the storm without seeing Georgia first made me frustrated. I had time for only one of two things: search for Georgia or pop by Mat's house while he was at work.

I didn't know what I wanted to gain from going there. It wasn't like I'd find any proof that he was abusing Georgia. Was that what I sought after? Proof of his bad character? Because what would I do if I did find that out?

Either way, I'd be on my bike tonight, and his place wasn't far from my own, so I'd allow myself to gain a little insight.

I left my parents to settle into first-hurricane mode. They were deep in conversation and didn't even notice when I told them over my shoulder that I'd be back soon. *Just as well*, I thought. I didn't want them to try to stop me.

But, once I was on my way there in the dark night, I wasn't sure that anything could've stopped me from riding to Shell Way and figuring out what Logan meant by saying Mat had something wrong with him.

Something wrong in the head.

Something that turned Georgia's skin purple.

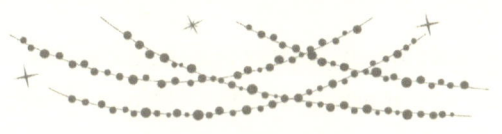

CHAPTER 9

Mat's house was stashed away in the moss-covered woods, nothing more than a wooden shack with a rusty, blue, tin roof warped by the heat and littered with the debris falling from the oaks that surrounded it.

His red crap-car was parked outside. When did he get off work?

Logan had told me that Mat lived alone. It scared me to think of the possible things Mat did here by himself all the time. There was still just enough daylight left to see, but on its heels would be a brighter light from the crescent moon. I walked down Mat's dirt driveway, pushing Red along beside me by the handlebars.

Yellow light blazed out from his glass windows, and I could see the flash of a television flaming from inside. I stopped when I reached the side of the house, pressing my body flat against the wall, and I pulled Red close beside me.

"Stop being so tense. You're freaking me out," I whispered to him.

The window was higher than it seemed from the driveway, so I stood on my tiptoes to try to see inside. A tickle of fear crept up my spine, and I wondered what Mat would do if he found me lurking here.

The snap of a branch in the distance made an accidental gasp escape me, and I thumped my back against the vinyl siding of his house.

I stayed pressed to the wall, waiting for Mat to open the window above me and check out what that noise was. But minutes passed with no suspicion from inside.

Though I could barely see through the dirty glass, I peered above the windowsill and found that I was looking through his kitchen and into the living room. He sat, drinking a beer with his back to me, attention focused to the TV from the comfort of his camouflage recliner.

Since I assumed he was drunk and distracted, I browsed through the items strewn across the floor that covered every surface I could see.

Dirty dishes cluttered his kitchen counter, and the living room carpet was tattered with age, spotted with brown stains. The refrigerator, half open, was stocked full of milk cartons and beer cans.

Another rustle of leaves caught my attention, and I slumped back to my heels, almost falling over Red. My vision was spotty from the lights inside the house, but a few deep blinks corrected it.

Nothing but the black woods stretched out in front of me. At my feet, a fat, gray cat slithered by, giving me an eye. He rubbed his tail against Ole Red's front tire, so I shoved him away with my foot. He sauntered toward the tree line in the distance.

I took a final peep inside. Mat hadn't moved at all.

If he'd still been at work, I'd have checked to see whether his door was unlocked or his windows would open, but with him sitting in there, I couldn't do much.

I stood there for minutes, watching him do nothing, waiting for him to do something, and, just when I turned Ole Red toward the driveway to leave, a motor started rumbling down the drive. Headlights sliced through the trees like knives, giving everything an ominous shadow, including me. Red and I ducked behind a scrawny bush at the far corner of Mat's house. I couldn't make out any details of the car or its driver as it pulled to a stop in the dust. The roaring engine turned off.

The faint lights from Mat's window shined on the driver, and Georgia stepped out, slinging her bouncy curls behind her. She breezed up the front steps to the porch, and I closed my eyes. *If you can't see her, she can't see you.*

From behind the bush, I lost sight of her, but I could still hear her every step. Finally, the door creaked open, and Mat called for her.

I inched with stealth precision back to my spot at the window and sucked in a breath, trying to make myself taller.

They stood next to the recliner, and Mat unscrewed the lid to a small bottle—a pill bottle— then shook out two little white dots, placing them on his tongue and swallowing them with a swig of his beer. Georgia looked away, making two fists by her side as if to say, *You can handle this.*

Muffled through the cheap wall, I heard her say, "Well, I came over. What do you want?"

Mat tried to pull her toward him, pressing his tall body into her, but she backed away. Was this the same argument from the beach that day I met her? Or a new one?

"Don't play stupid, Georgia."

Her name was almost unrecognizable when he said it, spoken with such little mercy, with no purpose except to demand her attention.

He stepped toward her again, jerking up her arm in his grip. That bruise on her wrist—this must be how it had happened.

His lips pressed onto hers, and with her hands on his chest creating a small gap between them, she kissed him back.

Did she have a choice?

They shifted, and she strained against him, then they moved out of my line of sight. I shuffled through the shrubbery to the next window and stood high on my toes again to see inside.

Georgia came into view right away, restrained against the far wall. She pounded her fists in unsuccessful defiance against Mat's thick pecs, but he grabbed her hands and slammed them down. I wasn't close enough to hear them or read their lips, so I pinned my ear beside the window.

I don't want to, Mat... Let me go home.

Next thing I knew, he was kissing her again. Mat flipped the switch on the wall next to her, and the light went off. I waited, trying to hear beyond the drumming of my heartbeat, and counted to ten, longing to hear a sliver of hope that Mat stopped. That she was okay. That he wasn't hurting her. Touching her. Beating her. Bruising her.

I moved a few feet toward the front door, thinking I should pound on it to distract him or give Georgia a chance to escape, and then the crash of something shattering on the floor inside sucked me back to the window.

Glass. Someone had shattered glass. Then came the low mutters of both of their voices, blurred and thickened through the wall.

"Can't we just talk? Please, Mat."

An abrupt thump rattled the window, paired with a noise that I concluded was Georgia hitting the floor.

I put my fingertips to the vinyl, conveying some sort of invisible message to her that I was here, just outside, hearing her pain and suffering with her.

Helplessly.

Out of habit, I patted my pockets for my phone to call the police or somebody to help, but of course, a couch had to land on my only means of contacting anyone.

Another body hit the floor; it must have been Mat. I backed away from the wall and glanced inside. While Mat was down, Georgia scrambled to her feet near the lamp that lay there in pieces.

"Get away from me," she screamed at him. "You're scum. You can't control me forever."

Mat rubbed the back of his head, rolling onto his side, and Georgia ran out of the room. I heard her go all the way through the hall, the living room. The front door didn't slam shut like I expected. She must've left it wide open because, a split second later, she was in her car and speeding away, and I was left pressed against Mat's house, trying to catch my breath.

CHAPTER 10

In some way, I had been changed by the horror of what I'd heard the night before. I could see it all over my pale face this morning when I looked in the mirror. I could see it when I put her ring on my pinky, rubbed my thumb over it, and took it back off. I could feel it when I tried to eat breakfast and lost my appetite.

She had run away. If she hadn't knocked him to the ground and gotten away, she might not have had the chance to run away.

How many times had this happened to her? How many times had she not had that chance to save herself?

And me. I just sat there phoneless, about to throw myself into Mat's home and probably get my butt kicked. But she'd gotten him to the floor, and she'd managed to escape his advances. I think she knew it was only temporary. He would drag her back again soon.

I was scared for her, but, more than that, I was impressed that she could handle herself. Would she be able to next time?

These are Ophelia's monsters, I thought.

I went to the beach around two o'clock. It was still crowded despite the storm warnings that had ramped up in intensity as the storm spun closer. I looked forward to the quiet solitude of wintertime, when Logan and Dad had assured me that Ophelia would be deserted except for year-round residents. Summertime hustle was fun for the tourists and great for local businesses, but the idea of just me and Georgia hanging out on the island, owning it, excited me.

There was no real reason to think that would ever happen. Where would that leave Mat?

I hadn't come to this island seeking a girl. I came here thinking I'd be miserable, and, in some sense, perhaps I was.

I disregarded my fantasy and spread my towel away from the throng of tourists trying to enjoy the last rays of sun before the storm. Tuning out the sounds of the crowds, I lay down and closed my eyes, allowing the heat to press into my skin.

Logan didn't show up on the beach, and neither did Georgia.

Within minutes, my resting turned into an unpleasant dream of Mat's fists deepening the bruising on Georgia's arm, digging into her tissue, and burying his handprint into her.

***

A blast of icy cold air met me when I opened the door to the ice cream shop, a welcome sensation that cooled my warm skin. There were already six people in line in front of me, most with children, so I used my rolled-up towel to claim the first seat that emptied—a white chair by the front window—and got back in line to wait for what I hoped was a good scoop of cookie dough.

The bell on the door chimed, and I turned to see Georgia, who popped up in line behind me. She flashed me her biggest smile and stuffed her hands into the pockets of her shorts.

Taken by surprise, I stepped back. *Perks of a small island.*

She flipped her hair in her customary way.

"Hi there." Half smiling, always.

"Hey." Happier than I should have been, I took another step away and almost knocked into the children in front of me who were shoving each other. I tried to disguise my surprised expression and searched for something to say.

"Here for ice cream?" I said.

I glanced at her wrists. They were still circled with a yellow healing bruise, so I moved my attention up, surveying her chest and arms for more signs of Mat's abuse last night. Since she was wearing a tank top, I would've seen any mark his violence had left behind on her skin.

She jumped in front of me to take the spot behind the kids in line.

"Nah, I just come sometimes to stand in line," she teased. "Yeah, of course I'm here for ice cream. What are you here for?" Every word was slow, taunting me, luring me.

"I'm glad I ran into you."

"I think I'm the one who ran into you." She chuckled, and we fell into a quick laughing fit.

Outsmarted, I returned her smile.

The family in front of us collected their orders, and we walked to the counter.

"We do seem to run into one another a lot," I said.

"Yeah, we do. But I'm pretty sure it was intentional those first few times." Trying to conceal another laugh, she nudged me with her elbow. "I'm almost positive you were following me." She looked right at me, awaiting my response.

Despite wanting to come back with something witty, all I could do to save my dignity was to deny. "I wasn't following you."

But I was definitely following your boyfriend last night. I flashed her my own small grin, absorbed in shame and in my memory of Mat pinning her to the wall. I looked away for a moment and cringed at the thought.

"Oh, then what were you doing?" she challenged again.

"It's a small island?" I guessed.

"Too small." Her giggle floated around the room like soap bubbles that I wanted to touch but couldn't because of their fragility.

Georgia ordered one scoop of strawberry and one scoop of peach, and I ordered two scoops of pistachio because they were out of cookie dough. I offered to pay for her cone, and she let me with ease. Then, I headed toward the chair I had saved, but she slid into the seat before I could, and I had no other option but to stand in the tight space beside her.

"Did you hear about the storm?" I said, keeping the conversation light, keeping both of us far away from what we experienced last night.

She licked a drip of pink ice cream that trickled down the side of her cone, and I found myself looking past my cone to watch her curve her tongue back into her mouth.

"Yeah. You scared?"

"No," I said. "It's just coming off Jacob's. Shouldn't be too bad." I hoped I sounded confident enough to convince her I believed that.

"Already starting to get cloudy." She looked out the window. Thick clouds blanketed the horizon, burying the sun.

"But isn't the storm supposed to hit tomorrow?" Fear took hold of me. She had to have heard it in my voice.

"The weathermen are never accurate," she said. "Are you staying on the island?"

I was glad she asked me before I had the opportunity to ask her first.

"Yeah. You?"

"Yes, of course," she said. "People overreact and evacuate like idiots, especially the tourists. I predict in about an hour from now, there'll be a traffic jam to make it back to the 'safety of the mainland.'" Georgia drew out that last part, making air quotes and rolling her eyes. She motioned to the family who had been in line in front of us, now seated at a table that ran the length of the wall. "People like that get really scared, and they drink up whatever the news tells them. This one won't be anything more than a little wind and rain. It'd be different if Anita was actually going to be hitting us."

Georgia's sharp certainty filled me in the places where I lacked. I knew nothing about hurricanes except what I had learned in school, but since I was a local now, maybe she didn't still think of me as some scared vacationer.

By the time we finished our cones, the shop was nearly empty, and Georgia's prediction had come true—cars lined up, one behind the other along Main Street. Beach gear and bicycles were strapped to the backs of almost every one of them. Georgia noticed me looking and laughed, loud enough to annoy the cashier, who glared at us as he wiped the counter clean.

Georgia batted her eyelashes at me in long, curious blinks. "Aren't your parents ever curious about where you go?"

"Not really," I said. "They like that I go out and do my own stuff."

"Your mom doesn't call?"

"My phone broke back in West Virginia while we were loading up the moving truck. The sofa leg landed on it, *agonizingly* cutting off all communication with my friends, which was perfect timing. Just haven't had the time to replace it yet. Don't really know anyone here to call, anyway, but I'll eventually get a new one."

"Don't your friends wanna talk to you?"

"I guess so. But they've all just graduated, so they're probably busy getting on with their lives."

I crossed my arms over the table.

"You seem to be out just as much as I am," I said before the topic strayed any further. "Does your mom ever wonder where you are?"

Immediate regret came up with my question. How could I forget what she had said about her mother?

"My mom doesn't care. Whatever I want to do, I do." But I saw right through her. Somehow, I knew that wasn't true, that she didn't do everything she wanted. If that were the case, what was she doing with someone like Mat? She hadn't wanted to sleep with him last night. She hadn't wanted to be there at all. What made her stay with him? A threat? Because he was bigger than she was?

The empty ice cream shop offered me enough privacy to broach the subject of him, but I wasn't bold enough to look straight at her.

"So how come I never see you out with your boyfriend?"

She delayed, picking at her broken cone. "We aren't together a lot."

That gave me some microscopic glimmer of hope, but he was still cheating on her. I knew that much, and I bet she knew it too. Knew about the girl from the grocery store parking lot.

"Does he live on Ophelia?" My question ended on a note too high, too forced.

"Yeah, he lives up by the shoals at the north end of the island. We just hang out sometimes. We aren't really all that close."

"Then why do you stay together?"

Instead of recoiling at what came across as my overstepping, she stared at me as if considering it. I could almost see her thinking it: *Why? Why do I stay with him?*

And my thoughts responded, *Because he's forcing you to.*

"Well," she said, "why shouldn't we? I mean, I'm here whenever he wants to hang out. He's usually available if I ever want him to be."

All I interpreted, though, was a much harsher rendering that truly said, *He calls me over when he wants to sleep with me. That's all.*

Her fingernails drummed on the table, and I noticed her pretty pink nail polish was chipped at the ends.

"Mat just gets on my nerves sometimes."

Although she probably already knew, the Piggly Wiggly parking lot incident sat right there at the edge of our conversation, but I couldn't bring myself to share something with such depth. It wasn't any of my business, and Georgia and I weren't close enough to talk about broken relationships. Spying on her boyfriend and contemplating breaking into his house was inexcusable too, but it had told me exactly how her skin became blemished and blue. That in itself replaced my guilt with a sense of justification.

I'd done the right thing. If she hadn't gotten away from him, I would've been there to make it all stop.

"Is he good to you?" I didn't even recognize my voice as the words came out before I thought better of it.

Georgia returned to her light and playful persona once more.

"Is your girlfriend good to you?"

I didn't have a girlfriend, and Georgia knew that. In fact, I was sure it was so apparent that everyone on Ophelia Island could surmise it.

"It's been since my sixth-grade science class, but Jennifer was pretty great." I glanced away just so I could avoid getting lost in a maze of embarrassment.

Georgia turned away and shook her head at my pathetic love life, pretending not to see.

Outside, night began to fall, and most of the stores had already boarded up their windows for the coming storm.

"It's getting dark," I said. "Like, crazy dark. How long have we been in here?"

The cashier said, "For a long, long, long time."

He flipped on a small radio with an antenna from behind the counter, and rather than the music I expected as he prepared to close the ice cream shop, the voice of a news reporter filled the small space. Georgia ignored it, tapping a finger to her chin, and I tried to make sense of the fuzzy words on the radio. He said something about Anita, the most popular name around.

Picking up speed as she nears the coast. Landfall is imminent...storm surges and heavy winds beginning sooner than expected...seek shelter...

I turned to look at Georgia, who was already fixated on me and still tapping her chin.

"Have you ever been on a sailboat, Sam?"

Chapter 11

The boats in the marina bobbed in the water, keeping time with the waves. The ocean thrashed, wild and awake, and the force of water crashing against the shoreline was very different than the lazy current that would be safer for sailing.

The entrance to the boardwalk was strapped with bright yellow caution tape that whipped around in the wind. Georgia told me that the beaches had been closed since four this afternoon, so, on the walk here, the streets were empty.

Seeing the island before a hurricane was eerie, like I was standing in the before picture that would soon pair with a tragic after picture. Maybe it was because I was new to the island or maybe it was because I was enveloped in storm-fueled paranoia, but I felt like Ophelia had an eye, situated above the trees and laser focused on me.

Georgia ducked under the caution tape and motioned for me to follow. Once again, I teetered on the dangerous edge of breaking the law. If I turned back, I'd forever regret the possibilities of what could happen if I followed Georgia under the caution tape. A world of hazard. Opportunity. Chance.

But I tailed Georgia anyway to a windowless shack made of battered wooden boards. Fishing poles, boat supplies, and life jackets were piled by the door, which, in my West Virginian mind, seemed like some sort of an effort to preserve them during the storm. I almost asked her why they hadn't been secured inside the building but needed to reduce my number of burning questions.

"What are we doing here?" I said.

"We have to get something here first."

We? "I think this is definitely breaking and entering."

She punched in a code to a keypad by the door, and it clicked open. We walked inside, but just over the threshold, I tripped in fishing net on the floor.

"Oh, watch your step."

"Perfect. Thanks." I untangled myself and said, "Um, Georgia?"

She turned to look at me.

"I think this is breaking and entering."

"I had the code to get in," she said.

"Did someone give that to you, or did you steal it?"

Spinning away from me, she shrugged. "I've had it forever, Sam. Relax."

More fishing poles inside were enclosed in a locked cabinet next to a case of dangling keys behind a small wall of glass. Following the squeak of a desk drawer opening and shutting again, Georgia appeared beside me with a round metal key ring hanging from her finger. She opened the glass case with expert precision and examined the lines of keys hanging on individual hooks, selecting a gold one with a tag on it.

"What does that say?"

"It doesn't matter." She looped the ring around her index finger, twirling it to expel a delicate chime as it brushed up against the master key.

She grabbed me by the hand and led me out of the building, before letting go so she could lock up behind us on the keypad. She walked fast, but I kept up behind her, making sure no one was watching us.

"Hey, I don't think we should do this. This is a bad idea."

"Stop worrying so much."

Her simplicity conflicted with my begging, my pleas to leave, but Georgia's persistence wouldn't allow my anxiety to keep us from moving forward.

She made it seem like there was no choice but the one she'd made for both of us. I knew that I didn't have to go along with her or to submit to the decisions she was making. I didn't know her well, but I knew that if I didn't go, she'd sail out to sea alone. After what happened last night, I couldn't just abandon her on the dark ocean. I had to go with her.

Georgia dangled the keys up to my face, and their cool metal reflected the dull light of the cloud-covered sky. "You can leave if you want, but I'm not turning back."

New place, new Sam.

"I didn't say I was leaving." Every inch she moved pulled me an inch closer to her like a magnet. "Don't you think you should ask the owner of the boat before you take it out on the water? Isn't this considered stealing?"

No matter what she was about to say, I'd already made up my mind to get on the sailboat. The effect she had on me—I couldn't shake it. Couldn't understand but didn't want to try to breathe without it.

Georgia led me down the wooden dock where motorboats and sailboats splashed in the water, tied to their posts to ride out the coming storm. The clouded sky hid everything under a dangerous canopy of darkness, but the wind slowed for the moment, and the ocean was calm and soft again.

"Which one is, um, our boat?"

She kept pace a few yards ahead of me but hunched over some, tiptoeing to lighten her steps.

"What?" she said.

"The boat you're stealing. Which one is it?" I came to a halt. *Who am I right now?* Sam Carter would most certainly not do anything like this, not even New Ophelia Sam.

Or would I?

"I'm not stealing it," she said.

"What is this, then?" I asked louder.

I fought an internal battle between knowing what was right and knowing what choice I would ultimately make. The devil on my shoulder tended to be the winner recently, and I knew that would not change here tonight.

"I know the owner from around the island." She turned around. "We're just borrowing it."

"I don't like it. Borrowing without permission seems the same as stealing to me. Does he know you're going to be taking his sailboat?"

Georgia paused at the side of the boat, running her hand across the bow.

Under my breath, I said, "This looks expensive." Precious as sterling silver.

I joined her. The sails were strapped to the poles, secured by thick rope, and the glossy wood of the bow twinkled in the water. Though the other sailboats in the marina were much larger and much flashier, her selection of this specific boat perplexed me. It wasn't the most impressive. It was a little rough around the edges. Some of the paint of the classic lines going down the stern was chipped. But it was still beautiful because it reminded me of Georgia. And if she was going to climb aboard, so was I.

Answering my question from moments ago, she said, "No." She scrambled onto the boat with ease, grabbing my hand to help me aboard. "He doesn't know."

The wood on the boat's main deck was slick with dew, causing me to slip. Georgia didn't see me catch myself on a rope that dangled from the mast, so I scurried to her side again.

"Are there cameras on this boat? Or anywhere around the marina, for that matter?" I scouted the tall poles around me but saw no surveillance angled down at us.

"Not that I know of." She grinned and began untying the rope that had the boat secured to the dock. "Relax, Sam. We're just going for a midnight sail."

"But it's not midnight."

Even through the shadows, I could see her flat expression. "Would you rather take a bike?"

If I could, I would.

"Fine," I replied instead.

Cool black water splashed against the back of the boat, and goose-bumps on my arms started to rise. The moon was gone under a blanket of clouds, but Georgia didn't fret about the dark like I wanted her to.

She didn't speak while she prepared us to sail out into the bay. I offered twice to help, which only made her laugh and point out what a useless noob I was.

"Do you trust me?"

I stared down into the water, thinking about how alone we would be out there in the ocean and then thinking that her boyfriend wouldn't appreciate this scenario.

"Depends," I said. "Do you know what you're doing?"

Like before, I chose to depend on her.

We set off from the dock in a slow glide, careful not to stir up the shallow water near the marina with our wake, but picked up speed as soon as we exited through the marsh. My knees buckled at the clap of wind above me. Georgia brought up the sails, and they caught wind, pushing us into the wide-open infinity of the ocean in front of me.

Seeing the sails fill up with wind left me feeling insignificant under them—just a tiny blip, a weakling in the face of the water's power. It controlled us, obliterating any pride I had left.

Georgia smiled up at me, and, out here, I could see a glimpse of freedom in her eyes that I hadn't noticed on land.

I bounced a smile right back at her, impressed by how well she handled the sails and all the complicated tasks that went along with them. Watching her work was a treasure because even in the pitch of night she moved with the confidence of someone who could see in the noon rays of day.

Helpless by her side, my nerves were calmed just by watching her proficiency at the helm. The lights from Ophelia became smaller behind us as the wind dragged us farther away from the shore until the lights were nothing more than tiny dots in the distance.

"Georgia?"

"Sam."

The way her voice sounded when she said my name—*Sam*—it was low and alluring. I wanted her to keep saying it. I wanted her to say it close to me, so close it'd be a whisper.

I searched her eyes again for that freedom so I could perhaps steal some and see what she was looking at out there beyond the bow. They were murky in the dark, but the dim light dancing off the water illuminated them just enough to see that she was actually looking at me.

"How much farther are we going?"

"Not that far. If you're scared, you can tell me," she said, and I was once again reminded of how alone we were out here.

"It's just—it's pretty late, and we're really far from shore."

"We can go back if you want."

Though the biggest part of me wanted to tell her the truth, I instead told her I wanted to stay.

She walked away, adjusted some ropes to lower the sails, and dropped the anchor. "We could just stay right here."

"Yeah. Here is good." I looked over the edge of the sailboat and tensed. I'd never been out this far in the ocean, not at night, not with a girl I barely knew.

When I turned back, I found Georgia lying flat on the floor of the boat. She patted the planks beside her.

"Come here."

Such a simple command, yet I would have died to obey it.

The miles of water around us disappeared as I lay down next to her. I didn't know how close she wanted me, so when she pulled her hands behind her head like a pillow, her elbows created a natural space between us that we both seemed comfortable keeping.

Georgia and I stared up at the sky in silence, in unusual silence. The wind slowed, and the waves were more tranquil. A couple of stars had broken through the clouds above us, hazy in the dense sky.

"Time slows down on the water," she said in a breathy exhale.

I looked over at her, studying the curvy line of her silhouette. For a fleeting moment, I considered telling her how beautiful she was.

Would she have wanted to hear that from me? Did her boyfriend tell her? Did her mom? It was the truth. The way her eyelashes fluttered when she shifted from star to cloud to star again just made me want to move closer to her, make her feel safe.

Georgia was right; time did slow down out here. And I could see the whole sky in her face while she was lost in the sky itself during this timeless hour, and I wanted to hand over the whole universe to her so she'd never have to stop sailing on the ocean. Her ocean.

"How many times have you done this?" The waves rocked the boat from side to side, and each time Georgia allowed herself to roll a bit closer to me.

She crossed her arms and faced me. "Whenever I feel like it."

Would I ever get a clear answer from her? "That's not very consistent."

"Consistency isn't spontaneous."

"Have you ever brought your boyfriend out here?"

"Mat? No."

"Why?"

Her enthusiasm fell away, and she turned again, directing her eyes toward the dark sky. "Where did all the stars go?"

"What?"

"It's so dark out here all of a sudden. Nothing but clouds now."

"Wasn't it already kind of that way?" My attention also shifted toward the sky and to the fierce wind that started fighting with our sails.

We both sat up, feeling the force of the breeze for ourselves.

She squinted with an unfamiliar concern, with an islander's judgement of the weather that I was learning to pick up from locals.

"It's really windy all of a sudden too. Is everything okay?" My core tightened with a knot of panic.

"These clouds," she whispered, searching for the stars, "they're thicker. Do you hear that noise?"

She stood, and I scrambled up, joining her at the helm.

"Hear what? All I can hear are the waves," I said.

The boat rocked from left to right, the sails snapping above us.

She said over the wind, "I hear rain."

The clap of the waves smacking against all sides of the boat sent spray from the ocean in all directions.

"Rain?" Crippling fear wobbled in my voice, too hard to disguise because I had to shout over the wind. "We have to—"

A wave slapped the side of the boat, tilting it, knocking us both down.

My face pressed against the floorboards, and shallow water gushed beneath me, trickling into my mouth. Instant pain swelled beneath my cheek, but I shot up, numb in my limbs, and Georgia was out of sight. I shouted her name, scouting the wet floor for a hint of her curls, and I screamed for her again, but it didn't matter. Every word got lost against the rushing wind.

The boat went dark, deepening in color, and all moonlit shadows had been cut off by the storm.

The sails flapped above me, loud snaps in my ears, a loss of all control.

I slipped again with the tilt of the boat, slamming into the floor, but down there, I could see Georgia tangled in the ropes by the stern. I rushed up to help her, unwrapping her ankle, and freed her.

Water poured down from the mast in heavy drops, pelting me, running straight down the back of my neck.

I pulled Georgia up by her hand, relieved that her ankle was able to bear pressure.

"It's the storm," she said, running past me. "Anita's here."

On smooth waters, the boat took great energy to maneuver, but on waters like these, I couldn't imagine a scenario where we'd make it back alive.

I met Georgia at the helm, desperate to busy my hands and get us back home.

"Let me help you," I shouted, the chaos of the storm sucking away almost all my voice.

"You don't know how."

Another wave collided with the side of the boat, sending a wall of water toppling over the deck, knocking both of us off our feet.

I pulled myself up using the railing on the edge of the deck and reached out to help Georgia up, but she had already scrambled up on her own.

Rain came down in heavy sheets, in fine shards of glass that carved me into jagged-edged ribbons.

Georgia ran to the bow and attempted to raise the sails, but the storm was too strong; she was no match for it. My feet slipped, and I was on the floor again, but I had to get to her. Help her. Make sure she wouldn't fall again. I grabbed the rail once more and made my way to her, the motion of the boat dizzying. I stood behind her to brace her against the railing.

"I think you should keep the sails down. The wind is too strong." But I couldn't tell if she heard me.

She had to yell at me, race the wind with demands to keep us afloat, duel head-on with the competitor.

"Go get the anchor. I can take care of this."

My dwindling faith in her strength weakened with each wave that rolled over us.

"No, you can't," I said.

"We aren't going to go anywhere with the anchor down, Sam. Go."

The wind stopped me in my tracks, and I pushed hard against it. "But what if we drift away?"

"Just *go*." She pulled on the ropes, and I skidded on my heels to the other side of the boat, losing all direction.

"Where is it?" I yelled.

"Behind me." Straining against the storm, her screaming broke into a desperate wail. "Pull, Sam. We have to raise it now."

I spotted the anchor, just in front of my position on the bow. My entire body shook with the boat, but adrenaline forced my tight hold on the reel. I pulled back on the handle, retracting the anchor until it surfaced, its rusty metal breaking through the black water.

Georgia made a noise behind me, and the boat jerked to the left. She'd managed to raise the sail and grant the wind control of the boat while she rested against the rail.

"Is the anchor up?" she shouted, and I sensed a miniscule hint of relief in her voice.

"Almost. It's coming."

The thrust of the boat launched me into the rail, forcing the air in my lungs out of me. I coughed, choking on a mixture of saltwater and rain pouring down from my nose.

Georgia appeared beside me, turning the reel while I strained over the edge and hauled the anchor over. A wave gushed over the boat, washing over my feet, so I turned to wrap my arms around Georgia, but another wave rushed in behind it, invading the boat and separating us in the flood. Water spilled up to my knees. The boat turned, tilting the other way, and I saw Georgia lose her balance, so I ran to her side just as she pulled herself back up.

She plunged through the river of water to navigate the boat and steer us back to shore, but the driving rain poured over us, distorting the scenery.

Her drenched curls hung straight now, sticking to her cheeks. I stayed behind her, grasping hold of the rails, able to catch my breath now that she was safe. Now that we were headed back.

The bow faced Ophelia now, and we made up some ground as the wind worked in our favor to drive us closer to shore than before.

Blowing rain made the lights from the beach difficult to find, appearing as simple yellow dots flickering at an immeasurable distance. *A functioning lighthouse would have been useful right now,* I thought, even though it wouldn't have helped us to overpower the storm's surge. It would've given us hope.

"*Sam,*" Georgia screamed.

But the moment I turned to respond, a wall of water hit me. A concrete sucker punch right in the face.

My back slammed against the railing, and the world went dark. The water swallowed me, and I floated in an abyss of blackness.

I couldn't see anything, couldn't hear. Up and down became unified, directionless. The sea won the race. It had hungered for me all night, and now it savored me.

Saltwater streamed up my nose, sending cool rivers shooting straight to my brain. The pressure from the water tugged at me, hauling me deeper than I had the endurance to fight. I thrashed against the force, stretching toward what I hoped was the surface.

Sight and sound softened until all was silent, obscured by the ocean above me.

My mind landed on Georgia, on her face, on her pleas for help, and my momentum returned. Kicking with a new resolve, I paddled up toward the faintest light.

Help me, Sam. Help me.

Sheer darkness and the sturdy current overpowered me. I needed something. Something to orient me, or to throw my body over, or to stand on once I got to the surface. Anything to stand on.

Anything to stand on.

A rock. I needed a piece of floating driftwood.

Something to stand on. Find something to lean on.

Anything to breathe on top of, to put my feet on.

It's fine, you're fine.

And then the pressure released from the depths of the ocean, and I broke through the surface. The boat appeared through the rain at least thirty feet away, collapsed onto its side, halfway under water, sinking. Silky flickers of light sprinkled through hairline fractures in the wet wood, and I splashed all the way to it.

Somewhere in the waves, Georgia called for me, but it echoed in my head over and over.

Help me, Sam. Help me.

I stopped pushing toward the capsized boat and searched the water around me.

Sam, help me.

I turned in a clumsy, frantic motion, slicing my way through the water to look behind me, screaming her name.

No answer.

Through the torrential rain and the force of the ocean spraying salty mist in my face, I could see nothing. My throat swelled with the rise of a panic attack, and my voice squeezed out of me in a tone I didn't recognize, escaping in a pathetic shriek.

My body contorted in the power of the current, but I made it to the wreckage of the boat and dragged myself up, my body dangling until I pulled myself aboard. The angle of the boat required that I took extra caution as I climbed higher, my arms desperate to cling to anything I could reach to stay above the waves that stirred around me.

The boat was taking on water, tilting farther, sinking downward.

I threw myself toward the wheel and spotted Georgia's still body on the elevated platform of the cabin. Unconscious.

I steadied one foot by wedging it against the railing and forced the other against the mast, then leaned my head down to her chest.

In the midst of the storm, her heart beat against my ear.

I maneuvered one arm under her shoulders while keeping the other secured to the railing and started to lift her into my safe grip.

But another wave struck the side of the boat, engulfing us in a sheath of heavy water that sucked us and the entire boat down with it.

CHAPTER 12

The ocean ripped Georgia from my arms, throwing us deep into the endless pool of water.

My hope for a chance at survival spiraled, and I felt her fall from my grasp.

The weight of the water was a metal plate against my body, coming to rest on top of me, constricting every bit of air out of me. I was propelled downward, lost in a hole, lost in space, weightless, floating into nothingness.

Under the water, everything slowed down.

And then.

Movement.

Noise.

The pounding sound of my own heartbeat.

It felt like a nightmare, the kind where you reach for something but seize nothing, where you're alive but can't move—where your mouth is open, but you're unable to scream.

You're fine. You're fine.

To minimize the sting of the saltwater, I pinched my eyes shut.

Georgia was gone, out of my reach, somewhere around me that I could not see. Water drew into my nose, and I held it there because if I let it out, all the air left in me would be gone. The suction of the boat plummeting into the water pushed me farther down, then something hard crashed into me, bumping into the center of my ribcage. The sudden soreness jerked me out of my daze, and I opened my eyes to an infinity of black enclosing me.

You're not fine.

All at once, adrenaline pulsed through me, throbbing in my veins. I needed air. I yearned to inhale. I pushed off whatever I had bumped into and soared upward. The water pressure freed me, and I surfaced, gulping in salty air to fill my lungs to their capacity. The distant lights on Ophelia had disappeared. The shore was nowhere in sight. But the lights must have been there, somewhere beyond the rain.

The waves made it difficult to see anything farther than a few yards ahead of me, Georgia lost somewhere in them. I screamed her name once more, my voice tired and waterlogged.

Help me, Sam. The echo, back in my head.

I summoned the strength from the echo to swim, searching for her, pulling myself across the waves and through the deafening rain blowing into my face.

The overturned sailboat floated close to me, and I made my way there. It was too slick and steep to climb now, but I kept my hand positioned against its splintered wood to keep my bearings as I scanned the water for her. I swam around the base, screaming her name, drifting with the boat along the current.

Over the waves, lights sparked on the island, so I was almost certain the beach was within swimming distance.

"Can you hear me? Georgia?" My shouts still went unanswered.

Inside the mouth of the ocean, at the lips of its entrance, the teeth of its yawn, I was a soundless speck of flesh.

A bright flash of lightning flashed across the dark sky and allowed me to see the shape of Georgia's crumpled body floating motionless through the surf. Then she was gone. Her name slipped out of me in a broken bellow, a whisper rather than a shout.

I kicked through the current, swimming toward where I last saw her. Lightning flashed again, revealing Georgia on the bumpy surface of the water. I found her facing upward, which gave me hope that she was still alive. But she floated among planks of broken wood and debris, showing no signs of the life I desired to see.

I reached for her, but a wave came from behind and swept me backward, putting Georgia just outside my grasp. Another bore over me, heaving me in the opposite direction. It thrashed me, lifting me to the tip of it, and crashed me right into Georgia's floating body.

I grabbed her arm and slipped down to her wrist, and I pulled the two of us together. Her face had submerged a little since the first time I had spotted her, so I dove underneath the waves and wrapped my free arm around her waist, launching us both toward the surface.

Her limp body was too unsteady on the water to revive her. I put my head on her chest to listen for her heart again.

A beat. Faint, but a beat.

On the shore just ahead, Ophelia's lights winked at me, a beacon of safety to guide me in. I headed in her direction, pulling Georgia along with me.

My left arm flopped over Georgia's midsection, and I let her head rest in the crook of my neck, struggling to stay afloat with her body pushing us both down.

The choppy waves sent us toward the shore, but water slapped down on us in a pattern I started to expect.

Then my feet hit something solid beneath me. Sand. Ground. My arms tingled with relief but still held Georgia in my weak embrace. I stood and carried her to shore, her legs dragging like dead weight when they hit the ground. I couldn't tell where on Ophelia we had washed ashore, but it didn't matter—we were safe, and we were on land.

I laid her body down in the sand, and through her tight shirt, I could still see her heart beating.

I turned away from her and vomited up a fusion of water and bile. Then I wiped my lip and turned back to Georgia.

"Wake up, Georgia. Wake up," I panted.

My vision was still blurred from the rain; I couldn't keep my eyes open long enough to look at her. I blinked, burning my tear ducts.

"Wake up." I patted her cheeks, urging her to move. "Can you hear me? Wake up, wake up."

A bit of movement swept under her closed eyelids.

"Can you hear me?"

I brushed the wet hair from her face and shouted her name once more.

Her breath hiccupped, and her mouth opened, a gurgling sound coming up her throat. She convulsed, coming back to life, coming back to me, rolling her head left and right. I followed her every movement, then brought her face toward me with my finger.

"Georgia?"

Her body tensed, and her shoulders went rigid with her sputtering, hacking up the ocean water from her lungs as she shot up. She grabbed her throat in a desperate clench and gagged on the ejecting liquid dripping from her mouth, coming to a final drip of slime that she swiped away.

Taking in seething breaths, she met my wide eyes, and I became aware of my hands—one still holding on to her abdomen, the other placed on her jawline. I didn't move them.

"Are you okay?"

Her arms swung around my neck and squeezed me in a feeble hug.

"Georgia, what happened?" I said between breaths. "You were unconscious. Are you okay now?"

"I think—" She rubbed the back of her head, slinking away from me. "I think I must've hit my head. That first big wave—"

"Are you okay?"

I met her hands with mine on the back of her skull, trying to assess the damage but felt only a small bump. Then she pulled her hand away, taking mine with hers. Her cold fingers shivered, so I intertwined them with my own, but I was just as frigid as she was.

The rain still pounded, falling heavy over us, so I could only see her face between the bolts of lightning still flashing overhead. Around us, the sand chunked in piles of wet globs while the dunes eroded into cliffs.

"We need to find shelter," I said. "We've got to get out of here."

"You're right."

"But are you okay, Georgia?"

"It's fine, I'm fine. We're safe now. Are you okay?" Her words tumbled fast, and she checked my neck, my ears, my ribs, moving her hands up and down my body as if to make sure this was real.

"Yeah, yeah, I'm okay. We're okay now."

"What happened? How'd we get back?" she said. Panic cracked her voice, and her tough exterior fell away. "Where's the boat?"

She clambered up and ran to the edge of the harsh tide, scouring the waves for the boat she had stolen.

Thunder sounded overhead, the rumble stretching across the inky sky, too loud to speak over. I ran to her and pulled her to me.

"Georgia." I hesitated, deciding how to phrase it. "The boat capsized, and I lost you, but then I found you again, and you were barely breathing, so I swam you back to shore. The boat's gone."

She paused. "How'd you manage that?"

"You," I said without thinking about how it would sound.

Another pause. Nobody except Georgia could silence a moment like this. "You saved me?"

"Well, yeah." In nineteen years, I'd never been a hero.

Her glossy lips begged for me to kiss them. But it was just my imagination playing tricks on me. It had to be.

"Thank you, Sam." Her hand grazed my arm, and a brief second of agonizing hunger pumped through me, all the way to where she was touching me. I grabbed her wrist, ready to draw her to me, to let her collapse into me and surrender to a moment of weakness, a moment in which Mat didn't exist.

But he did. And his girlfriend was standing in front of me.

"Of course," I said. "I'd do it all over again." The impulsive desire I had drained from me, stealing away my energy, so I couldn't fight my nerves any longer. "The boat is gone." I rubbed my eyes, my face. "What are we going to do? It wasn't ours."

She glared at the ocean. "We should get out of here."

"Where are we going to go? Home?" I couldn't stay out all night, and I knew my parents were freaking out, but telling them about tonight and how it all unfolded in a hurricane was off the table.

"You don't want to go home?" she said.

"We stole a boat, Georgia, and it sank in the ocean. I can't tell my parents that." The wind blew the rain sideways at us, so we turned our backs to it, but no matter how I tried to shield myself, the water persisted, slashing my skin.

"Don't tell them," she said. "Just say…say you went swimming with me. Do they know anything about me?"

Her question put me on the spot. I hadn't exactly been sneaking around with her, but I hadn't been completely honest about her either. We weren't a couple, so why did that question make it sound as if we were? If I answered yes, she would know that I had talked about her to my family, but if I answered no, then wouldn't that have made me sound like I didn't want to talk about her to my family?

She reminded me that she had already met my dad a few mornings before while she was working at the diner.

"Right," I said. "Yeah, they know about you."

"Just tell them we went swimming together, and you were out really late and walked me home or something."

Her color fell ashen, opposing her usual summer glow, and I wondered how pale and scared I looked. Fear was something I hadn't expected to see on her face but was a look I wore far too often.

A streak of white lightning blazed across the sky, giving perfect but momentary light to the beach before thunder roared again.

"Okay, okay," I repeated. "Whose boat was that? Georgia, will he know that it was me and you who took it?"

"He'll never know. It belongs to some guy named Johnson. I swear, he won't know anything. Come on, we have to get off the beach. The storm is too dangerous."

***

I did end up walking her home, so it wouldn't be a lie to tell my parents that. Georgia knew the location that we had washed up to be the south beach, but Ophelia was small, and it didn't matter since the island was walkable from end to end. My house was on the north side, and I still had no idea where she lived.

We'd snuck off the beach in a hurry, but once we were on the deserted road, we slowed our pace. The rain hadn't let up, and thunder sounded closer with each rumble, louder now that the ocean wasn't growling in my ears.

We walked side by side, but I let Georgia stay one step ahead, leading the way to her house. We didn't say much, partially because it was difficult to hear each other in the storm, but also because it was too stressful to think of anything useful to say. I wanted to reach out and grab her hand, get nearer to her, and make sure the storm wouldn't steal her away from me again.

Her house was tucked away on the north tip of the island, my side of the island. Branches and tree limbs gathered at the foundation of her house, and a floodlight dangled from one corner. One side of the gutters sloped to the ground, crumpled and twisted from the wind.

We took shelter from the storm under her front porch awning, an escape from the showering rain. A tiny light beside the front door cast eerie shadows on her, flickering, but through the little window on the door, it was dark inside. I doubted anyone was home. Her mom would've waited up for her, or her brother would've left a light on. *Right?*

We turned to face each other.

"Are you sure you're okay?" I said.

My desire came back with an overwhelming urgency to pull her to me, into me, onto me, a need that had lingered since we washed overboard.

"I'm sure. I promise I'm fine," she said, removing her wet hair from her jawline. "Are you?"

"Yeah, I'm okay too. Promise." Water dripped from her clothes, caressing every one of her curves. "Are you going to tell anyone about this?"

"No, and you have to swear—"

"I won't," I said, holding my hand over my heart. "Honest. Promise."

I met her gaze and held it for longer than I intended, falling prey to the spell she cast on me. Her wet shirt made it difficult to avoid sneaking a look at the unintentional curve of her breasts, but I kept my eyes up, and the height of my adrenaline bled through to this moment, and I wanted more than anything to kiss her. To really kiss her, the way they did in the movies. The way a guy is brave enough to forget about all the reasons not to and whisk her into a new life.

Why shouldn't I? I'd just saved her life. She could've died. I could've died. And Mat could definitely end both of our lives if he ever found out about this.

My opportunity to kiss her perched right in front of me, unsteady in the wind, and could've taken flight at any moment.

But still, I waited.

Settling for the next best thing, I threw myself around her in an urgent hug, harder than the one we shared on the beach, and, this time, we didn't part. She wrapped her arms around my neck and squeezed me, burrowing her face into my sandy shirt. For the first time, she seemed to grasp the danger of what we had found our way through, and I relished the way she clung to me, the way she started to relax against me. Her hand slid to the back of my neck, and she ran her fingers through my matted hair.

"Thank you," she said into my damp shirt.

The sky sent a snarling stretch of thunder through the distance.

I gave her a final squeeze and then let her go. She twisted away from me, and her shirt rose just enough over her waist to reveal a glimpse of her bare skin. My eyes latched onto a yellowish-green splotch of discoloration just above her hip bone, but she caught me about to inquire and yanked her shirt down to cover it, her hands lingering there for a moment.

Before she could make an excuse, I said, "Did you get hurt tonight on the boat?"

An injury from the shipwreck would still be black and blue. That bruise—it wasn't fresh. The center bloomed with a yellow knot and spread into a green puddle surrounding the injury, healing.

With a minor gasp, Georgia looked right at me, but she knew better than to tell me it was the accident that caused it. It couldn't have been from last night, either. While that thought made me feel a bit better, I recalled seeing Mat grab her and knew that there was bound to be another mark of a deeper color somewhere else on her body.

Georgia hesitated, tugging at her shirt a little more and then closing her arms to cover herself.

"I had an accident at the diner."

Her practiced nonchalance demonstrated years of painful rehearsal when asked a question about her bruises, but she mirrored a fragile girl who was tired of lying, tired of covering for Mat.

"It's getting better."

I looked down at her wound once more, then back at her drooping face to convince her that I knew the unavoidable truth.

"Thank you," she said. "I'll see you soon. Maybe when the storm is over."

Over.

The night was over, a night I hadn't wanted to be over when we were eating ice cream before the storm, but this ending—this, I was fine with.

"Maybe," I said. "I'll be around."

"Get home safe, Sam. You better hurry."

"Of course."

We didn't say "goodnight," not even "goodbye." She simply walked into her house without looking back, shutting the door behind her, and I exited the porch and entered the hurricane, wondering where on Georgia's flesh Mat had touched her and left his mark.

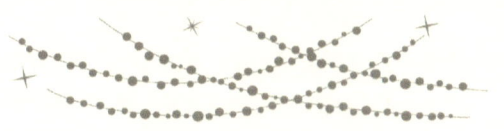

Chapter 13

I opened the front door to see my parents huddled together in the living room. Mom was honed in on the TV while Dad was pressed against the back window. I dragged myself inside and collapsed in a heap on the floor. My saturated clothes weighed on my shaking muscles, which gave out the moment I shut the door behind me.

Mom raced over to me, concern crumpling her face.

"Oh, Sam, where have you been? Are you hurt? We've been so worried. I can't believe you didn't call, but how could you call? You have to get a cell phone once these storms end. Are you okay? Honey, you have to drive Sam to get a cell phone soon."

Her barrage of questions flew at me one after the other. I didn't even know the answers to them. Was I hurt? Was I okay? *Where have you been?*

The lie trapped in my subconscious stuck on the tip of my tongue.

You went swimming with me, Georgia had said.

"I can drive," was all I could muster between breaths, but they didn't hear me.

"Where did you go? You should have known better than to be out in this weather. I can't believe the storm came sooner than they said." She hooked her arm under mine to help me up. She gave it a tight squeeze, and water pooled onto the wood floor as a result.

Dad came over to lay a hand on my back. "These hurricanes can be so sudden, kiddo."

I repressed my guilt long enough to plow through the conversation with them with an urge to blurt out: *I'm a liar, and I like a girl who's trapped.*

"Yeah, I know," I said.

Mom felt my other sleeve, which led to another puddle of sea water ending up at my feet. "At least this storm wasn't as bad as they thought it could've been."

"Yeah, thank goodness it isn't hitting Ophelia directly," Dad said.

They stepped back to assess my condition. Asserting confidence during a lie is the key, so I pulled together my best poker face.

"Do you remember that girl Georgia? The one you met at the diner, Dad."

He crossed his arms and zeroed in on me. "Yeah, yeah, of course."

"I ran into her, and we ended up hanging out for a while. We went swimming until the storm hit and then I walked her home. That's why I'm so wet." I removed my shoes and wrung out the excess water from my socks.

Dad laughed. "Son, it's no surprise you're soaking wet. Look what you just walked through to get here."

My breathing quickened into a wild pant. I avoided his gaze and his hurried look at Mom.

"Yeah, I know. That's what I meant," I said.

I made a show of examining the water still dripping from my clothes, making the puddles below me grow.

"Sorry for the mess, Mom. I think I need to change. Then I'll get this mess cleaned up."

"Honey, don't worry about it. You just get some dry clothes on, and I'll take care of it."

She turned to head upstairs for a towel but stopped by the window when a clap of thunder shook the house. Then she left me alone with Dad.

"So you walked her home. Where does she live?"

I tried to disguise my silence as exhaustion, but I really was considering how much to tell him.

"She's not too far from here. Just up the road, at the tip of the island."

"You get her home safely?" Dad was a sucker for old-fashioned romance. Did valiant heroics fall into that category? Not that I was a valiant hero. I couldn't even kiss her.

"Yeah, she's home. She's not afraid of hurricanes. Not afraid of much, actually."

And it was suddenly one of my favorite things about her, even witnessing her intense fear in the water tonight.

Mom came back and wrapped a towel around me, handing me a dry set of gym shorts and a T-shirt.

"I was so worried about you being out there all alone in this storm," she said. "I don't want you to leave the house again until this is over. Okay, Sammie?"

"Sure," I said. But I couldn't tell my own truths from my own lies. "When will it be over?"

Dad walked to the sofa, relaxing down into the cushions. "Probably by tomorrow evening. These storms usually blow through in less than twenty-four hours."

Mom said, "The weather improves quickly after a hurricane, I think. Read that on the internet."

I patted myself dry with the towel Mom had handed me and peeled off my heavy, wet shirt.

Then Dad said, "You're spending a lot of time with this girl."

Mom perked up at Dad's line of questioning and fired off one of her own. "Yeah, what's her story, Sam?"

"Well, I—I don't even know her last name." It was a weak answer, and one they weren't satisfied to hear. Shouldn't I have known that little detail?

"Her first name is Georgia," I continued. "She lives at the top of the island, and she has a little brother, and she moved here when she was twelve, I think." I couldn't come up with anything nice to say about her mother, so I said nothing. Nothing about Mat either. "She works at the diner in town."

"Have you met her family?" Dad said.

"No."

Mom said, "You should bring her by, Sammie. I would love to meet her."

I busied myself with the towel. "Oh, but we're not—"

She cut in before I could finish. "Well, yeah, but do you like her?"

By accident, I dropped the towel and stared down at it absorbing the puddle at my bare feet. After a sigh, I muttered, "She has a boyfriend." Saying it out loud frustrated me, heated up my jealousy.

"That doesn't mean you can't like her," Dad said.

"Her boyfriend is such a jerk too."

I didn't want to say anything more, but a fusion of anger and pride and secrecy and bravery came spilling out before I could stop it.

"He cheats on her and lies, and he hurts her. I know he does. I've heard bad things about him, so I know he's not a good guy. My friend Logan says the same thing. We just—we care about her, you know? I just want to help her, and I feel like I can't."

Mom's expression softened, and she adopted a more understanding tone. "Then why do you think she stays with him?"

She waited for me to answer, but I couldn't say more without revealing myself as the boat-stealing, breaking-and-entering son that I'd become. My silence seemed to speak volumes to them.

"Do you think she likes you?" Dad's question put me in a head-lock, and I felt like I was under water again, unable to breathe. It was scolding me, poking me in my ribs with its skinny finger, saying, *Well, do you? Do you?*

In my embarrassment, I felt Georgia's head on my chest again at the lighthouse the night of the party, but like my truths and lies, I couldn't decide whether there had been something between us or it had just been my imagination hoping for more.

Georgia.

She tricked me into thinking she was invincible, but, on the inside, she was a weak, scared girl. Still, she took me by the hand and led me to take chances that I'd never been willing to take in West Virginia. Veiled in a code I couldn't crack, she made me wonder how she balanced it all.

"She has a boyfriend," I repeated. It was the only thing I could say without giving away everything clawing in my body to come out.

"Still doesn't mean anything," Dad said, waving me over to the sofa.

I stayed in my pathetic puddle, melting.

Mom offered me a friendly smile. "Keep seeing her, Sam. She won't be able to help herself once she gets to know you better. You know that old saying…oh, babe, what is it?"

She snapped her fingers at Dad.

"'Better to have something?'" Dad tapered off as he tried to remember.

"'Better to have loved and lost than never to have loved at all.'" She clapped her hands.

"Right, that's it. Alfred, Lord Tennyson," Dad said.

But what the magnificent Alfred, Lord Tennyson failed to mention was the part that comes after the losing.

I could relate to Tennyson because the truth was, I lost something every time I saw Georgia. My mind, perhaps. My awareness of anything at all surrounding me. My ability to see past the summer, past her face, past any of her flaws. I hated myself for that; I'd known her for only a few weeks.

"How'd you know that?" I asked.

"English class, son. Can't remember where the quote came from, but it's one that sticks with me after all this time." He winked at me and then at Mom.

"You need to rest, Sammie," she said.

For the moment, the news had stopped reporting on the storm, so Dad flipped off the TV, and he and Mom headed upstairs to try and get some sleep.

Yeah, that old saying. *Is it better, though?*

I needed a distraction. I needed to think of something other than Georgia and my feelings for her. I needed to disturb every settled thought of all that happened at the lighthouse and over the course of the night.

Thinking a shower would clear my head, I heated the water to the hottest level I could stand and tried to scrub off the entirety of tonight. When I finally fell into bed, I couldn't sleep for thinking about Georgia, and, after hours of repositioning, I shot up and snatched the ring she gave me from my nightstand. I held it high above me, wondering if it would've been lost in the sea had she worn it tonight. Staring at it, memorizing it, I saw all of our interactions before the shipwreck. I saw her licking the ice cream cone. I saw her at the window in the lighthouse that first time. Then I saw her bruises. On her waist. Her chest. Her wrist.

I shifted focus to how much I regretted not kissing her. Why did I back out? The opportunity had been there, and it seemed appropriate because, in that moment, Mat didn't exist. If I had made the move to kiss her, would she have tried to stop me?

I set the ring back on my nightstand, and it spun in tiny circles until it finally came to rest.

Then I whispered to myself, "You suck, Sam."

Mat was still her boyfriend, no matter who Georgia had chosen to take on the sailboat. To put her in the position to cheat on him turned me into a horrible person. Just because Mat was a cheater didn't mean she would do the same to him. Didn't mean she *should* do the same.

Where was Mat tonight, anyway? Did he call her only when he wanted sex? Or did he call her each time he wanted to take out his frustrations on something?

I finally drifted off to sleep with my thoughts floating around in my brain like my mind was the ocean, everything jumbled together under the brackish water.

The rain fell in severe showers on the roof, and the wind gusts made the house creak, clapping the shutters open and shut against the windows. A bad dream startled me awake, and I sat up, realizing that my nose was still stinging from the saltwater I had inhaled, and my eyes still burned from a thousand little sand grains that were still stuck there.

In my dreamlike state, the only thing I could hear was gurgling groans coming from the boat as it tipped and sank below the surface. The splash was still resounding in my mind, and the power of the waves sucked me underneath and jarred me awake every time I drifted off. I tried to go back to sleep after each loud reminder, but the darkness of my closed eyes suffocated me. The last time I saw such a defeating gloom, I was under water.

The last thing I remembered was the sound of Georgia's broken scream for me, and I was out.

***

Two days after our sailboat incident, I went to visit her.

Damage from the hurricane tore up our front yard, bringing down tree branches and blowing trash and debris everywhere, so I had spent all of the previous day helping Mom and Dad dig out from the mess. But one whole day without seeing Georgia was enough. Today, I'd find her.

I had yet to hear anything about a stolen sailboat. Maybe no one would ever find out, and maybe, even if they did, we would get off easy. But I was prepared for a police officer to drive up to my house to arrest me. Lucky for me, it would probably have been the same one who stuffed me in his car that night we broke into the lighthouse.

No one ever showed.

Yesterday, the storm had weakened, the only remnants brief showers and a few lingering thunderstorms. The wind was still whirling, turning the island upside down, but the rain was starting to head north, away from us.

Ophelia's weatherman said that Hurricane Anita had made her way to the Georgia and South Carolina coasts, so any remaining storms should be gone by morning.

My body ached from head to toe, and the soreness in my arms caused them to shake when I picked up anything. Taking a deep breath hurt my chafed throat and throbbing lungs, and working in the yard only overused my torn muscles more.

I headed out the front door, pedaling to Georgia's house to check on her. Knowing where she lived made me feel closer to her, if for no other reason than to assure me that I could get to her if she were in danger.

Her mother answered the door, and a puffy cloud of cigarette smoke pushed me back a step. She had high cheeks like her daughter, but her thin skin drooped and hung from her bones, and her dirty-blonde hair was tied back in a saggy ponytail.

"Can I help you?" Her tone suggested that she didn't care whether she could help me.

"Hi," I said, clearing my throat. "Hi, I'm here to see Georgia. Is she home?"

"She's not here right now." That was it. All she gave me.

A boy with sandy blond hair and bright baby blues peeked at me from behind their sofa. Jeffery.

"Well, do you know where she is?"

She covered her mouth to let out a throaty cough, then put her hand back on the knob. "I don't know. Prob'ly with that young man, Mat. Wanna leave her a message?"

Don't you care who she's with?

"No, thanks."

As I stepped off their porch, she called, "Hey, you."

"Yeah?" I spun around.

"Try again later."

She blew another puff of smoke at me and flashed me a yellow smile, then shut the door.

***

Trying twice in one day to find her would've seemed desperate, so I chose to give it up and try again the next day. Meanwhile, I tried to ignore my gut, which told me, *Go back to Mat's house.* To see what kind of pills he had popped the other night. To see if there was evidence of... cheating? Lying? I didn't know. Petty crime, maybe?

It wasn't the sordid details I pined for. It was his intentions. It was Mat's capability of putting Georgia in danger that I wanted to understand.

I parked myself by the dunes on the beach for the day with Ole Red in the sand right beside me. My plan took no time to perfect; I'd wait among the dunes across the street from the gas station for Mat to arrive at work before I started out for his place.

New island. New Sam.

The creak of Mat's brakes squeaked down Main Street before I saw him drive his red car into the gas station parking lot. He sat behind the wheel for the last drag of his cigarette, so I moved closer and huddled underneath a group of palm trees, ignoring the drops of rainwater that fell every so often from their branches. The sand was still damp from the storm, and it piled together in chunks that stuck to my skin.

I waited for at least half an hour, taking mental notes of Mat's actions through the big window while several people filed in and out of the store, pumped gas, and went in empty-handed and left with two cases of beer, box wine, and lottery tickets. Since Hurricane Anita hit the island, Ophelia moved more slowly, accommodating locals instead of the throngs of tourists who'd left for the storm.

Mat took his break as soon as there was an opportunity, and he held his phone to his ear the moment he stepped out the doors. Was it Georgia on the other end of that call? Was it the girl from the Piggly Wiggly parking lot?

He looked around the building and, satisfied that no one else would need his help, he climbed back into the driver's seat. Mat folded himself behind the wheel, too big for his car, smooshing himself into the tight space which, with the seats bent over, was just open enough to fit both himself and a girl in there.

Lighting another cigarette, he rolled down his window. Just then, another car pulled into the lot and parked beside him. From my spot under the palm trees, I could hear Mat's annoyance as he slammed his car door shut and headed back inside.

So I made my move.

Shell Way seemed forgotten, older than the rest of Ophelia somehow; the trees here were leafless, as though they'd been burned by lightning. In the daytime, there were fewer places to hide, less darkness to shield me if I needed it.

I hopped off Ole Red.

Rust streaked down Mat's blue roof, and tree branches hung from his gutters. His house was close to the marsh, a fact that had escaped me the last time I was here, distracted and in the dark. Just when I was surprised Mat's house hadn't flooded, my flip-flop sloshed in a puddle concealed in his unkept, grassy lawn. I shook the water off my foot and continued to the front porch, leaving Red by the base stairs.

Of course I knew the door wouldn't be unlocked, but I tried it anyway. When that didn't work, I left his porch and moved Red with me to the kitchen window. Standing on my toes, I gave the window a push, but it was locked up by two latches, so I tried the back sliding glass door.

Not a budge anywhere.

I muttered to myself and Red, "What is he hiding in there?"

I put my face to the door and looked inside to be certain that no one else was there.

Logan was right; Mat lived alone.

Red and I walked over to the bedroom window, the same one where I had watched as Georgia tried to push Mat away from her. Her distressed voice replayed in my head, every word I'd heard as I bit down on my shirt hem from the other side of the wall—*I don't want to, Mat. Can't we just talk? You can't control me forever.*

I pushed on his bedroom window, and it unleashed a shrill squeak. The potential consequences of pulling myself through this window exploded in my brain: I was about to break into Mat's house and rifle through his medicine cabinet.

I really don't want to go back to the police department.

But... *Georgia.*

Just do it. You'll be fine. Now go.

Once the window was halfway open, it stopped, lodged by years of idle mildew. I measured the size of the opening, trying to decide whether it was worth trying to squeeze myself through.

But I didn't give myself a choice.

Bracing Ole Red against the house, I crawled atop his seat to wrench myself face first through to the other side, but, partway through, I got trapped at my hips.

I reached down as far as I could stretch, hoping to find something to grab on to, but there was nothing. Instead, I lay both hands flat against the inside of the wall and pushed, slinging myself inside and landing on Mat's thin bedroom carpet with a thud.

I froze, listening, waiting to get caught, and, when no one came, I stood and brushed myself off.

The bedroom smelled of dirty sheets, stale beer, and leftover remnants from a week's worth of microwave dinners. His bedding lay in a wrinkled pile, and his pillow had been tossed to the floor, covered with stains that I could only assume were sweat and other bodily fluids. The closet was open, and the doors were hanging loose on their hinges, revealing another mass of dirty laundry.

One of those guys, I thought.

I tried to breathe through my mouth and crept further inside in slow, silent strides.

There was a dragon somewhere nearby, and I was going to be the one to wake it, to slay it. At least for Georgia's sake.

His kitchen smelled of garbage, and a layer of grime blanketed every flat surface in sight. Trying not to disturb his mess, I searched the countertop for his pill bottles, but they were not apparent in the mountains of dishes and trash.

In the living room, I kicked through empty beer cans that cluttered the stained floor and snorted at his filth.

Then, I found it. The tiny orange pill bottle stared up at me from next to the TV, marked Matthew J. Corbin, Ziprasidone. The name of the medicine didn't ring a bell, and I wouldn't remember it long enough to go back home and type it into Google. I removed the lid and peeked inside. There were only about ten pills left in the bottle. Keeping the bottle in my tight hold, I snatched up a pen on top of a wrinkled newspaper in his camouflage recliner, thinking Mat didn't seem like a crossword puzzle kind of guy.

Zipra—what?

I scribbled the name of the prescription on the back of my hand, and the moment I set down the pen, tires screeched outside the door. I dropped the bottle, startled, and it rattled on the carpet, so I darted for Mat's bedroom through the hallway. In my panic, I was louder than I'd hoped to be, but angry screams booming from the front porch masked my hurried escape through his bedroom. At the window, I heard the front door swing open and hit the wall with a loud bang, and people shuffled inside. I scurried out the window headfirst, trying to balance on Red's seat but falling over, bringing him down to the moist dirt with me.

Amid Mat's shouting, a second voice shouted back.

Georgia.

I stayed parked just under the window, my stomach clenched. The front door slammed again, and from down here against the wall, I felt the vibration in my skull. Unsettled dirt from Mat's angry drive home still clouded the air around his car, drifting toward me, prompting me to rise above it and look up.

Overhead, I had left his bedroom window open.

Nothing I can do about it now, I thought. *But I've got to get out from under it.* I couldn't have closed it from down here anyway, so I crossed my fingers that Mat would assume he'd left it up the last time he had gotten drunk.

The sounds of their screaming grew louder as I edged through the shrubs, Red's gears clicking along beside me.

Then Georgia's voice came through the wall below the kitchen window, all the way from the front-door area.

"So what if I got in late? Why do you care? It's not like you were worrying about me being out in the hurricane."

I pressed my ear against the wall, which shook with the vibration of Mat's heavy stomps. "Were you with that guy from the police department?"

Me? Was I the one causing this argument?

"Georgia, tell me the truth," he demanded. "Don't you lie to me."

Without realizing it, I was holding my breath deep in my lungs, waiting to hear the slap of his palm on her face. Just like last time, I reached for my phone in my pocket and came out empty-handed. Phone or no phone, I'd break into his house again in order to save her from Mat if she needed it.

"I'm not. I went swimming late, okay? Back off," she said.

That night I dropped her off at her house, Mat must've been there.

I heard the clatter of her feet moving to another room and traced their noise to the living room, just a wall away. Dragging Red as close to me as he could be, I used his handlebars to help balance me while I stretched up to see through the window and find them in the living room, the same spot where I'd been standing just a few moments ago. They would never have suspected that I had been there, but I did a quick scan to check for any evidence I might have left behind.

"Mat, stop."

She backed away from him, and he rushed toward her and raised his fist. I clutched my ears and sank below the window to avoid seeing the inevitable.

"You disgust me," he said.

I swallowed the urge to vomit into the bushes and forced myself back up to get another look.

Georgia held her hand to her cheek, rubbing it where a red mark was starting to form. From my place under the window, I could feel her hate for him diffusing around the room. Could see it in her eyes. Mat grabbed her shoulder, forced her to face him, and kissed her, hard.

It was better than hitting her, but I imagined either deed presented her with equivalent pain.

Mat pushed her out of sight, and I was met with abrupt silence, the implication that she had quit fighting.

From the window, I saw him plop into the camo recliner and snap his fingers at Georgia, who rested her weight on the kitchen doorway. Still touching her cheek, she walked to the fridge and grabbed him a beer.

For the next few minutes, they didn't speak. Georgia curled onto his sofa, and Mat watched TV in his chair.

I started to sneak away with Ole Red, but my foot caught on a branch leftover from the storm, which sent me sprawling over Red and landing just in front of Mat's car.

Mat's voice shot straight through his thin walls. "Do you hear something outside?"

His footsteps stomped to the kitchen and then through the house. Criminal regret immobilized me.

"Why is this window open? Was somebody in here?"

Georgia stayed quiet.

I got up, my knees wobbling, and sprinted behind Mat's car, pulling Red with me. His chain dragged; I must've yanked it during my fall and unhooked it from his underside.

"I'm stuck," I whispered to myself. "I'm stuck. Okay. Okay, don't panic."

I glanced back at the house and to the open window but didn't see any signs of Mat headed my way. My shaky fingers tried to hook the chain back on, but they kept slipping from the black grease.

"Come on, Sam," I said. "Come on, come on."

"What's going on here?" Mat shouted from the open window. Red's chain slipped to the ground again.

I didn't have time to keep trying. Giving up on the chains, I picked up Red by the bars underneath his seat and ran across the yard and into the woods. Red and I dove behind the trunk of the biggest tree I could find, and I went to work messing with the loose chain again.

"Six years in a bike shop has to pay off sometime," I told myself and finally hooked the chain back into its rightful position.

"If anyone's out there, you better leave now or I'm shooting," Mat yelled, and I took note that he had a gun somewhere in there.

For what seemed like minutes, hours, decades, I stayed hidden behind the tree until I heard the window slam shut, then I spun the pedals around on Red for good measure. I peeked around the tree one last time toward the house. The window was closed.

Pushing Red out of the trees, I sped out of there, clicking him up to eighth gear for a quick escape.

***

Up in my room, I turned on my laptop, disconnected from the entirety of the world except what I had just seen.

Mat had hit Georgia because of me, because we had been together a couple nights ago. But Mat had no proof; he had nothing to go on. There was no way he could have found out about us being together unless someone told him.

What if Georgia told him? Everything about that night was her idea, though. She knew that, at some point, she would face repercussions if Mat had suspected she was out with someone else. Yet she still took the chance.

Get out of her life, something told me. *You're the reason he hurt her today. Leave.*

The ink from Mat's pen had smeared a little on my skin during my frantic ride home.

Leave. Don't make it worse.

I shook away the thoughts because only Mat was responsible for the actions he was taking. Mat was the bad guy, not me. *I think.*

Even though I was quite certain that it had been me that had driven him to do it.

There was no leaving her now, now that Mat knew about me, now that I was stuck on a small island with no escape.

Still able to make out the name on my hand—Ziprasidone—I typed it into the search bar on Google and scanned through the first page of results. Results for side effects, usage, and warnings appeared, so I clicked on the Wikipedia link and read that Ziprasidone treats schizophrenia and bipolar disorder.

Wikipedia kept calling it an "antipsychotic drug."

Strings connected in my mind, intertwining, all making sense now.

What Logan had told me was right after all. Something truly was wrong with Mat.

I continued reading: "Schizophrenia: A mental disorder regarded as behaving abnormally, confused thinking, and false beliefs."

This wasn't Mat's main issue. It was his moods that made him furious, abusive. He must have been on this medication for bipolar disorder. I searched the internet again for more information. "Bipolar Disorder: A mood swing that can last from days up to months causing depression, emotional highs, and extreme manic behavior. Suicidal thoughts can occur."

Extreme manic behavior. The strings in my mind formed a concise web of answers.

I scrolled down. "Patients taking Ziprasidone should limit their alcohol intake, as it can cause impairment in thinking or judgement."

Clicking back on the search bar, I typed "Alcohol and Schizophrenia."

The screen refreshed to show a new list of links about what can happen when alcohol is involved, so I clicked on a link with the most promising title: "How Alcohol Affects Schizophrenia: What You Don't Know."

A few paragraphs down from the introduction by Dr. Kail, the article explained that alcohol can make schizophrenic symptoms worsen, sometimes causing hallucinations.

"Likewise," Dr. Kail wrote, "the use of alcohol will likely be the cause of failure to keep up with a medication regimen."

If I'd checked the date on which Mat's medicine was prescribed, I would've known if he had been taking it consistently. I closed my eyes, hearing him slap her all over again, hearing his screaming at her about who she was with.

The strings—they made a thick rope around my neck.

My mom interrupted my research, calling for me to come downstairs. I logged out of my search, erased the history, and turned off my laptop. Ophelia Island was home to abounding secrets, apparently, and I just added one more.

Downstairs, my parents were watching The Weather Channel again, and I took a seat on the arm of the sofa, listening in on the report.

Another hurricane had formed just off the coast, according to the meteorologist. This one was expected to go one of two ways: up north to the coast of South Carolina or straight for a direct hit on northern Florida.

"This is a fast-moving storm, so we're keeping careful watch and will continue to update the path of Hurricane Boris to predict where it will be making landfall. Stay tuned for more updates," the meteorologist said.

Later that night, we found out that Boris had become a Category 4 storm and was coming right for Ophelia.

That meant several things.

Evacuation for all residents of the island.

Georgia had to get out of here. She would probably evacuate with Mat.

We all had two days to pack up and leave.

And Boris would be devastating.

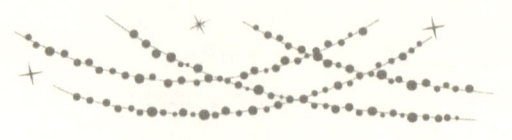

Chapter 14

Day one.

Ole Red and I went for a joy ride around the island, hoping to run into Georgia, still stuck thinking about the way she looked standing in Mat's living room the night before and how she must have felt under the weight of his hands as he held her against his body.

I spent all afternoon with Red, but even after I had ridden by the ice cream shop, the cabana, all of the beach entrances, and even the driveway to the lighthouse, I hadn't found her. My last option was to head to the diner.

I stuffed Ole Red in the bike rack between two other bikes that were locked in place. My lock had gotten lost sometime between ninth grade and the move to Ophelia, so I had to trust that Red would put up a fight if someone tried to steal him.

"Make some friends," I whispered to him before I walked through the double doors of the diner.

Right away, I scanned the dining room for Georgia's familiar ponytail of blonde curls. The older lady who waited on me the last time I was here stood up front with the register and asked me if I was dining alone.

"Yes," I said.

Unamused, she seated me in a booth next to the window. She handed me a menu, but before she could walk away, I said, "Is Georgia working tonight?"

The waitress blinked at me and analyzed my intent, pressing her lips together. "Yeah. Give me a moment."

"No, no, I wasn't asking for her."

But she was already walking away.

I breathed a heavy sigh and put my elbows on the table. When I went to college, I'd have to stop being so nervous, so clumsy, so *idiotic*.

Waiting for Georgia to pop up at my table exhausted me, so I opened the menu and pretended to study it, getting to the omelet section before Georgia made it to my table.

"Hey, stranger. A little bird told me that you were asking for me."

Her flirtatious tone made her seem so…normal. So okay. Like nothing bad had ever happened to her.

I unraveled in my seat as if I hadn't expected to see her alive after last night. She was too unpredictable, too good at hiding any clues I was seeking, for anyone to suspect she had fought with Mat. Perhaps there was more to her, to her relationship with Mat, than what I understood.

"I wasn't asking for you. I just told you I'd see you after the storm, and I'm a man of my word."

Quick save. My attempt at flirting back was rather impressive. At least in my mind.

She took a seat in front of me, grinning. "Ah, I thought you were following me once more."

"I didn't follow you here," I said, "but I did want to make sure you were okay after the other night. You know, the storm. Your head and all."

She rubbed the injury. Her hair was pulled back halfway, held in place by a neon-pink bow.

"It's okay," she said. "I can still feel the bruise, though. Thank you for asking."

"Good. I'm glad you're fine."

"And thank you again, Sam, for what you did." Her sincere stare bore right into me.

What I did? I started reminding myself that she didn't know I had witnessed her latest fight with Mat, but it took a second to register that she was talking about how I had saved her life. The one thing I couldn't do was save her from Mat. I had done nothing but run away.

"Yes, of course," I said, returning her stare.

We gazed at each other, both lost in some other time and place. Georgia looked away first, but it was I who broke the silence.

"There's another big hurricane coming straight for us. Did you hear?"

Her attitude shifted back to that catlike manner that I first noticed at the lighthouse. "Yeah, I did. I heard it's supposed to be a big one."

"Everyone on Ophelia will have to evacuate."

"Where will you go?" she said.

"My parents were able to book a hotel room somewhere on the mainland in Fay County. I'm not sure where." It didn't matter where it was; I just knew I wanted her to follow. "What about you?"

Georgia looked out the window. "I don't know. I haven't really thought about it."

That urgent need to protect her engulfed me again, like we were sinking in water, and I had to catch her hand and swim with her to the surface.

"Are you planning on leaving the island? Georgia, you have to. It's too dangerous to stay."

"Yeah, I'll be fine. I doubt evacuation is really necessary."

"Yes, it is definitely necessary. You have to leave, Georgia. I mean, maybe you could even come with me."

"Oh, I'll be safe wherever I go."

"Okay, but you do have to leave. That's what the news is saying."

Dismissing me, she gave me a flippant "Okay" and stood from the booth. "Now, what can I get you to eat?" She got her pen and pad from her apron pocket, poised to take my order.

I smiled, and a heat wave simmered on my skin. "You're my waitress?" It was a dumb thing to say, but the words just slipped out.

"Today, I am," she said.

I thought for a moment before I continued. "First, I'd like to know your last name."

She hummed a pleasant hum. "It's Gabehart. Yours?" She bit down on her bottom lip, drawing my attention to her mouth.

"Carter," I said, still focused on her lips. "So, what's the best thing on this menu?"

Georgia took her time to answer, looking me up and down. "I have something in mind."

I couldn't summon my own words, or any communication at all, that would convey what I wanted to say to her.

Snapping my attention back to the conversation, she said, "I'll surprise you. How about that?"

"That's…that's fine with me."

Ten minutes later, she was back with a waffle. Her other hand held a cup of vanilla ice cream.

"It might not be the best thing, but it's my favorite," she said with a wink. "A waffle and vanilla ice cream."

"Certainly looks great. Thanks." Before I took a bite, I decided this would be my favorite too.

"My pleasure." She flashed me another sly grin and then left to check on another table.

When I finished, she sat down again and slid my plate away.

"Don't you ever work?" I laughed.

"Sure, if I have to. Does this place look busy to you?"

She was right. Not one person had entered the diner the entire time I'd been there. Just as the thought crossed my mind, the door opened, and two uniformed police officers sauntered through. One of them I recognized from the ride I took in the back of his cruiser. My heart skipped a beat.

"That's the cop that caught us at the lighthouse," I said.

"He's harmless. He was just trying to scare us."

While he accomplished his goal when it came to me, he had been unsuccessful in scaring Georgia.

The officers bellied up to the milkshake counter, and another waitress greeted them and took their order.

"Do you think he remembers us?"

"Of course he remembers us. He probably doesn't see many new faces on an island this size. Tourists don't typically break into the lighthouse, and I guarantee he knew all about your family the minute you crossed the bridge and officially became Ophelia residents," she scoffed back.

"I hope he doesn't see us."

"They're both pretty focused on what to have for dinner. Have you seen these guys? They live on coffee and doughnuts, that's for sure." She laughed.

The diner was quiet enough for me to pick up on their conversation. "You know, the boat that washed up this morning hasn't budged, but that Johnson fellow came by to claim it yesterday." Without looking, I recognized the voice of the bald cop.

Does he mean that *boat?*

"Yeah?" the other one said.

I nudged Georgia under the table, pointing in their direction.

She caught my eye, then sank into her seat, giggling, and I shot her a dirty look to shush her.

"I think it's just gonna have to stay then. Boris is going to wash it away in a few days anyway. It's already destroyed."

I opened my mouth to say something, but Georgia lifted her finger to her lips to shush me this time, so we strained to keep listening.

"I think you're right. Boris is going to do a number on this island. But boy, those other boats Anita got a hold of got pretty messed up too. Now this new storm is coming through. It wasn't just the Johnsons' boat that got smashed up. You hear about the McMillians'?"

The other cop shifted on his stool, causing the keys on his belt to chime together. "I can't imagine what a second hurricane is going to do." Then he changed the subject, wondering how he would meet his quota of parking tickets without any tourists on the island.

Georgia turned to me, unwinding a little. "These guys don't know it was us. Oh my gosh, Sam." Her cheeks flushed with relief, though I hadn't known she was afraid. "They don't know," she said again. "The cops have no idea. They think it was the storm."

The gaping hole in my chest, present since we had left the boat's wreckage behind, was closing again.

"Such idiots," she said. "Sam, we're safe."

I collapsed, dropping my head onto the table in relief. "This is the best day of my life."

"Hey." She leaned across the table. "My shift ends in fifteen minutes. If you wait, I'll show you the top of the lighthouse. We can see all the damage Anita did to the island from there. We can see the beach, maybe even the boat. *If* you're interested."

"Back to the place where they almost arrested us? Again?"

"Consider it a celebratory win against Ophelia police."

"Then, yes." My answer came out quicker than I intended, but not before I remembered the last time we were there. She had given me her ring. Did she even remember that?

"Definitely," I added. "I'll wait for you. I want to."

"Great. See you in fifteen minutes, after I get out of this uniform," she said and walked away.

And every step she took fascinated me.

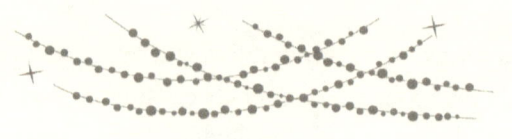

CHAPTER 15

At the tip of the lighthouse, I could see the beach from just above the tree line. We searched the sand for the shipwreck but weren't able to locate it from here. The waves rolled onto shore, crashing with white foam, and, from our vantage point, it was a painting of a faraway paradise.

Georgia locked her gaze on the ocean as if it were calling her and I couldn't hear it. I wanted to feel what she felt. Wanted to see what she saw.

She was impossible to pin. Too *Georgia* to ever give a straight answer, too endless, too beautiful. Her hair was messy, but she made it look good. Her smile was mysterious but never gave a hint to any clues. She was the kind of girl who could play with knives yet never get cut. She was so easy to fall in love with, but I understood why people held her at bay.

Georgia was as far away as the stars and as deep as the ocean. I wanted to grasp both—the stars and the sea—but nobody can hold on to light or water. No other girl could ever compare to Georgia's infinity and depth, and I was never more sure of anything in my life.

"Life is so easy up here." She didn't look away from the ocean; she was fixated on the tides. I realized she was right, that depending on the direction of the wind, just as soon as bad things washed up on the shore, they were picked up and carried right back to the sea.

A symbol of her life. A constant tide of good and bad, routines that she had just come to accept. I wanted to show her that there was more to life than what she knew on Ophelia. But she already knew life was better elsewhere. That was why she wanted to get away. This island wasn't fooling anyone.

"Life is easy everywhere," I said, thinking that wherever she was, it *would* be easy. "It should be, I mean."

"If life were a book, it'd be a tragedy."

If life were a book, huh?

I studied her expression for a long time, searching for whatever it was that gave her such a negative outlook on life and seeing Mat written all over her face. Tragedy was what he was doing to her. Tragedy was him.

My fingers gripped the wooden railing to keep me from wrapping my arms around her, but I released it, knowing, at least for now, I had the strength to deny my urge.

"If life were a book, it wouldn't be that bad," I said. "Come on, it could be a comedy."

The tension in her shoulders began to drop.

"See?" I said, coaxing a grin to appear.

"That's not funny."

"Then why are you laughing?"

"You," she answered. "You're always so—I don't know." Her eyes darted around, bouncing from me back to the ocean. "So content."

What could possibly give her that impression?

"Well, yeah," I said. "I'm not tragic. But neither are you."

"You're right. I know I'm not, but what I mean is tragedy impacts life more than happiness. Tragedy bleeds into everything."

I waited, hoping she would go on.

"It just does."

That's all I was going to get from her.

I looked out at the ocean and tried to come up with something to say, something that could heal her pain. Her suffering.

"Even in a tragedy, there's happiness in the beginning, at least," I said. "I mean, to lose means you had to have something in the first place."

"Exactly."

"If life were a book, it would read like one. Books are everything, all kinds of emotions rolled up in one."

Georgia was burning a hole in me; I could sense the heat from her stare. "Love is the reason we have tragedy," she said.

Being bold was my only option. If life was a tragedy, then I should've made the happy moments count. I took the chance before I lost my nerve.

"Are you afraid of ending things with Mat?"

I took a couple of steps backward, fearing that I had picked too hard at her scab, just waiting to see how much she was going to bleed. But, to some strange degree, I still wanted to know everything about him. About them. I wanted to know what kinds of things he did to her and how he got away with doing them. I wanted to absorb every ounce of their relationship so I could interpret it, analyze it, and maybe, just maybe, make it all better somehow. Save her from Mat and show her a life that she looked forward to living. Even if she didn't let me be her hero, I would settle for less.

If he could be her tragedy, I could be a better one. If she allowed Mat that much, I should have gotten more.

Georgia shot me a look as if to say, "I see what you're doing," and turned away from me. She made her way back to the stairs that led down to the main house, and I followed her to the bottom, still waiting for my answer. On the main floor, she walked backward down the hall and didn't stop until she reached the first doorway.

"You know, I don't think I've ever shown you around," she said, tossing her curls over her shoulder.

One curl that was shorter than the rest bounced beside her eye, always there, never tamed, never able to be pinned back. I loved it.

Taking me by the hand, Georgia led me into a room on the upper level that had pastel wallpaper covering its paneled walls. In the center of the room was a shaggy pink rug with a little white crib sitting on top of it.

"Doesn't look like the people who lived here stayed long after they had a baby," I said, but it came out more like a question.

"The lighthouse keeper died a few months after she was born, so the family moved in with the wife's parents." Georgia knew a lot about this place, convincing me that maybe she felt less alone surrounded by the history of a family who had a sad ending. She wandered around the room, taken by the history of this lighthouse, her fingers trailing along the crib's railing, dragging a layer of dust off in the process. "It's sad. The father died in a hurricane, left a family of three."

"He had another kid?"

"An older daughter."

"Why couldn't the family stay here?"

"No income," she said. "Back then, women didn't have jobs, and lighthouse keepers weren't paid that much to begin with, so the family couldn't afford to stay. Plus, they built a new one on Jacobs, and this one was just forgotten."

I took my time circling the room, noticing the thick layers of settled dust, which gave everything a gray tinge.

But I couldn't focus. Not with Georgia standing here alone with me.

"What a shame that Boris might damage this place," I said.

"This lighthouse has held up pretty well through the years. She's not going anywhere."

I tried to imagine what kind of attachment Georgia felt for this place or what kinds of things she came here to think about. Ophelia Island saw it as a forgotten lighthouse, but maybe, in her world of catastrophe, it was a beacon of light, guiding her through the dark to find safety.

Now that she was comfortable inside her safe house, I was comfortable enough to demand an answer to my tireless question.

"Where are you planning on going during the storm? You have to leave, Georgia. I know I'm new here, and I don't know anything about hurricanes, but everyone on Ophelia is being asked to evacuate."

Georgia gnawed at the inside of her cheek and kicked up the edge of the rug with her flip-flop.

"I'm just going to stay, I think. Mat and I will ride out the storm. Maybe at his place. It's at the top of the island, and he thinks we'll be safe enough."

"Listen, I don't think that's smart. I think—"

"Don't worry about it," she interrupted. "I've been through a million hurricanes. I'll be fine, and this is none of your concern."

"The news is reporting that Boris is going to be really bad, so it's my concern if I don't think you'll be safe."

What did I know? I'd been living on an island for only a few weeks. I was hardly an expert like she was.

"Mat and I will be fine. You should—"

"Mat isn't the one I'm worried about," I said.

She blinked at me, stunned.

I'd finally made her speechless. My body begged me to sweep her out of harm's way and into a sheltering hug.

This is getting out of hand, I told myself. Because I wanted to kiss her.

Neither of us said anything to fill the silence that had settled around us like all the dust in this twilight hue.

Any other time, I would have rushed to apologize for breaking these rules, but truth dominated the lies Mat was feeding her. In this case, I'd never apologize for my honesty.

"Sam, it's not your problem. I'll be safe."

Promise?

I'd offended her, it appeared, but she let it go, pushing past me back into the hallway.

"Shall we carry on with our tour?"

Considering the subject closed, she led me to one more bedroom upstairs, then showed me the master bedroom downstairs. From the doorway, I had a view of a large picture window, overlooking the backyard that got swallowed up by the tall, mossy trees.

Georgia walked straight to the window but said nothing.

Why do you always lose yourself in your daydreams? I wanted to ask.

I met her at the window and pretended to see whatever it was that held her attention there.

"Is this the husband and wife's room?" I cringed. *Husband and wife? So awkward.*

She turned toward me. "Yes."

Having her so close to me, I had to snap out of it before I did something Mat would make me regret.

The seconds hurtled by, burning my skin as they passed.

Leaning in, closing in, the moment swelling around me—someone had to say something.

"Is this the end of the tour?" I whispered as not to disturb the silence.

I looked down into her emerald eyes, then shifted south, locking onto her lips. It was the soft curve of pink. The way they turned up at the edges.

"Do you want to see more?" she asked.

I didn't care about seeing anything else in the lighthouse, and I couldn't think about anything other than how it would feel to kiss her. My conscience screamed at me to slow down, that she wasn't mine, that this might not be what she wanted.

But I wasn't strong enough to stop, even though nothing about it was right.

The small gap between us closed, and I let myself surrender to the kiss I wanted.

I could taste the beach on her, the salt, the water, and I wanted to taste more.

After our night on the sailboat, after our very first night in the lighthouse, the only thing I wanted to do was to protect her, to keep her from harm and whatever was hurting her. Now, at last, she was letting me.

I placed my palms against her cheeks and held the kiss, firm, willing it to translate everything I wanted her to know because God knew I could never say those words.

Before I could take it in, finish drinking until my thirst went away, before my fingers could wrap around her waist, she pushed herself away from me.

I froze, and the ghost of her soft lips lingered on mine. A pool of emotions leaked into the back of my mind. Regret. Fear. Thinking I'd misread the situation, blood rushed through my ears, making everything sound fuzzy. I had just messed everything up for good.

Of course you have.

We didn't look at each other. There was no noise, no movement. The moment was a picture of uncertainty. Framed and nailed to a wall. She was going to leave or never speak to me again or slap my face or some combination of all three that would break through her concrete stillness.

"Sam…"

I waited, ready for whatever she was going to dole out, but before I could even comprehend what was happening, she was kissing me again.

Georgia moved her hands to the back of my neck, and I pulled her as close to me as I could. But I still wanted her closer; I wanted to feel her entire body with my body all at once. I gripped her waist, her skin, and the hem of her shirt fell over my knuckles.

She flinched; I had pressed on her yellow bruise. The very last thing I meant to do was hurt her, even if through a fervent craving I skimmed over an old battle wound.

"I'm sorry," I whispered almost inaudibly.

Returning my hands to the curve of her waist, I moved my lips back to hers.

They were warm and full between mine, hungry for my own, and we kissed until the sun went down.

Georgia pressed against me, and the blaze in my fingers moved up, covering almost her entire back. The three weeks we'd known each other had come to this moment—this starving moment—with a force that jolted me into the present, forgetting all about the anguish I went through to get here.

She pushed me backwards, feet stepping on feet, and I fell onto the edge of the bed, pulling her down with me. Without losing our pace, she tugged up my shirt and slid her hand under it, working her way up my back, and using the other to hold my face to hers. My skin tingled in every place she touched.

We fumbled together in a frantic effort to take my shirt off, tossing it to the floor. My body wasn't as muscular as I wanted it to be, and I didn't have a summer tan like I should have by this point in the summer, but she didn't stop to examine me.

I got nervous about the fact that I was a virgin, and she definitely was not, about being inexperienced when she was quite educated, about wanting to keep going and having no idea what she wanted beyond that.

My arms wrapped around her waist, hugging her closer as she laid me down. I nudged my knee in between her legs and rolled her on top of me, slipping my hands up the back of her shirt, exploring, memorizing every bend and arch of her body. The fear I'd been holding on to since we got to the lighthouse fell away; it wasn't her first time with a guy, so there was no reason to be self-conscious about her feeling all of me or the fact that my body was unable to hide its cravings.

Finding their way back to Georgia's stomach, my fingers trailed upward, crawling up her skin, flushed with heat and passion. I stopped when I got to the edge of her bra.

Do you want to see more? echoed through my mind.

Inching up her back, my palms smoothed out over the clasp.

Just then, she broke away from me, a blast of cool air spilling between us. I reached for her despite the apology I was putting together for kissing her in the first place.

"What is it? Georgia, what's wrong?" I gasped.

"Nothing." She smoothed her wrinkled shirt and pulled her hair back out of her face. "It's nothing." Her loose curl fell, shielding her eyes so I couldn't read them.

That one curl.

In a flash, she was off me and on her feet. "I can't do this. I need to get out of here."

I propped myself up on one elbow, feeling exposed without my shirt. "Georgia, if I—"

"Sorry, Sam. I'm so sorry." She bolted out of the room. "I'll see you later." Then, she was gone. She ran through the hallway and into the living room.

I heard the creak of the front window as she shoved it open. The loud thud as she climbed through it to the porch below. And silence as everything seemed to fall darker than before.

I retrieved my shirt from the floor and sank back down into the pillows, alone, humiliated, wishing I could vanish into thin air, wishing I could think of any scenario that didn't end with Mat murdering me.

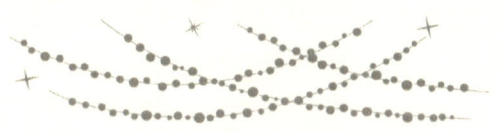

Chapter 16

Day two. Who cared about Boris anyway?

The hurricane was heading straight for Ophelia, barreling at us with full force. Mom and Dad were in panic mode, preparing for the evacuation, and I couldn't do anything except mope while I tossed random items from my bedroom into my overnight bag. All that made the cut were some clean clothing, an extra pair of shoes, and my ratty BMX magazine. I hadn't quite finished unpacking from the move, so there were plenty of empty boxes lying around to repack.

Dad was busy boarding up the windows of our house while Mom was busy storing as much as she could on the second floor. Everything she could manage to lift was moved upstairs into closets and bathrooms, away from windows and safe from potential flooding on the first floor. I should have been helping them both, but Georgia stole every ounce of my energy the second she ran out of the lighthouse and never returned.

Her purple ring lay on my nightstand, white dust beginning to encircle it. I picked it up, held it to the light, blew it off, and, just for the sake of comfort, let it fall down my pinkie finger, the same one that had promised her I wouldn't share her secret. Then I took it off and stashed it in the buttoned pocket of my cargo shorts.

Later that afternoon, I snuck out and took Ole Red to the beach for a moment of peace after the previous night—a night which my parents knew nothing about. I'd driven myself crazy for the past twelve hours.

Stop thinking about this in hours, Sam.

Since last night, it'd been nothing but *One hour since I kissed Georgia. Five hours until daylight. Four hours until I can look for her. One hour until I can leave this house. Just a few more hours until Boris.*

I hadn't slept at all.

The Johnson sailboat had washed up on the beach and was still there, lying on its side. Its sail was tattered and ripped, its bow split open, cracked like an egg having poured out a mess of splintered wood and ropes.

A crowd had gathered around it. Teenagers and families elbowed each other to catch a glimpse of the wreckage that Hurricane Anita was believed to have swallowed and spat out. Muffled chatter revolved around how the sailboat managed to wash ashore here, how the storm brought it all the way to the opposite end of the island.

I made my way to the back of the gathering, seeing a handful of summer breakers, squeezing in the last bit of beach time before Boris.

Catching sight of the sailboat, I was taken right back to the middle of the storm—the overwhelming blackness, the burning saltwater, and, more painful than my stinging senses, the sound of Georgia's erratic screaming.

Help me, Sam.

Yellow tape wrapped all angles of the boat. *Caution, she's dangerous.* Georgia would've looked good in yellow.

Any evidence that the two of us had been on the boat was long gone, washed away with the storm, but I couldn't help but check for anything that could pin the wreck on us. I craned my neck to see over the heads of the other bystanders, but there was no indication that we had been the last two souls on board or anything to suggest how close we had lain as we searched for the stars that dark night.

My relief was interrupted by a heavy slap on my back.

"Hey, dude."

Logan swished his wet hair out of his face, spraying my cheek with water.

"Hey."

"This shipwreck is pretty dang crazy, right? Anita was one insane storm, man."

"Tell me about it." Memories of the past few days flashed through my head.

"That Johnson fella who owns this heap is so pissed right now, I bet," said Logan. "I know I would be."

"Well, nothing he can do to control what happened during the storm." Anxiety clogged my lungs, making it hard to breathe. "If it survived Anita, it would probably get destroyed anyway by Boris."

Logan shrugged and stepped back out of the crowd, and we headed down the beach together.

"Been with that girl from the party lately?" he said.

Last night boomed to the front of my mind. "Yeah, I've seen her around."

"Nice, Sam. She's a wonder. One of the feisty ones back in grade school."

Though I wanted to ask for details, I didn't want to talk about Georgia, and I thought he sensed that because he didn't press.

"Ready for the storm? I'm headed off the island today," he said.

"Yeah, me too. My parents and I are leaving in a little bit to stay in a hotel on the mainland. We're heading out as soon as Dad finishes boarding up the new house."

"Man, I hope it holds up. Boris is supposed to be a monster. I'm headed to my cousin's place in Georgia until it passes. Should come home a couple days after, if the bridge doesn't wash out. The island is going to be wrecked, dude."

The sky was bright despite the overcast cloud cover, and the dead, still, humid air was simply a preview of Boris.

It was weird to hear Logan talk about going to Georgia, a state with both beaches and mountains, a place with the threat of both hurricanes and tornadoes, where people from Florida ran for safety. My Georgia urged the same fear and respect from me.

I started picking the skin around my nails. Georgia's lack of evacuation plans threw me into a state of panic. It was enough to push me to try looking for her one last time.

"Hey, I think I'm going to head out. I have some things to do, but be safe during the storm. I'll see you when we get back," I said.

"Yeah, you too, Sam. We'll hang after the storm."

He jogged away, and I ran to get Ole Red, pedaling hard toward the diner, the only place I had faith in finding Georgia this time of day.

It was already three in the afternoon, and my parents wanted to leave before sunset, so I felt a bit rushed. The island seemed harsh and big when I was trying to find something tender and small.

Cars were lining up in the direction of the bridge, evidence that Ophelia's residents were heeding the storm warnings. That would be me and my parents in the Bronco soon, so I pushed Ole Red to his limit. Sweat dampened my face, but I didn't stop. I needed to find Georgia to try and convince her one last time to leave the island, but what I wanted even more than that was to tell her how I felt, that the night before hadn't been just some kiss in the heat of the moment. I needed her to know that I wasn't Mat, not even close.

I'd find her, beg her to come with me, to escape Ophelia before it was too late, and I'd do it right away, at the diner, before I lost my nerve.

I pushed through the doors at Joe's.

That same older waitress stood there, organizing the menus and ignoring me.

I tapped my foot, but she didn't look up.

"Don't tell me," she said, unphased. "Georgia."

I searched the dining room, filled with the hope that Georgia would jump at the chance to leave Ophelia with me, but didn't see her. In fact, the entire place was empty. I stood on my toes and wiped the sweat from my brow, surveying the dining room, waiting for her to appear, to call out my name.

"Well, she's not here, sweetheart. No one is anymore. We're shuttin' down for the storm." She stuffed the menus back into place under the register.

"Seriously?"

The waitress started wiping the counter but paused when she realized I wasn't going anywhere. She put her hands on her wide hips.

"You look a little, uh…tense."

"This is important," I said. "It's urgent that I find her. Do you know where she is?"

"Not a clue, kid. Didn't come in for her morning shift. That's all I can tell you." Smoothing down her apron, she went back to wiping the counter.

Outside, the gray clouds were followed by a black tide of thick gloom. Boris. The storm blew closer every second I stood here wondering where to find her.

The waitress exhaled a deep puff of annoyance at me. "You need her address? I'm not supposed to but—"

Her address. I didn't need it. I knew exactly where Georgia lived. I'd memorized a path to her house and was already out the door before I called over my shoulder, "Thank you, thank you, thank you."

Ole Red and I sped to her house, weaving through evacuation traffic, and I threw him down halfway up her driveway, running the rest of the way. Red's front wheel was still turning, so I shot him a silent apology. Taking the porch steps two at a time, I realized I hadn't seen any cars parked outside. I peeked through the window in the front door and found no lights on, no people, no life inside. Nervous sweat began to puddle in every crease of my body, and a brick of disappointment crushed my hope of finding her before the storm and bringing her with me to the hotel.

You need to go home, I thought.

No. I needed to find her.

I rang her doorbell, pushing it over and over, going unanswered each time. The dings resonated through the empty house until I finally gave up. I retrieved Ole Red and started toward home, fighting against Boris's Category 4 winds.

It was almost four o'clock, and traffic was at a near standstill when I cut through Main Street. My parents would be eager to leave soon because it was going to be a long and difficult evacuation from Ophelia. But I wouldn't be ready to leave until I knew Georgia was safe, until she knew that I wanted to keep kissing her, until we had talked about why she left me lying there.

I pedaled Red up my drive, about to ask if I could use the car before we left the island, prepared to beg if I had to. To my dismay, my parents were already busy packing it.

Making a quick U-turn, I yelled back to them, "Guys, I'm going out on my bike for a little longer. I'll be back in an hour."

I must have looked desperate and disgusting with sweat because they stood by the porch stairs, cupping their chins and demanding that I stop.

"Why are you so red, son?" Dad asked. "Come sit down. We're just about to leave."

With another reluctant U-turn, I parked Ole Red and took a seat on the front step.

"Yeah, honey," Mom said, "I'm sorry, but you can't go back out now. It's just not safe. We need to get off the island. It's going to start raining any second."

"You guys don't understand. I need to go because the hurricane is coming, and my friend—she's not leaving, and I need to talk to her and tell her about some other stuff so—"

A drizzle of rain began to sprinkle, falling in heavy droplets against the porch roof.

"Please, Dad, I have to find her. She's—"

"Wait, who? Do you mean the girl from the diner?"

"Oh, it's her?" Mom jumped in.

"Yes, yes, it's her, and she's not evacuating, and I need to talk to her. I have to find her. I think she's upset with me, and she definitely cannot stay on this island."

Mom shifted her weight from one leg to the other, pressing her lips together. "I'm sorry, Sam. It's too late now. We can't stay. The traffic is going to be bad enough as it is. If we leave any later, we'll risk not getting off the island ourselves."

She loaded one last box into the trunk and slammed it shut, motioning for me to get in.

"It's okay," she said. "We've already packed your duffle bag, and we'll hook up your bike to the bike rack."

"Why is she staying?" Dad said. "She's had all the time in the world to leave."

"Exactly. I don't know. I don't know. Probably because her stupid boyfriend doesn't want her to go."

I opened the car door, but I didn't get in. The drizzle coming down was still light, hardly noticeable. It wasn't too late.

"What's she upset about?" Mom's empathy failed to soothe me. "Her boyfriend won't let her leave?"

I slammed the car door shut and stumbled back to Red, trying to find the best way to paint the picture and build the courage to defy my parents.

A streak of lightening flashed across the dark sky above our yard's canopy of oak trees, but all I saw in that split second was Georgia's face leaning over mine, her curls brushing my cheeks and then disappearing with the white light.

"She's just—I don't know." My frantic words ran together. "She kind of likes me, and I think she's upset about it, and I want to tell her how I feel before I leave. And I know it's going to be dangerous staying here, so I have to tell her that she has to get off the island and forget about her stupid boyfriend who's only trying to control her."

I hesitated, wondering whether I had made my point.

"She could die if she stays here," I added, thinking, *It might not be the hurricane that does it.*

My parents shared a glance but didn't waiver.

"Sammy," Mom said, "there isn't time. I promise you can take the car as soon as we get home, just as soon as the roads are safe. But it's time to go now. You'll find her after the storm, and you can tell her whatever you want to then, okay?"

It was not okay.

"And as for her boyfriend, well, maybe she'll come to her senses."

***

We tied Ole Red to the back of the Bronco, and then we were off. The island had turned gray and dark, but the only thing I could see from my spot in the back seat was Ophelia, shrinking smaller in the hazy rain as we drove farther away. All my optimism about finding Georgia faded with it.

My stomach acid swirled in my gut. The whole way to the bridge, I kept my eyes peeled, on alert for Georgia, who I expected to find wandering down the street. Thunder boomed overhead, and my fantasy dwindled away to nothing.

"Sunshine all year long," I reminded Mom.

Her stoic face cracked a small smile in the rearview mirror.

"This is just part of island life, Sam. You'll get used to it."

I sulked in my seat.

The interstate was backed up for miles, so it took us almost three hours to get to our hotel, a drive that should have taken less than an hour. By the time we arrived, the rain was pouring, relentless against the hood of the Bronco. Boris was on its way, arriving full force tomorrow night. The dark clouds flashed with vivid streaks of color, lightning dancing across the sky, my only entertainment. I started to track the storm by counting the seconds between each clap of thunder and the next bolt of lightning.

I closed my eyes and put myself back in the lighthouse with Georgia, hoping she was remembering the same thing, and I tried to *feel* her thinking of me, just as I was thinking of her. But it bothered me to recall the way she had deserted me last night. The way she stopped kissing me, pulled away, and left me. Was it out of guilt because she had a boyfriend? She could have told me that, she could have asked me to stop, but she didn't. She'd confused me every waking second after I'd found her being hurt by Mat.

I was none other than the hopeless mouse that got caught in her flirtatious trap.

Maybe she hadn't expected me to take her seriously. Maybe she was friendly and flirtatious with everyone, and I caught her off guard when I kissed her. But she had kissed me back. I could feel her body responding to mine, wrapping around me, letting me have it to myself.

I sat in the car while my mom checked us into a room at the Comfort Inn. It took forever, which I had expected, given that it was fully booked. Our room was on the fourth floor, but I didn't bother waiting for an elevator; a line was forming all the way through the lobby. Our room was basic and small, with two beds too close to each other. The walls were closing in on me already.

I would go insane confined to this room, sick about Georgia.

Mom unloaded sandwiches from the cooler and handed me a bottle of water. I wasn't at all hungry, even though the last time I ate was at breakfast. I tossed the water to the side and popped open a can of soda that I had bought from the machine down the hall.

Mom and Dad felt sorry for me, so they let me choose which bed I wanted for the next couple of nights. I flopped down on the bed closest to the door because I didn't want the lightning flashes to disturb me while I slept. But I was never going to be able to sleep. Even after pulling the curtains from wall to wall, there was still a half inch gap that remained open. Every flash of lightning lit up the entire room.

I lay in bed, restless until five thirty in the morning.

An hour till sunrise.

My parents were heavy sleepers who snored, and I knew they would sleep until around nine o'clock in the morning. I had slept in my clothes and had stashed my shoes just beside my bed, the car keys within reach.

The outer bands of the storm were just beginning to reach Ophelia. Boris was not holding back, but there were still a few hours until the island took on the brunt of its force.

Georgia.

She was out there on that island. Was she tucked in bed at Mat's house? Was she having trouble sleeping? Could she be thinking about me?

Eight o'clock in the morning. Sunrise was two hours ago.

I pictured her kissing Mat goodbye as he slept and throwing on a jacket to hide her bruises. Slipping on her shoes. Grabbing the car keys. Running out into the storm to find me, to do anything to make sure I was okay and tell me she was in love with me.

Just like I was doing.

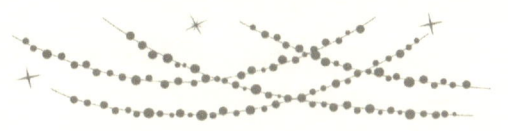

CHAPTER 17

Guys, I'm on my way back to Ophelia, but don't worry. Boris won't hit for a few more hours, so I'll be okay. I took the car, but I promise I will be back long before it gets dangerous to drive. I'm going to find Georgia because it's not safe on the island, and I have to tell her something very important. I'll be back as soon as I can.

I'm sorry. Love you, Sam.

I left the note on the coffee maker and patted my shorts pocket. Her ring, which I'd placed there yesterday, made a faint impression on my hand. It was still there, and it was going back with me to Ophelia as my good luck charm.

Sunrise wasn't anything like a sunrise this morning. It just got a little bit less dark outside.

The interstate back to Ophelia wasn't busy. No one was headed south. No one but me.

Ole Red was having a rough ride back there, strapped to the back of the car. I watched in the rearview mirror as the wind picked him up, and he was wobbling back and forth, banging against the Bronco. Both of his tires spun in endless circles, but he was secure; I'd tightened the straps myself.

Back in fifth grade, I rode Red across town to declare my love for Jennifer Corrine. Now, here he was with me again as I was about to do the same thing with Georgia. Funny how some things never change.

"Close your eyes," Jennifer had told me at recess. The slides were as tall as the clouds back then.

"I am, I am," I'd said.

"Okay, now imagine you're at the most beautiful place in the world."

"Fine, okay."

At the time, I wasn't thinking about paradise on the beach or a candy shop or even my latest *Transformers* car. I had been thinking about Georgia. I just hadn't known it. The girl in my head was a nameless, faceless image, but I was certain now it had been her.

That memory had been long gone, lost in the back of my mind until now. It was Georgia who was responsible for bringing it back.

"What do you see?" asked Jennifer.

"I don't see anything yet."

"You have to tell me what you see."

"I can't see anyplace."

"Tell me what you're seeing."

"I just see a person."

"Who is it?"

Jennifer assumed that I was talking about her. I didn't correct her, but then she hugged me, so I let her go on thinking that, and the next school year, she was my actual girlfriend for a couple weeks.

Georgia—a girl I was afraid to touch, who I had already risked my life for once—I loved her. She was a life I had saved.

Heavy sheets of rain blew onto the car when I reached the bridge to Ophelia, and I gripped the wheel with white knuckles to keep the car on course. I exited the bridge and headed toward Main Street, the trees giving me a bit of cover, acting as a barrier to the blustering wind and rain.

The island was deserted. Downed tree branches were strewn across the road, and I maneuvered around them, forcing me to drive though large puddles that were already starting to flood the empty sidewalks.

Evidence of anyone who had stayed behind had been blown away. Joe's Pancakes was locked up tight, ominous and empty, shut down like the rest of the ghost town Ophelia Island had become. The diner's windows were boarded up, so I was unable to see inside, but still, an image of Georgia roamed through my mind. But there was no time for daydreams now.

I turned on Shell Way and headed straight to Mat's house.

That ugly blue roof came into view. Water streamed off it in heavy rivers.

Mat's car sat parked in the driveway. Doubt made me pause, but the sight of Ole Red in the rearview reminded me why I was here. So, I put the Bronco in park and raced through the rain to the front door, but I kept the engine running in case I needed to make a quick escape.

The skin on my knuckles fractured with each loud bang as I pounded on Mat's door, but I didn't care. Light from the TV flashed through the tiny diamond-shaped window on the door, and a can of beer sat in a ring of condensation on a table beside the recliner. In case Mat was in the bathroom, I waited a minute, trying to shield myself from the blowing rain before I knocked again.

Inside, everything was still. Mat had to be here, and, if he wasn't, Georgia should've been. Why wasn't she coming to the door? If they were in bed, wouldn't they at least try to see who was caught outside in the storm? Biting my lip, hoping I wouldn't find them in bed together, I sloshed through the mud to the bedroom window to get a look inside. The light was off, and Mat's mattress was just the same as it had been the last time. Nothing more than a sloppy mess of covers. It didn't look as if Mat had even slept here. Just as I started to wonder where he had been the past few nights, I remembered the girl he was cheating on Georgia with.

Where would they go without a car in this weather?

I slipped on my way back to the Bronco and soaked my clothes with mud, but I shook it off and climbed into the driver's seat, throwing a spew of muddy droplets in every direction. The wipers couldn't keep up with the pace at which the rain was falling, so I depended on my memory to remind me where to turn.

At the end of his driveway, I stopped. Where was I going to go? She was supposed to be with Mat, and now they were both gone without a car. Were they moving on foot somewhere?

The only other place Georgia could have been was the lighthouse. Just the thought of her taking Mat there made jealousy boil under my skin. The lighthouse was *our* place. Her thinking place. At least that's what she had told me. It was not a place where she would have taken Mat.

But I steered the clunky Bronco toward the lighthouse anyway, swerving to avoid the maze of trash cans, shingles, and tree limbs that littered the street. The beach flew past in a blurry, dark-gray streak, and just as I passed by beach entrance seventeen, I caught sight of something moving—a person marching alongside the swirling waves on the raving shore. I slammed on my brakes, but the water on the road caused me to skid, nearly running the Bronco into a tree.

I looked back at the beach. In the dark and the haze of the wind and rain, the figure had almost disappeared.

But I knew that walk. It was tattooed in my memory from the first time I saw her.

I opened my door, catching it just as a gust of wind blew it back toward my face, but I pressed on, forcing my body forward against the wind and pelting rain until I made it to the beach. Yellow caution tape at the entrance had torn, now in tattered pieces, shredded at the ends where it had been tied to close off the beach.

I ran to the water to reach her, sprinting through the hard sand that had been packed down by the showers.

Each drop of rain felt like a dagger, splitting my flesh wide open, my discomfort made worse by the wind lashing at my open wounds.

I called for her from the splintering boardwalk, but her name evaporated in the roaring storm.

No visible line separated the clouds from the ocean. One lay on top of the other, blending into a black blur, spinning together in darkness.

The ocean in the sky, and the sky in the ocean, and here we were, stuck between them.

Her back was to me when I finally got to her.

"Georgia," I screamed, but she didn't turn around. "What are you doing out here? Are you crazy?"

I placed both hands on her shoulders and forced her to look at me. Georgia's ferocious mane of wet curls spun to me against the wind's will, smacking me right in the face, and another strong gust pushed us against each other. I wrapped one arm around her, determined to help her get off the beach, but she fought against me.

She paused in confusion, brushing my hands away from her.

"Following me again?" Her sharp-edged anger cut me to the bone.

"What's going on with you? Georgia, you need to get off the island." I had to shout just so she would hear me, but it didn't matter. Nothing mattered except getting her off this island, and screaming, I realized, was the only way to communicate with her. To really, truly get her to listen. "Haven't you seen the news? Take a look around."

Detached from the weather around us, she became her own storm of emotions. "Everything is fine." Then she lowered her voice until I could hardly hear her. "I'm staying with Mat."

"Mat won't keep you safe."

"And you will?"

"Yes, I swear I will if you'll just leave the island with me. Georgia, you're risking your safety—your life—just being here. Why would you do that for him?"

"Sam, I'll be fine." It was a blatant lie, and she knew it. "What are you even doing here? You're not supposed to be on the island. I thought you left."

"I did. But I came back. And I couldn't find you at Mat's house where you said you'd be."

"Why'd you come back?" I wasn't sure she was ready to hear my answer.

"You know why. Georgia—"

A wave crashed at our feet, exploding like a cannon, and, as an instinct, I turned her toward shore, shielding her with my body. Water splashed up to our waists, and we both lost our footing, so I grabbed her arm to help steady her in the rumbling surf. Waves bit at our legs, tugging at our bodies, begging us to venture deeper out to sea. The ocean wanted us.

"Come back to the mainland with me, Georgia. This isn't safe."

"You can't take me with you, Sam." She jerked her arm back, pulling it out of my grip. "I'm staying here."

God, I wanted to rip my hair out of my scalp, pick her up, carry her to my car, make her listen. "Mat doesn't deserve you, Georgia. Leave him. Leave him here and come with me."

She looked at me hard but said nothing.

"He lies to you. Georgia, I saw him with someone else. Mat doesn't love you. He couldn't. He cheats on you."

"I cheated on *him*. I was with you, remember?" Her voice kept breaking with obvious pain. Something in the way the words toppled out felt raw and true, like maybe this was the first time she was admitting to herself that she had any kind of feelings for me. That she was relieved to have been with me on that bed instead of Mat.

"He hurts you," I said. "I've seen it. Georgia, I've seen everything. I know what he does to you, and I can't stand by and watch. I know how mad he gets, and I've seen him hit you, and—"

My chest caved. We stood there in the rain, attacked by the storm, defeated by things much bigger than we were.

Though her face was wet from the hurricane, I could tell her eyes filled with tears.

"Just leave, Sam," she said. "We'll talk after the storm. I promise."

Promise.

Promises break.

"Talk to me now, Georgia. I need to know. Why did you run out and leave me last night at the lighthouse? Was it guilt for being there with me? Did you even care about me at all? Because that's why I'm here, Georgia, because I care about you."

The storm raged on around us, pressing into me.

She spun on her heels. "Just leave, Sam. I can take care of myself."

"No." I trailed right behind her. "I'm not leaving again without you. I'm not leaving you the way—"

The way you left me last night. I wanted to say it but couldn't.

I knew the exact reason she had left me. Georgia had run from the lighthouse because she was afraid that I would become one more in the line of people who left her. She left me because her father left her mother, and her mother didn't care about her, and Mat mistreated her, and everyone in her life was ruthless.

"Just go." She began to run, so I followed her.

The wind hurled itself into me, but I charged forward after her. I grabbed her by her bruised wrist and spun her around, so close that I knew she could hear me this time. The pale color of her face was gone. She was no longer lifeless, but alive—her eyes, her nose, her lips, all full of color again.

"Listen to me."

I latched on to her waist, pulling her to me. The wind beat down against my face, tossing Georgia's curls around my neck like a lasso. I wanted to kiss her, but it wasn't the time for that yet. Not until I made her understand.

"I came back to make sure you were safe, and I didn't do that for nothing. I'm not letting you get hurt; you've been too hurt for too long, and I'm fixing that. Today. The first time I saw you, you wore your hair down like this, you had on a pink tank top, and I hadn't seen you smile yet, but I knew it was going to be beautiful. Georgia, you take my breath away." I meant it. I meant all of it, and I didn't know why I mentioned those small details, but it felt right.

"And I know how screwed up things must be for you. I know how screwed up Mat's brain is and...please, just come back with me. I can't let you stay on Ophelia. I won't."

Water spilled from our faces, puddling between our chests.

"And I did follow you that day," I continued.

Her facial expression remained hidden behind a layer of ocean and storm and wind, but even through all of that, she was still a flame. If she went away, I would be left with a body covered in burns.

For a moment, I thought she was going to give me everything I wanted. Let me sweep her off her feet. Let me take her home with me. But the moment my words registered with her, she stiffened with shock because I remembered all of that, because I even *knew* some of it.

"To be honest, I did follow you," I admitted again. "I was wondering if you were okay. And I don't know everything about you, Georgia. I've only known you for a few weeks, but I know I love you. I know I'm in love with you."

She held my gaze. I waited for her to try to escape my hold on her just so I could reel her back to me again, but my silence allowed my words to sink in. I wasn't letting her go in this storm.

Georgia was crying now, a soundless cry, and I couldn't tell whether the drops on her cheeks were rain or tears, but I knew she was crying. Crumbling.

"No, you don't," she said.

"Yes, I do."

"You don't even know me."

"Yes—"

"Why do you keep saying that?" She wriggled out of my grip and started to back away.

I'm not the bad guy, I wanted to scream after her.

"Why are you so convinced that I don't love you?"

"I love someone else." Though her words penetrated right through my heart, I knew it was an excuse. Georgia didn't love him. She knew that. I knew that.

"So?" I stepped toward her again. "That doesn't mean I can't love you."

"How can you love someone who doesn't love you back, Sam?" The question was more for her than for me.

"You would know; you say you love Mat."

She looked away. Georgia had no idea how to be honest with herself, how to see the truth for what it was, without all the lies tainting it.

Betrayal. Truth. She embraced them as one—one single essence—because the truth felt like a lie to her.

"You don't love him." I shook my head and nudged her face back toward mine. "Georgia, you don't love him."

The wind pushed her against me, but she resisted and kept me at arm's distance this time.

"I just want it to be over," she said. "With him. With everything."

She sounded so small, so taken over. We were both just ships in a tsunami. The chaos of the storm made it difficult to hear her, but I understood her perfectly. She wanted it to be over, and so did I. She could end it if she would only trust me. I wanted to cry for her because she was being torn apart piece by piece, dissolving in the murky water, and I wanted to gather her up in my arms and place the pieces of her back together.

"I love you, Georgia. Why is that so hard for you to believe?"

She bit her bottom lip, and I could see a growing sob building in her lungs.

"I don't know what love is." A distinct tear split through the rainwater on her cheek. "I don't know how to love you."

"It's so easy."

With that, Georgia let me pick up her pieces. I tipped her chin toward mine and cupped her neck in my hands, then her cheeks, and I kissed her. As I tightened my grip on her, she grimaced. I must have rubbed another bruise.

I'm sorry, I mouthed. *I won't hurt you. I'll never hurt you.* Then I started saying it out loud, and she stood on her toes and wrapped her arms around my neck, collapsing against my body.

"Take me to the lighthouse," she said, her face buried in my soaked shirt.

"What about Mat's?" I thought maybe she would explain where he was and why he wasn't at home to begin with, but she remained silent.

"I just want to go to the lighthouse tonight." Her thinking place. I couldn't say no.

"Why didn't you go there first?"

She moved her foot in a tiny circle while she thought about how to answer. Her focus shifted to the mark it had left in the wet sand. "I don't know."

"Does Mat know about this?"

Her green eyes darted once more to the ocean.

"Is he home? I went there to find you, but no one answered the door. I saw his car parked in the driveway."

Nestling into the crook of my shoulder, she pressed farther into my drenched shirt. "He's..." If she said anything more, I wasn't able to hear.

"Where? What?" I asked again.

"He's passed out."

When I'd peeked through his window, Mat wasn't on his bed or in his chair. "But he wasn't in his room."

"He's on the floor. Let's go," she said. "Don't worry about Mat. He's fine. If I don't care, then you shouldn't."

The lighthouse was the safest place for us to be during the storm. Georgia had said that this lighthouse had survived many hurricanes already, and the intensity of the wind and rain had picked up, so I didn't argue about going there instead of insisting that we leave Ophelia in the height of the storm. I thought of my parents and wished that there were some way I could reach them. They must have found my note, and I was sure they were worried sick. There would be some kind of punishment coming my way, but I couldn't do anything about it at this point. I did exactly what I needed to do, and any punishment—except for losing Georgia—would be worth it.

Georgia propped her elbow against the door and stared out the window for the entire ride, clenching her seatbelt every time we had to swerve. Time warped with our distress, and it took us twice as long as it should have to arrive at the lighthouse thanks to all the storm damage. I hated to think about how much more damage was still to come.

A hundred questions about Mat whirled together in my brain, ready to come out, but the words just floated in a misspelled puddle on my tongue. Boris was the only thing that filled the silence.

I parked the Bronco in front of the porch stairs at the lighthouse. We counted to three and made a run for the window, and I helped Georgia in first, then launched myself through, pulling hard to close it behind us. Rain pounded against the roof, but the storm became muffled through the walls of the living room.

Georgia and I stood there in the lighthouse, breathing. Dripping. She shivered, but there was no way to dry off. The commotion of getting here had settled, and there was a peaceful quiet between us, which made the moment seem almost cozy. In my fantasy, Georgia and I should have had a fire crackling in the fireplace. In our reality, water puddled around our feet, and the darkness pushed us close together.

She made no movement when she said, "I'm going to stay here."

I traced her face with four fingers. "Are you safe here?"

"Yes," she said, taking my elbows in her small hands. "I will be."

"What if Mat wakes up? Won't he come looking for you?"

Despite the present dangers of the weather, Mat still seemed more of a threat than Boris.

"I don't want to leave you," I said. "I'm not leaving you."

"Mat won't come back."

Lightning struck somewhere close, and the whole room lit up in a bleached flash. In the briefest of moments, I could see the exhausted purple rings under her eyes. And I could feel the purple ring in my pocket.

"How do you know he won't?"

"When Mat drinks enough, he's out for an entire day." That seemed believable, but her statement was weak, and I didn't want to question her honesty with me. Georgia was a good liar, but I buried my suspicion and decided to trust her.

"I'll be safe here," she said again.

"Let me stay with you."

"Sam, then your parents will freak out and—"

"And that doesn't matter. Just let me be with you."

"Do you trust what I'm telling you, Sam?" she said.

I closed my eyes and nodded.

"Then leave me, and trust that I'll be okay."

Waiting for her to expand on how she could ever be okay in this storm, even if she was protected by the strong lighthouse, I knew she'd say as little as possible.

"Is there any way to contact you? I want to be positive you're okay," I said.

"Of course, I'm going to be okay." She forced a fake smile. "You don't need to call. I'll see you when this blows over."

Over.

"I think you'll be safe here. I'm just worried about you. I'd like to be able to find you," I said.

"But you don't need to find me."

Her stubbornness channeled my inner Logan, making me want to curse, but I was able to regain control of my words and my emotions.

"Georgia, I'm so sorry for everything—"

"Sam, you didn't do anything bad." She paused, then out of nowhere, she thanked me.

"You're welcome," I said. "I'll be back soon. For you."

We shared a cold, wet hug, but the next booming crash of thunder was my cue to go. Our wet clothes clung to our bodies and stuck together as we tried to pull apart. It reminded me of our first hug on her front porch the night of the sailing accident. When I wanted to kiss her but didn't. With the storm swirling outside, I chose to be brave.

Our lips came together in a frenzy of uncontrolled exhilaration. "I want to stay," I whispered to her.

"Go back to your family," she said, kissing me again. "They would worry. I'll be perfectly safe here until you get back."

She'll be safe, she'll be safe, I kept repeating. "Are you sure?"

"Yes."

"Why didn't you leave Ophelia with your mom and brother?"

Our gaze shattered, and she grew distant again. "I didn't want to shack up with my mom's boyfriend through the storm. Jeffery likes him. He's too young to know any better."

"When I get back," I said, "I'll come. I'll be back tomorrow morning. It's just one night in the hotel, and I'll be back. I'll come back for you."

"I want you to come," she said, admitting it for the first time. "If you can catch me." She grinned, the same crooked smile that did me in from the start.

"I'll follow you." I flashed her a weak smile.

"Bye, Sam. Be safe out there."

Love while you still can. I wanted to tell her one more time that I was in love with her, but I didn't want to be a cliché, throwing those words around like a cheap phrase.

Instead, I grabbed her face and kissed her, better than the first time, deeper than we had experienced before. I pulled back just before I got carried away and planted one more kiss on the tip of her nose.

"Bye, Georgia. I'll be back soon," I said, blowing her one final kiss as I climbed through the window.

I'll come find you.

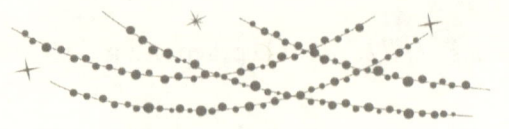

CHAPTER 18

B oris was gone.

It had flooded the marina, washed away boats, and its winds had raised the roof off most of the houses on Ophelia. It had also broken the windows at the gas station where Mat worked, even though they had been boarded up with haphazard plywood. Mobile homes were toppled on their sides or simply gone altogether. Most of the shop owners on Main Street had been lucky, but a few would have to deal with the broken glass that now littered the sidewalk. I wondered how our house had fared in the storm, but, like the lighthouse, it had been there for years. The side roads were still flooded, so we had to take the long way around to get home.

I shrank in the back seat, absorbing the damage, wondering how Georgia survived unharmed. *If* she survived unharmed.

When I'd gotten back to the hotel, my parents had been furious. I understood why. I apologized and swore I would never do something that stupid ever again. After they had given me both a lecture and a guilt trip, they asked if I had been able to find Georgia. And they seemed happy for me when they heard that my mission to tell her how I felt had been successful. They also knew that I planned on heading straight to the lighthouse the moment we parked the car at home.

They wanted to argue but didn't. I think it was because they knew their arguments would fall on deaf ears. They had been most angry about the fact that I'd risked my safety, but they seemed to understand my urgency after I explained how I'd found her strolling along the beach. I also told them that Mat wasn't trying to find her and that he didn't answer his door.

Devastating scenes met us at every turn as we drove across Ophelia early this morning. While the day before had blanketed the island in a black downpour, the sun was shining once more, and everything was colorful again. The sky wasn't in the ocean anymore.

Our home still stood under the soggy trees, and the roof was still intact, but several of the boards Dad had nailed up to protect the windows were either hanging down or missing. The greenery around the house drooped left and right in a temporary windblown wilt, though a few trees had fallen. One big tree had taken out the driveway, its trunk uprooted, its exposed root system caked in heavy balls of muck.

I'd expected it to be worse, but if my house was still standing, the lighthouse would be too. My parents were relieved to discover we still had power, as did the rest of our end of the island, but I wouldn't feel an ounce of relief until I laid my eyes on Georgia.

To my dismay, Red would have to sit out because the sidewalks were still too muddy and wet for a bicycle. I would have to drive there instead. So I tucked Red in the garage and threw our baggage in there too, resolving to help my parents clean up the mess when I returned.

I peeled out of our road, spraying mud everywhere, and sped up when I reached the driveway to the lighthouse. It was still standing, bold and stately, but, right away, I saw remnants of a shattered window on the lawn and a chunk of railing that had broken off from the tower above. Anxiety pulsed through me.

I raced to the window and banged on the heavy wooden door, calling for her on my way to the window. Shoving open the front window, I climbed inside to the living room.

"Georgia?" I called but got nothing in return.

The dining room was empty, and so was the den. I went to the bedroom where we had shared our first kiss, expecting to find her asleep on the bed. But it was empty, still wrinkled from where we had almost taken things too far, a crumpled reminder of our brief moment there.

Her name came off my lips with more insistence now, but I received no response.

Upstairs, the two other bedrooms were neat, undisturbed, untouched. Empty. With little motivation, I climbed the spiral staircase to the top of the tower, but she wasn't there either.

Before I lost all hope, I told myself she must have gone back home. I ran down the tower steps and jumped back in the Bronco. When I got to her house, I was greeted with a wave by a man who was clearing fallen tree branches from the front yard. I stepped out of the car.

"Excuse me?"

The man threw another large branch to the top of his growing pile. He stopped what he was doing and turned to me. His face was scruffy with a five o'clock shadow, and unwashed hair covered his forehead. "Yeah?"

"Um, I just came by to see if Georgia was here."

He turned back to his brush pile, hesitating for a moment. "Georgia?"

Her name didn't register with him. *Georgia who?* This must have been her mother's boyfriend. The man her brother Jeffery loved.

"Nope," he said, coughing to hide his blunder. "No, she's not been around here for a few days that I know of."

"Do you know where she might be?"

He threw his hands in the air and shrugged before going back to the tree limbs. "I don't know where she is. What's your business with her?"

Why did he care? "She's my friend, and I want to make sure she's made it through the storm okay. You were aware that she stayed on the island, right?"

"Did she? I told her momma that girl was crazy." He shook his head. The guy had no idea she had stayed on Ophelia.

"Thanks anyway," I said and left him to his wood pile.

If Georgia wasn't at the lighthouse and she wasn't at her own house, she would have to be at Mat Corbin's house. I reasoned that he had probably come after her when he woke up from his drunken state and forced her to come back to his house with him. Her skin, I imagined, would be peppered with new hues of blue and purple.

Mat's car was still in the same spot it had been yesterday. In fact, it looked like it hadn't moved. I parked the Bronco in front of his house and kept the engine running like I had the last time I was here.

The boards on Mat's front porch had started to bow, and the awning had blown away. Water from the porch was seeping inside his house from underneath the door. His living room carpet had no doubt flooded. Its foul smell wafted toward me.

I knocked on the door, giving Mat plenty of time to answer before I started pounding. Any second, the door would swing open, and I would have to face Mat and tell him I have to see Georgia. But no one answered.

I peeked through the window. The TV flashed a wrestling match, though Mat was not sitting in his recliner. A can of beer sat on the table beside it. The same beer from yesterday.

I ran to the side of Mat's house, avoiding thick, leaf-covered puddles, and looked through his bedroom window. His mattress was sloppy with the same tangled covers that I'd seen the last time I peered through his window.

Nothing from Mat's house had changed at all since I was here last. Since I found Georgia out on the beach and she told me he was in there, passed out on the floor.

***

"She's nowhere," I wailed when I got back to the house. "She's not at the lighthouse where I left her, not at her house, and she's not at her boyfriend's house either."

I wished I'd run into Logan on my way home to complain to him instead of my parents, since he knew a little more about Georgia and Mat.

If Mat had forced Georgia to go somewhere after the storm, she wouldn't have had time to leave me any kind of note. But Mat's car was still in his driveway. Did Georgia have a car to her name? I didn't know. The first night I snooped around Mat's house, she had driven up in a black car. There had been a black car sitting in the driveway at her mother's house earlier.

Mom was in the kitchen chopping fresh veggies for our dinner salad while Dad set the table.

"Well, did she mention she might have to leave Ophelia for some reason?" Mom asked.

Dad had removed the remaining boards from our house, and Mom had already unpacked. They'd already called and scheduled a tree-removal service to come take care of the oak that fell in the yard too. I felt a little guilty for being out all day, searching yet again for the elusive Georgia. I had circled the island and retraced my steps, which meant that I'd also escaped my family's second move-in.

"No, nothing, not a word. I mean, she promised me she'd stay at the lighthouse where she would be safe. She asked me to take her there, even. Why would she leave?"

"Perhaps she left with her boyfriend." Mom tried to keep her tone even, though I wished she would have expressed my level of concern.

"She wouldn't leave with him. She doesn't even like him."

Mom took a break from her chopping. "What do you mean by that?"

"Yeah, I already told you. He's not a good guy," I said for the millionth time. Mom nodded with a sympathetic pout.

"You think she'll show up?" she asked.

I concentrated on rubbing my fingers across the countertop to keep myself grounded.

"It's possible. I just want to know why she left. Also—this is another weird thing that happened yesterday—I first went to her boyfriend's house to find her, right? And he didn't answer the door or anything, but his car was there, and he had a beer on the table. She was at the beach, out in the storm when I found her because—well, I don't know why—and so, if she wasn't with him, and he was home, why wouldn't he answer the door? For all he knew, it was her wanting in. And, I mean, she did say that he was passed out drunk, but—"

"They could've had a fight or something," Mom said.

"He wasn't there," I said. "At least I don't think he was. You can basically see right through his house from his windows, and I didn't see him on the floor. What if he decided to get off the island at the last minute, and Georgia decided that she wanted to stay?"

"Why would she want to stay here all alone? I just don't know if that makes sense, honey."

"Because I already know that she didn't want to go with her mother, and she might not have wanted to go with Mat either."

"Mat?"

"The boyfriend."

"Oh."

"Even if he were passed out last night, that doesn't explain why he wouldn't be answering the door today," I said. "And, also, I don't think she would've gone back to him today."

I left it at that, though I wanted to tell my mom everything. But, if I did, my parents might've decided to get the police involved, especially if they thought Mat was missing. I didn't want to get Georgia involved with the police in any way. Not until that was my last resort. Georgia could've skipped town and not told me. But that was impossible.

Possible.

I shushed the voice in my head.

Anything was possible at this point.

Dad joined us in the kitchen. He took off his fisherman's hat and wiped his head. "Was the lighthouse damaged? I don't want to be negative about this, but…" He brought his hat to his chest, holding it there. "Do you think maybe she was…that the hurricane…"

Mom froze mid-chop, and Dad glanced at her, sharing a moment of unease.

"No, no, that's not possible," I said. "No way. The lighthouse survived the storm."

Georgia hadn't slept in the bed that night, and she wouldn't have slept on the couch right next to the windows. Was it possible that she had been injured by the storm from inside?

"Son, I really wish there were something we could do to help," Dad said.

But all I could hear was Georgia's screams becoming a breathy whisper in my ear: *Help me, Sam.*

"Have you tried the place she works? That diner?"

"Yes. I went by there earlier, but the diner was closed today."

I had driven by Joe's Pancakes a thousand times, hoping to see the light on inside, but, each time I passed, the darkness behind those windows disappointed me. "That'll be the first place I check tomorrow morning."

After a quick dinner, I sat on my bed with my laptop open and pulled up an ariel view of Ophelia Island on Google Maps. It was a slender slice of land that Boris could've sucked up through the eye of its hurricane. We were outlined by a thick border of marshland followed by white sand that disappeared in the green trees and residential lawns in the center of the island.

I found Main Street and traced the road all the way past Joe's to the path that led to the lighthouse. Surrounding the lighthouse were tall oaks. I moved my cursor to the marsh a quarter mile behind them and came across a web of streams that wove through the brown swamps.

The storm could have carried her from the lighthouse to the deserted marshland in a flood of water that she couldn't escape. She could have stepped outside for the briefest of moments and been blown away by the ruthless breath of Boris. In that marsh right now, her body could've been ripped and bruised by a force stronger than Mat, caught in the swampy grass, bent and broken.

My salad inched up the back of my throat. She wasn't dead. Couldn't be.

I closed my laptop and tried to forget that I had ever speculated Georgia was a corpse.

In my shorts pocket, her ring pressed into my outer thigh, so I picked it out and set it on my nightstand, bending down level to look at it.

"I'll find you," I murmured. "I'll find you."

Dead or alive.

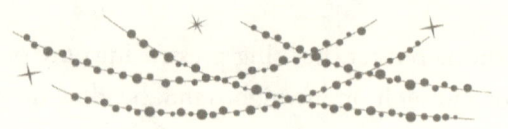

CHAPTER 19

I barged into the dining room of Joe's Pancakes and was surprised to find that all the tables were empty. Movement shuffled through the kitchen, but I didn't spot Georgia.

I stood, waiting in a puddle of my own sweat dripping beside the Please Wait to Be Seated sign. Music played from the speakers above me, mocking my impatience.

Georgia wasn't here. I could already feel it in the hollowness of the diner, even though everyone had returned to the island yesterday and all last night. But I needed to know when she worked again just to put my mind at ease. That is, *if* she worked again. I recalled that Georgia hadn't come in to work on the morning of the hurricane. Maybe she got fired.

Of course it was the older waitress who discovered me at the front doors.

"Back so soon." She restacked the menus, popping them down in their designated bin.

"Yeah, is—"

"Nope. Haven't seen her since before Boris."

"Do you know where she is? I mean, I've been looking for her because she's disappeared." It stung to say it out loud. "So has her, um, boyfriend."

The woman stared at me, scrutiny blazing across the whites of her eyes. She shoved her hands inside her apron pockets, fed up—with what, I couldn't be certain.

162

"Why're you out lookin' for that boy?"

Her foot tapped the ground, her hostile tone catching me off guard.

"Her boyfriend?" I said. "Look, I just need to find Georgia. I thought if I found him, I might find her too."

She made a low humming noise behind her lips and messed with the buttons on the cash register to avoid looking at me. "That boy is no good for her."

An instant connection linked us; this woman knew everything I did. She had to have seen Georgia's bruises, and she might have seen her scars too.

Her black eyes settled on my face, waiting for me to say something.

"Well, have you seen him?" I said. I thought of Georgia's plea for release the night she gave me her ring, and her insistence that she wanted the relationship with Mat to be over.

"I couldn't tell you," the lady said. She was done being helpful.

I tried a different tactic. "Do you know when Georgia is scheduled to work again?"

She looked up again. I tried to sneak a peek at her nametag, but she wasn't wearing one. "Not sure, hon."

I cringed, and my jaw clenched.

Together, in the silence, we both zoned out, contemplating Georgia. Perhaps she had opened up to this woman about everything. About Mat. His violence. His hate. His sex. His alcoholism. His illness.

"What's your name?" I asked.

"Sonya," she said. "And you're Sam."

I couldn't remember if I had told her my name, but I gathered that she could have heard it from Georgia.

"Yeah."

She busied herself with the register and ignored the thick silence between us. We were finished.

"Anyway, thanks." I reached for the door, but she called me back.

"Hey, kid."

I turned around.

"Georgia wouldn't leave for good without telling you goodbye," Sonya said. "If she were going somewhere, she would've told you goodbye."

***

After I left the diner, Ole Red and I headed down to the beach to survey the damage from Boris up close.

The ocean spewed up on the sand, but cleanup was in full swing. The wreckage of our sailboat, which had washed ashore after Anita, was no longer there. Boris had eaten it. The storm had gulped down the island then coughed up the splinters.

Out of ideas, I steered Red back home.

For the rest of the day, I sat alone on the couch and watched TV. The sun began to set, shifting the island into night, but I barely noticed. I didn't even look up when Dad plopped down beside me in his fisherman's hat.

"Holding up okay?"

"Eh," I said, very *not* okay. Very un-okay, if that was even a word.

Dad removed his hat, squeezing its soft canvas into a ball. "You wanna talk about it?"

I muted the television. Did I want to talk about it? Was I actually ready to discuss the Georgia-sized hole that had formed inside my heart?

"She still hasn't come home, and I've checked everywhere. I'm so confused. Even her friend from the diner doesn't know anything, and even she knows that Georgia's boyfriend is a total creep."

Dad stayed silent, waiting for me to continue.

"Her boyfriend isn't a good boyfriend. I haven't told you this, but I think the guy's bipolar and schizophrenic. He takes medication to control it, but he drinks with it, which causes him to—"

I couldn't say it.

We crossed our arms and tucked our hands in our pits in the same swift motion.

"Does her boyfriend hurt her?"

Painting Georgia as a girl who tolerated abuse wasn't what I wanted to do. The concept of something so ugly associated with someone so beautiful just didn't make any sense.

That word *abuse* strangled me. My neck felt knotted in a sailor's complex tangle.

Dad let out a loud breath. "How do you know?"

"Logan told me some things, and I just figured some things out for myself. I caught her a few times covering bruises with her jacket."

"Does she know that you know?"

"She does now."

"You think she might have run off with him?" He held his chin.

That familiar anchor in my chest sank deep into my stomach. "I think if they left Ophelia together, it was because he forced her."

Dad considered this for a moment, then furrowed his eyebrows. "Think she'll be coming back?" Concern contorted his face, which made my anxiety about her disappearance worse. He had touched on my biggest fear: Georgia and Mat were gone, and they would never come back. Unless she was floating in the marsh.

The replay of Sonya's last words boomed in my brain: *Georgia wouldn't leave for good without telling you goodbye.* I chose to believe that.

"Yeah, I think she will be."

There was nothing left to say. I couldn't force Georgia to appear, but I wouldn't rest again until I found her.

We settled back on the couch and unmuted the TV with a mutual hope that Georgia would appear on the island soon.

According to the local Fay County news, Boris had spared Ophelia from its worst. By the time its biggest storm bands had begun to hit the island, he had weakened a little, which is how we still had power. Neighboring islands to the south hadn't been so lucky. The weatherman noted that because there was a last-second change in the storm track, Boris detoured and didn't score a direct hit on Ophelia as expected.

"Twenty-one-year-old Matthew Corbin, Ophelia Island resident, is reported missing after Hurricane Boris tore through Ophelia Island."

I didn't realize what the news anchor had said until Mat's name flashed on the screen.

Gasping for air, for words, I flew out of my seat. "Dad, that's him. That's Georgia's boyfriend."

"What?" He rushed to my side.

I rewound the broadcast to hear it again. Mat's name and photo popped up on the screen.

Then I let the story play on.

"Corbin was last seen at work earlier in the day and claimed he was not planning on evacuating before the storm."

I turned up the volume. "This is him, Dad."

"After a short investigation, it appears Corbin was in his home around the time of his disappearance but possibly left his home on foot in treacherous conditions. Rescuers have no leads and, at this point, have not discovered any evidence of foul play. If you have any tips on the whereabouts of Matthew Corbin, please contact the Ophelia Police Department, which is currently conducting the investigation and considers this as an active missing person case. They have stated that they believe Corbin, like others who did not evacuate for Hurricane Boris, suffered from fatal flooding. Currently, there have been nine persons confirmed dead since the storm."

The reporter cut to another topic, and Dad grabbed the remote from my trembling hands. He turned the TV off and put his arm around my frozen shoulders.

He couldn't have died from flooding. His house was fine. Unless, of course, he did leave on foot. But that meant he could have kidnapped her. If the police were wrong, and he wasn't dead, then there would be no other explanation as to why Georgia was also gone.

"Matthew Corbin was Georgia's boyfriend?"

"Yes."

Dad rotated to face me now, and his fishing hat dropped to the floor, forgotten. "Did you see him on the island the night of the storm?"

"No, no, I didn't. When I got here, he wasn't home. His car was still there, but he was nowhere. He had to have left on foot." Theories streamed together, forming a flood in my head. I sat down again and put my head in my hands. "Dad."

"What is it, son?" he asked.

"Mat was gone before the storm. I swear he was. Oh, my God." Georgia couldn't have been with Mat. She wasn't kidnapped. He didn't take her. "I don't know if he left the island or if he's dead or if he left Georgia behind or what, but he was gone by the time I got there that day, and I don't think he's been back."

His car was parked in the same spot. His television was still on, his beer untouched. He wasn't at home when I found Georgia on the beach.

"She couldn't be with him," I said.

My legs were weighted down with an iron truth. I couldn't move if I'd tried.

"If she isn't with him, why did she leave?" I said.

"And where is the boyfriend? Do you think it's possible he could be dead?"

That question landed square on my shoulders. Concrete, hard, and already set in an unmovable place. Hearing someone else say it—asking me the question—sounded different. Dead? For a split second, I wanted to celebrate Georgia's potential liberation. But no, no. Dead? I hadn't wanted that.

Dad paced around the coffee table. "I don't know, but do you think that's why she left?" he said. "To go looking for him?"

"He may have had one of those bipolar episodes, and something happened with his meds and his drinking."

I recalled the results of my Google search: *Schizophrenia: A mental disorder regarded as behaving abnormally, confused thinking, and false beliefs.*

"Yes. His medicine treats schizophrenia too. He can have confused thoughts and behave weird and stuff. Mat drank. A lot. What if he got drunk and—"

"Do you think Mat's disappearance might explain why Georgia wanted to go to the lighthouse instead of his house?" Dad asked. It was a loaded question. Heavy as a loaded gun.

Georgia had never told me the reason she was on the beach during the storm. She could have gone looking for him. I supposed that was a realistic possibility. But if that had been her motive, she was fast to give in and didn't argue about leaving the beach to go to the lighthouse with me. She had told me he was passed out at his house. Was she lying? I had been suspicious, so should I have paid better attention? Georgia could've been out looking for him. But if Mat was gone and possibly dead, wouldn't that be a relief to her? His abuse would be over, and she would be free.

"Maybe," I said. "Maybe she wanted to get away. All I know is they didn't disappear together."

And I had a feeling she knew where he was.

Chapter 20

A bluvion.

It's a rare word, meaning "that which has been washed away." A flood. Uncountable.

I learned it in a book when I was a child, and I woke up with that word buzzing in my memory, awakened by Georgia's voice.

Help me, Sam.

I pictured her body washing away. I saw Mat drowning in the waves. I imagined her in the storm, running from Ophelia and all her madness.

Instead of going into the diner, I pedaled past it. The black car wasn't there, so Georgia wouldn't be there either. Heading back to the lighthouse, I pedaled faster. Part of me wanted to go back and talk to Sonya again, to see what else she could tell me about Mat, but that wouldn't help me anymore.

There were new tire tracks imprinted into the muddy driveway that hadn't been there yesterday. Someone had been here, and I hoped it was only to check on the place, to make sure it hadn't sustained major damage from Boris. I judged by the thickness of the muddy puddles that I would have to roll Red along beside me. He was already dirty, but I promised him I would wash him as soon as my search was all over.

The front window on the lighthouse porch had been shoved open, but there were no cars here. When I had been here the day before, I'd checked the window twice to be certain I had closed everything back down. I stopped to listen, but everything was quiet, was still, and I didn't sense any movement inside. Searching the drive one last time to be sure no one was here, I confirmed there were no cars parked anywhere that I could see.

Weren't Georgia and I the only ones who climbed through the window? Who hung out at the lighthouse at all?

For a moment, I worried it might be Mat, hiding out here, waiting for me or waiting for Georgia. But I determined it had to be her.

I ran up the creaky porch stairs, taking two at a time. Muddy shoe prints lined the porch leading to the window, small, smaller than mine. My feet clapped across the living room floor as I ran through the house.

"Hello?" I called. Silence.

In the dining room to my left, I heard a commanding stomp that vibrated through both the air and the floor. Fearing the worst, I backed against the wall. The voice in my head said, *Mat is here*, but I was too close. I pressed on, creeping behind the dusty antique chair. Another loud clatter came from the next room, and I paused. It wasn't Georgia; it was too careless of a noise. She wasn't sloppy. I peered around the corner from my hiding spot and saw Logan messing around with something in the china cabinet.

"Holy sh—" he stopped himself. "Shoot." He relaxed when he realized it was me, dropping an antique blue plate in the process. It fell to the wooden floor and cracked in two.

I bent down to pick up the pieces. "Nice job."

"Dude, this place is sick," Logan said. "But not in a good way. Like, in a disgusting old way, right? But it's cool. Haven't been here in so many years."

I filled my palms with the two pieces of blue and white porcelain, but it slipped from my hand, and a hundred more scattered around us, so I gave up and started stacking the bigger ones on the table.

"You could've made your presence known," I said.

"Dang, dude. You wake up in a bad mood or something?"

"Sorry. Just thought you were someone else."

His skateboard deck leaned against the table, scratching up the antique wood with its tattered grip tape.

"Who'd you think I was?" When I didn't answer, he said, "Oh, never mind. You hoped I was Georgia?"

I moved his board on the floor. "Yeah."

"Then no worries. Apology not necessary. Hey, have you been here before?"

"I've been here. Got busted by the police and had to go down to the station."

"Holy crap. Did you get in trouble?" *Crap* was an obvious improvement from what he wanted to say, but his voice was still riddled with amusement.

"No, he just told us not to come back. But I've been back a few times."

"'Us?'"

"Me and Georgia. We were here together."

"Nice, Sam. I knew you had it in you." He chuckled under his breath.

Logan, while exploring, had probably seen the wrinkles Georgia and I had left there on the bed and assumed that Georgia and I had come here to have sex. Though I'd wanted to, the truth was, even if she hadn't cut things off and left when she did, I still wouldn't have slept with her that night. I couldn't sleep with someone else's girlfriend, no matter the circumstances, and I would have backed off, no matter how hard that would've been.

"So where is she?" Logan said.

I followed him to the kitchen where he continued to rifle through the cabinets.

"I don't have a clue. Have you seen her around?"

"What makes you think I would have seen her? She's not my girlfriend."

"Well, she's not mine either. Georgia's been gone since the storm. She disappeared right after it hit the island. I've been searching every day since, and I can't find her."

"You sure?" He continued through to the kitchen. "Probably went off with that loser boyfriend."

"Didn't you hear? Mat's gone missing too."

I explained my theory, that wherever they were, they hadn't gone together. Logan asked all the same questions that Dad had asked me, and, eventually, I spelled out everything that I knew. Every bruise, every kiss, every touch.

Logan seemed mesmerized by the story. "Oh, my word. Dude, this sucks." He ran his hands through his dark hair, considering all that I had shared. He promised he would volunteer to help locate her if I wanted him to.

"If I could just contact her," I said.

"You didn't get her number?" He slouched down onto the dusty couch. A cloud bloomed all around him, and he jumped up to wave it away.

I stepped back, trying to avoid breathing it in. "No, I don't even have a phone yet. My cell broke before the move, and then all this with the storms and moving and stuff, I just haven't had the time to get a new one yet."

"How did you ever meet up with her then?"

"By chance," I said. "Everything that's happened—it's all been by chance."

"Well, someone at the diner has to have her number," he said.

***

Logan followed Red and me to the diner on his skateboard. When we arrived, I parked Red in the bike rack, but Logan insisted that he bring his skateboard inside with him.

For once, there was no sign of Sonya. Someone new welcomed us, and I recognized him as the owner. He ducked below the register to grab two menus for us.

"Hey," I said, "we're not eating today. I just need to ask about someone who works here."

He returned the menus to their cubby and rested his body against the front counter. "Sure. What can I help you with?"

So far, so good.

"Well," I started, "Georgia Gabehart, one of the waitresses here—I just really need to contact her, and I lost her number and was hoping you could help. Maybe you could give it to me?"

"Sorry, guys, I can't give away that kind of employee information." He puckered his lips with artificial compassion. "Have you checked with her parents? Or maybe her friends? I can tell you she didn't show for work a few days ago. She hasn't been back since. I figured she might've run out on us. She does have a bit of a rebellious streak in her, you know."

Yes, I did know.

He turned on his heels, finished with our pointless questions, and left Logan and me standing alone at the diner's entrance.

Asking Georgia's mother for help in finding her seemed like the only option I had left.

We pushed through the doors, and I retrieved Ole Red from the bike rack.

"This blows," Logan said, and I had to agree. "*Gone?* Georgia?" He shook his head. "Man, I hope she's okay."

"She's probably okay, right?" I asked.

"After everything you told me? Probably not, Sam."

"It looks like I'm going to have to get the number from her mom," I said, "but I really don't want to do that."

Dropping his skateboard to the ground, Logan attempted a few tricks by the sidewalk, while he contemplated what to do next. A car turned in to the parking lot, and Logan picked up his board.

"We could try. We can't just not do what's necessary if she's in danger."

"I don't know. I've already bothered them enough. They claim they don't know where she is; they say they haven't even seen her. Have you met her family?"

"No," he said, and we sat on the curb. He tossed back a streak of hair that had fallen in his face.

"Her mom is nice enough on the surface, but the live-in boyfriend was really rude when I went by their house yesterday. It's like they don't even care where she is, and they don't seem to be worried that they can't find her."

Logan didn't say anything.

Another car pulled into the parking lot and came to a creaky stop in a space beside us. The door opened, and Sonya's legs popped out. She slung her purse over her arm and smoothed the skirt of waitress uniform before pulling herself out of her car and reporting for her shift. I jumped up and waved her down before she could go inside. Logan stayed behind, watching from his skateboard.

"Excuse me, Sonya?"

"Hi, Sam," she said, her voice deep with sleep and dread.

"This might be a weird question, but would you consider yourself a friend of Georgia's?"

My hands pressed against my lips in a praying position. Sonya's blank stare gave nothing away, and my confidence dwindled.

"What are you talking about?"

"Okay, I still haven't found Georgia, and I don't have any way to contact her, and I just spoke to your boss, but he wouldn't give me any information. So, as a favor, do you think you could give me her phone number? It has to be in there somewhere. In the diner."

She shifted, resting her heavy weight on one leg, and stared at me, then at the diner, and back to me again.

"You and your friend wait in the back by the dumpster. I'll be a minute." She shoved past me on her way through the door.

Logan and I walked to the back of Joe's and stood there, holding our noses against the offensive aroma of the trash. Pacing back and forth, I contemplated what I was going to do with Georgia's phone number.

I turned to Logan. "You have a phone that we can call her from, right?"

"Do I look like I'm from the 1800s? No offense."

I waved it away.

"So you and this girl. I've never gotten an answer. Is she your girlfriend or what, dude?"

My head spun in frantic circles around a track, racing to find the answer I wanted. "I don't know. Probably not. I've kissed her, but that's about it."

"That's it?"

"Yeah," I said.

"Don't you spend a lot of time with her?"

"Sort of." Flashbacks to every moment we spent together played like a movie reel inside my brain.

"Does she like you?"

"Well, she kissed me, so I guess it's possible. I mean, I think she does."

"Kissing doesn't mean a girl likes you."

"Then what does?"

"You would know if you know," he said.

"How are you so educated on this?"

"Dude, I have three sisters. I know all about girls."

"Well," I said, "what do you know about Georgia?"

He shrugged. "She's a tough one to crack. Always running around the island, partying. The boys like her; the girls don't."

I waited for more.

"In school, she could outsmart anyone, dude. She never got in trouble. If she wanted to pull the fire alarm, she'd do it without getting caught."

"How do you know that?"

"The only people she had to fool were adults. And, just for the record, she never pulled the fire alarm. That's just an example. I'm just saying, I don't think anyone on this island knows a lot about her."

"Yeah, but why?" I pushed.

"Because," he said, "she doesn't get very close to people. She and I have been on this island for years together, and we're only . . . acquaintances. What does that tell you?"

"Well, it makes me wonder how Mat got ahold of someone so hard to catch."

"He's huge," Logan said. "He could trap anyone he wanted."

Sonya swung the back door open, disrupting the conversation, and handed me a sticky note without saying a word.

"Thank you," I said. "Thank you so much." My first instinct was to hug her, but I knew better.

"Listen to me, Sam." She pointed straight to my eyes. "If you find her, you tell me."

"Yes, I will, I swear." Her narrowing gaze held mine a little longer, then she left, and the door slammed behind her.

I didn't wait to get somewhere private. Logan tossed me his phone right there by the dumpster, and I dialed Georgia's number with my shaking fingers. Logan turned on the speaker function, and we hovered over it together, waiting for her to pick up. Between rings, I could hear the gap between Georgia and me. I could feel the expanse of empty space, the silence between each ring while I waited for her to come back. She didn't answer any of my calls. If Georgia were determined to disappear, my attempts to reach her would mean nothing.

I gave Logan the number for our house phone and told him to call me immediately if Georgia called back. He promised he would, and he promised that he wouldn't stop trying her. We walked down the sidewalk through town, Red by my side, and Logan said, "Maybe her phone is just off."

But we both knew it would have gone straight to voicemail as soon as we called if the phone was dead. I shrugged, shrinking into my shirt, some subconscious way of trying to hide from the facts. Of disappearing too.

"She probably left it behind," I said.

"Some people just don't answer numbers they don't know."

"Yeah, maybe. But, come to think of it, I haven't seen her with a cell phone."

"Maybe she doesn't have one," he said.

I perked up, thinking that could be true. "Maybe if she does, she just doesn't use it a lot."

Maybe, maybe, maybe.

Logan stopped in front of an Asian restaurant. "Well, this is my stop."

I looked above to the sign: China Grill. "This is your place?"

"It's my dad's. Our family place, actually. I'll definitely be inheriting it someday."

I grimaced at the thought of staying on Ophelia Island just to keep a restaurant open. If Georgia hadn't been keeping me on my toes, I'd have already been second guessing my choice to commute to college on the mainland instead of living on campus.

"Let me know if you hear anything. I'll see you later," he said.

On the ride home, I reshaped everything I heard, smelled, or saw into Georgia. Each ugly mud puddle became a bruise, and every symbol of life transformed into her. Even the death of a palm tree branch twisted my thoughts back to her. When I rode over it, the sharp leaves grazed my ankle and left me with a thin, bleeding cut.

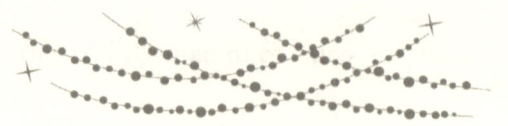

CHAPTER 21

Another day came and went.

There was still no sign of Georgia, no returned phone calls, and nothing new from Logan either. Keeping up the search effort, while also keeping track of the local news, where they were still reporting on the search for Mat, made eating and sleeping difficult. Two more people turned up dead from the storm. That made the number of deaths eleven.

No dead body had washed up on Ophelia beaches, and there were no reports of the fact that Georgia was also missing. Why hadn't her mother reported her missing? Why hadn't anyone? Maybe since everyone on Ophelia knew her character better than I did, they knew she'd reappear or thought that she wasn't in danger.

Ugh, I thought. I'd look insane if I got the police involved and then found out she was totally fine. Plus, I knew that she hadn't gone missing during the hurricane. I had clues of my own that could lead to her. Possibly. But there was a big, empty gap between the moment I had left her and the moment I realized she was gone. Had she stayed awake all night pacing? I would have if I'd been her. There hadn't been any food or water at the lighthouse, but it was only one night. Georgia was alive somewhere, and I'd told her that I would come back for her.

If you can catch me. Had she been planning to leave all along?

I want you to, she'd told me.

As a last resort after Georgia didn't answer any of my morning calls, I phoned Logan from our house phone. I felt lame every time I had to dial a number instead of tapping a contact on my iPhone.

"There has to be some sort of record of her somewhere, like, a money trail or something," he said. A loud beeping noise in the background kept interrupting my thoughts and was working its way through the phone.

"Unless she's crashing somewhere for free," I said. It was an option I hadn't before considered.

"So sorry, Ma'am," he replied.

"Where are you?"

"At work. But the police can find out if she's using a credit card, right? They can track her that way or something."

No police. "Hey, I can let you go if you're working."

"Nah, you're good, you're good. Anyway, with the credit card stuff, I bet you could go to the cops."

An idea fell into my open hands. "Can the phone company track her cell?"

"Yeah, you know, most cell phones can be tracked if the owner has it set up that way."

"Wouldn't you need a password?" I asked.

"Probably."

"Maybe they can still track it somehow without one."

"Sure, but I bet then you gotta involve the police and stuff. That'll be fifty-eight twenty-two."

"Right, yeah, no. I mean, I'm not even positive she's in trouble. Imagine if she wasn't in trouble. I'd look crazy."

"You're not wrong, dude."

"If I did go to the police, think her family would find out?"

"Um, I don't know." He mumbled to himself, counting change, I assumed. "Shoot, I'm sorry. Not the best at counting change. Gah, I thought plastic was on its way in. Thank you, have a nice day."

"I just didn't want to bring the cops into this, you know? What if it isn't that serious?" I said.

"Dude, listen to me. She hasn't made contact with anyone in—how many days after a massive hurricane? And her boyfriend, or ex-boyfriend, whatever—he's still missing. You're desperate, aren't you?"

Georgia was worth the risk of trying to shut down whatever was making me so afraid.

"I guess I'm going to the police department, then," I said.

"Hold on, I'll come. I get off in thirty minutes. Can you wait?"

"You want to come with me?" I asked.

"Yeah, of course I do. It's Georgia, dude. The only girl on the island no one can crack, remember? And if she's in danger—which she might not be, so don't flip out—then I want to help. And I want to figure out how the heck she's vanished into thin air."

Something about his statement relieved me. I wasn't the only one who thought of Georgia as *vanished.* "Oh," I said. "Okay, that's great. Thanks."

"So you can wait for me?"

New Island Sam wanted to venture this road alone, but a sliver of me knew I needed a friend around to keep me afloat. Otherwise, I'd have kept drifting into oblivion.

"Sure, I'll pick you up. I'll be in the white Bronco."

***

While I was waiting for Logan to come out, I took the crumpled sticky note with Georgia's number out of my pocket. *This is it,* I thought. *Your last option.* Logan stalked out of Piggly Wiggly three minutes after four, his hair slicked back, and he jumped in and buckled his belt.

"Sup?" he said. "You ready?"

"As I'll ever be," I said, speeding off. "Thanks for coming with me, by the way."

"Yeah, duh. Anything for the new kid." He laughed.

I tried to laugh with him but choked on my frail attempt.

Over at the police department, the pace was slow and quiet. Phones weren't ringing, criminals weren't scattered everywhere, but there weren't many visitors on Ophelia after the hurricane either.

The lady at the front desk greeted us with a warm smile. "Hi. What can I do for you boys?"

"Hi. Um, I have a question," I said, my voice shaking.

Logan broke in, saving me. "We were wondering if it's possible to track a cell phone if we give you the number?"

My armpits started to dampen with sweat.

He continued, "Not you, of course, but maybe one of the officers?"

The receptionist cocked her head. False sympathy oozed from her gentle grin.

"You know what? I believe we can. Let me just go ask one of our officers if he has a moment to speak with you."

She rolled her chair back and walked down the hall toward an open doorway, her ballet flats making light taps against the floor. Her manicured fingernails ticked on the officer's door, and in a loud whisper, she said, "I have two young men out here asking if they can get a cell phone tracked. Do you have just a moment?"

Their quiet mumbles drifted back and forth behind the door, and then he said louder, "Send them in."

The receptionist walked back to her desk. "He said you could head in."

She pointed us to the door, and we were met by a skinny, fresh-faced officer who couldn't have been much older than we were. He ushered Logan and me inside and motioned for us to sit. I was confident that he was a rookie on the force.

"Hello, I'm Officer Palmer Woods."

I'd half expected to be having this conversation with the bald cop who found me at the lighthouse, so Officer Woods was a welcome relief.

My hands were damp with sweat, so I wiped them on the back of my shorts before the cop reached out to shake mine and Logan's.

"I'm Sam Carter."

"Logan Pointer."

Woods looped his thumbs through his belt. "How can I help you guys today?"

"We wanted to know if you could locate a cell phone for us," I said.

He took a seat behind his desk. "Sure thing. One of you lose it in the hurricane?"

"You could say that," Logan muttered.

"Well, not lost in the hurricane, just gone since then," I added.

"If the hurricane got it, then I'm sorry, boys, it's likely to be destroyed." Woods's attention was glued to his computer screen. "Plus, I'd need a warrant to do any tracking."

Destroyed. It strangled me yet widened the gaping hole I was falling into.

"A warrant?" I said.

"Right. Unless this were an emergency."

Logan and I glanced at each other. I'd been telling myself this wasn't an emergency. And it wasn't. Was it?

Logan was thinking the same thing. He said, "It kind of is, actually."

"It's kind of an emergency?" Woods said.

"My friend," I blurted. "It's her phone. She's been gone since the hurricane, and I thought that if we could track her phone, we'd be able to find her."

"He's right," Logan said. "We think she might be gone. Like, *gone* gone."

Woods adjusted his jaw and looked from me to Logan. "What do you mean, *gone* gone?"

I swallowed. "Well."

"No, no." He held up his hand. "I think I understand. Why do you two believe that?"

"Because she hasn't contacted us since the storm, and the last time I saw her was right beforehand."

"Has she been gone more than forty-eight hours?"

"Yes. She disappeared after the hurricane, but I know she didn't go missing during the storm."

"What do you know about her disappearance?" He was starting to sound more like a cop.

My natural aversion to public speaking defeated me, but Logan picked up on my struggle and took over at just the right time.

"We have reason to believe that she's missing because of multiple absences at work and no communication with her family or her friends. We don't know for sure what happened after the hurricane—we think if her phone is still ringing, then someone must still be charging it. If she's dead, we think her phone would be too, given that it would've probably been close to her at the time of her disappearance."

Woods locked his fingers and rested his chin on them, putting the pieces of our story together. He was hooked on the word *disappearance*.

"And no one has filed a missing person report on her? Not her family?"

I bit the inside of my lip. This answer was tricky. "Officer Woods—"

"Just call me Palmer."

"Okay, Palmer," I said. "She doesn't come from the best family." I tasted my own blood as it spread over my tongue.

He puffed out his cheeks, deep in thought, and slumped back in his chair. Palmer put the tip of his pen between his teeth and thought for a moment before he spoke again.

"We're searching for another young man who's also been missing since the storm came through. I think he's close to your age." He paused. "Do you two know anything about that?"

"I've heard about him on the news. I don't really know him, but I've seen him around the island. I know he works at the gas station." I trailed off, not knowing what else I could add.

Palmer made a note on his screen, and I could feel his stare. "Do you know any reason why these two disappearances would be related? Was there a relationship between your friend and Mat Corbin? Were they involved?"

I don't know what they were, I wanted to say. "Maybe. I'm not sure what their involvement was." I tried to play it off, and Logan stepped in.

"Their disappearances aren't related."

Palmer shot us a strange glance before he turned back to his screen and typed again.

I added, "I saw Georgia the day of the hurricane. She was safe, and she was alone."

"And you've had no contact or anything from her? No calls, nothing?"

"Yeah, we've tried that, and I've spent days looking everywhere on the island for her," I said. "I've talked to her family and her coworkers, and no one has seen or talked to her, but they don't seem to be concerned."

Palmer narrowed his eyes and shook his head. "Why wouldn't Georgia's boss report her as a missing person? Mat Corbin's boss called us the first day he didn't make his shift."

His suspicious tone deepened. I couldn't say anything to make Georgia look bad. I couldn't say that I dropped her off at the lighthouse. I couldn't tell him I fumbled through Mat's medicine and discovered he was mixing medication and alcohol, skipping doses, and the side effects resulted in hurting Georgia. Then she would look like she had a motive to make Mat disappear. And a reason to run away.

But she was too weak under his authority. No matter how hard she tried, she'd never have been able to fight him off.

"Georgia isn't the most reliable employee when it comes to her attendance," I said. "She didn't show up for her morning shift the day Boris started, but they were going to close the diner early anyway, so they didn't think it was a big deal."

"But what about after the storm? I thought you mentioned that she hadn't been back to the diner at all. Is it not a big deal for her to miss several shifts in a row? I would think this would raise some level of concern for her employer."

I looked over at Logan, and he gave me a discreet shrug. Palmer's focus was a hot laser beam pointed in my direction. I had nothing to say, so I kept my mouth shut and gripped the armrests of my chair. It would not go unnoticed to the eye of a trained officer that I was acting too nervous and definitely not being forthcoming with the information I held about either disappearance.

Palmer didn't take his eyes off me but kept typing. When he finished whatever he had added to his file, he picked up his pen again, this time tapping it against the edge of his desk. Tap, tap, tap, tap. It was enough to drive anyone crazy, but, in my agitated state, it was worse. His silence implicated he was formulating a theory of his own, with me as his person of interest.

Then the tapping stopped.

"Okay, boys, here's where we are." Palmer stiffened, straight and formal. "You need to do the best you can to locate this girl tonight. If you aren't able to contact her by tomorrow afternoon, I'm going to file the missing person report, and the department will have no choice but to get involved. We'll have a warrant to do so."

Instant regret suffocated me.

"When you do find her, you will need to bring her by the station. We're going to need to ask her a few questions about the Corbin case. *Pressing* questions. She and Mat went missing at the same time. They could have been together or she could at least have an idea about where he is."

Even if I were able to track Georgia down in the next twenty-four hours, there was no way I would be able to get her to agree to come answer questions about Mat.

Palmer sensed my hesitation. "Don't worry, Sam. Your friend isn't in trouble. I'm just trying to connect the dots. Ophelia isn't known for people going missing, and now, in the course of a few days, we have two gone. By your own admission, they knew each other, and we just need to dig a little deeper to see if these cases are in fact connected. Just want to make sure they're both alive and well and haven't been harmed by the hurricane. They really should have evacuated. It's strange that they were presumably the only two on the island during the storm."

I swallowed, my vision narrowing into a tight scope that could see only Palmer's curious eyes on me.

Palmer stood, and I took that as a hint that he was ready for Logan and me to leave him alone.

"Also," he said, "I'm going to have to have permission from the owner of that phone in order to run an official search for it. Unfortunately, until you obtain that in writing, I'm not going to be able to help you unless you would be willing to file a missing person report. In doing so, this will be considered an emergency."

That was not an option.

"Doing so would provide us with a reason to ping the phone, especially if you're convinced she has it in her possession. If you think she might be in some kind of danger, this is going to be your best option."

"Thanks, Palmer, but I think I'll wait one more day and see if I can track her down on my own before I do anything like that." I could only hope I sounded confident enough to convince him of my innocence.

Logan and I followed Palmer's lead and shuffled through the door of his office and back down the hallway. We had our assignment. We would have to track Georgia down in mere hours and then figure out a way to bring her in front of Palmer for questioning. Logan and I didn't speak, but I knew that we were both racking our brains for another option.

Palmer stood in his doorway, intent on watching us walk away.

Logan pushed through the station doors with me right behind him. We had one more day. Though I didn't like it, this sounded better to me than the alternative and getting the police involved.

I looked over at Logan who had already climbed into the Bronco. "What do you think?"

His face flushed white. "We should've done it. Why didn't you?"

Taken aback, I said, "Do what?"

"File a missing person report, Sam."

"I don't know. What if she ends up hating me? If we file a report, then we find her after we track her phone—you think she might be pissed?"

"The thing is, Sam—I hate to burst your bubble, dude—but you've been looking for Georgia on your own for how many days now? And you still haven't found her. Actually, the only thing you have found is a bunch of new questions that you don't have any answers for." Logan brushed his hair back. "I think you have to go back inside and file the report."

"No way, Logan," I said. "Absolutely not. I can't file a missing person report on Georgia if everyone on the island believes she left of her own free will. Also, Palmer definitely thinks I had something to do with this. I saw his face in there. He's weird about me knowing her and Mat." I cranked the car. "No. There's no way I can do it."

Logan climbed out of the Bronco and stood on the curb. "Sam, it's the only way," he said through the open door. "You heard Palmer. He can only track the phone with a missing person case. There's no other way, and you said you wouldn't stop until you found her. So here's your chance." He closed the car door and said through the window, "If you won't do it, then I will."

I jerked the key out of the ignition and got out of the car, meeting him on the other side.

"Fine," I said. "Fine."

Palmer would have more ammunition to use in the case he thought he was building against me. To my surprise, he was standing in the station lobby when we entered. It was almost as if he had anticipated our return.

"Listen, guys," Palmer said, leading us back toward the privacy of his small office once more, "I need you to tell me you officially want to file a missing person report on your friend, and I'll give you a paper to sign. But I'm willing to help you out a bit with your problem if you help me with mine. Go ahead and sign, which will give me permission to run the cell phone records. I'll give you your twenty-four hours to find her before I enter her information into my system. I'll track the phone and then, if you produce her within that time frame, I'll shred the paper you signed. But that's a big if. If you bring her to the station and prove you've found her. We'll assess her condition, and we will ask her a few questions, and then we'll release her. I can't do anything more than that for you right now."

"So if you track the phone, then we find her, all we have to do is bring her by to show she's not missing, and everything will be kept between us? Nothing after that?" I said.

"Correct, nothing after that but a few of my questions. Once I ping the phone's location, I'll drive you to wherever the phone is now. This could be serious."

"No," I snapped. "I mean, we know she's alive. We, we…" I spluttered, losing my focus. I couldn't risk bringing Palmer with me to find Georgia. She would run for sure if she thought there was a cop nosing around about Mat. She didn't even want to discuss that stuff with me. And besides that, *I* wanted to be the one to find her. *I* wanted to bring her home.

"Logan and I can handle going to wherever the ping takes us, and if she's not there with the phone, we can contact you about the more serious stuff. Is that fine?"

"Bro," Logan said to me, "this is like the smallest island ever. It's not NYPD, okay? They trust us. Right?"

Palmer's face tightened, and he blew a strange groan out of his nose. "All right. Yeah. This is a safe place. I'll agree to this, but only because I have a feeling that you're correct in assuming she's alive. Plus, I have a meeting in about ten seconds. What I'm going to do is send you the coordinates of the phone. But if she's not there, well, you know the rest." I wasn't sure that we did. "That means you bring her to the station, and this goes away. But if I don't see her by tomorrow, I'll have no choice but to bring both of you back in for questioning. Consider yourselves persons of interest if you don't find her."

Crystal clear. If I didn't find Georgia, I would be the one in trouble.

"I'll give you my card so if I'm not here, you can call me immediately." He pulled the card from his shirt pocket and handed it to me across his desk. "Am I understood?"

Logan and I nodded in agreement.

"Good."

Logan and I both had to verbally confirm that yes, we were aware that we were filing a missing person report on Georgia Gabehart, and we were certain that she had been gone for more than forty-eight hours. The form Palmer had me fill out asked questions about her appearance, her height, weight, eye color, and details about the last time I had seen her. He had Logan and I both sign the bottom. I gave him Georgia's phone number, and by five thirty, her phone was a bouncing little dot on his screen. The phone was at the marina, the dot floating in the harbor.

I jumped up and grabbed my keys. "Can I go now?" Stupid question.

"Yeah, go, go, and don't forget my card. Call me if she's at the marina, and don't forget to bring her back here. I'll be here for the rest of the night."

For good measure, Logan snapped a picture of the exact location of the phone, and we raced to the car.

"Floating in the marina?" I said. "That freaks me out, Logan."

"Me too. She's fine. I'm sure she's fine. Just get there. Let's get out of here. The phone won't have much time left if it is under water."

"You're right."

Maybe the phone had fallen out of her pocket or something or maybe it had been stolen, but the millions of possibilities smothered me.

I thought back to my search on Google Maps and pictured her body once more floating in the dirty ocean, washed up beside a boat in the clumps of trash and Boris's vomit, her chest swollen with water, her face dark with the discoloration of bloated tissue.

But I promised I'd find her, dead or alive.

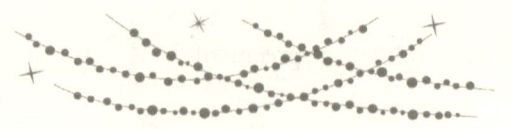

Chapter 22

There was a thirty-man cleanup crew working along the damaged marina. Broken boards and parts of boats were lined up on both sides of the sidewalks. Huge limbs and piles of wet leaves covered the concrete parking lot. The dirty water was littered with torn grocery bags and garbage that swirled all around the marina.

Georgia wouldn't be swimming there.

They wouldn't let anyone get in water that dirty.

She could have been hanging off the propeller blade of a boat, could have been pinned down under water by an errant tree branch. She could have decided to chuck her phone into the water and just walk away.

Logan and I threw ourselves out of the Bronco and sprinted across the hot asphalt lot, shouting her name the entire way. All the workers stopped and watched us run to the edge of the water.

Streaks of the late evening sun penetrated through my T-shirt, but I didn't care. I was too close now. I could feel her.

"She's this way, this way." Logan pointed toward the dock where the boats were harbored.

"Where?" I said. "Which one?" I swiveled my head around, trying to see something that seemed familiar, but the sun blinded me. Everything did.

He zoomed in on his phone and looked to the docks. "That one."

It led us to the fourth boat slip from the end, which housed a small sailboat that looked like a little version of the one Georgia and

190

I sank. I got on my knees, searching the water around the slip, but it was impossible to see below the dark current.

Some kind of noise came from inside the sailboat, so I pointed to Logan, motioning to him that I was going to climb aboard. Palmer's card had crinkled with my body's humidity; I handed it to Logan for safekeeping, for when I found Georgia and he could call Palmer.

I swung my leg over the boat's railing, and the door to the cabin swung open wide.

No one walked out, so I swung my other leg over, and my feet hit the deck with a *thunk*. I steadied myself and continued toward the open door.

Before I took the first step leading down to the boat's cabin, I called for Georgia but was met in the small stairwell with the odor of old wet towels and the smoke from a match.

When I reached the bottom of the stairs, I saw it. There, on a small wooden table was a cell phone lying face down beside a white candle.

"Georgia?" I said, and when I heard no answer, I reached for the phone with my shaky, but determined fingers.

"Hey." It was a voice I didn't recognize.

An old man appeared beside me and snatched the phone from my grip. He wore suspenders that wrapped over his bony body, and he carried a janitor's broom.

I held my arms above my head.

"I'm sorry, I'm sorry. I'm just looking for someone." Each sentence bled into the next, but he didn't want to hear anything I had to say.

He scrutinized me like he was a hawk, and I was his prey. "Who might that be?" His southern accent was rusty with his old age.

"Her name is Georgia," I said. "Georgia Gabehart, and I think she's in here somewhere." I lowered my hands but kept them close to my side. "Is she?"

He relaxed, straightening out the hunch in his back. "What's your business with her?"

"After the hurricane, I tried to find her but couldn't, and I ended up tracking her phone here. To this location. To your boat."

He rotated the phone in his hands in slow, deliberate turns, his face unresponsive.

"So is she? Here, I mean."

I heard Logan's voice shouting from somewhere above me. "Sam, she's here!"

"What? Logan?" I shouted back.

The old man shifted his position, prepared to use his broom to protect himself. "I don't put my nose in her b—"

"Sam?"

Georgia.

There it was, her voice, the one I had been searching for, bouncing around right behind me. A ray of sunshine after a long, cold winter. I turned around to find her standing in the doorway at the top of the stairs, flanked by the light from the setting sun, a halo of light around her vast array of sandy curls. She was dressed in an orange tank top and a form-fitting pair of denim shorts. My image of her had been grungy and dirty, but she was perfect. Alive.

A brown paper bag rested in her arm, holding groceries from the market next door.

"Georgia?" Her name rolled off my tongue as it had many times, but the taste had changed from sweet to tart.

She walked down the steps, her stride as effortless as it always was. "What are you doing here? Sam,"—she set down her bag—"you found me?"

"What's this boy doing here, Georgia?" the old man asked her.

"Mr. Harper, he's fine, he's fine. Would you give us a moment?"

The old man grunted but handed over the phone to her before walking up the stairs with his broom.

Face to face now, finally alone, Georgia and I stood staring at each other. Instead of giving her the long-desired hello kisses I had imagined, all I needed now were answers. I wanted them with a vicious urgency.

"Where have you been? I've looked for you everywhere."

"Sam."

"Is this where you've been the whole time? I've called you a hundred times. How could you let me be so worried about you?" My determination sounded like anger, but the answers—I craved the answers.

"Sam." She reached for me, but I took a step backward. "I'm sorry for worrying you. I was...I was going through some things, and I just needed some time. I couldn't stay at the lighthouse after the storm, and going home wasn't an option either." A blaring silence hung in the air between us. "Sam, I'm sorry. I didn't mean to worry you. I think it's been long enough now, and I'm just so sorry for everything."

The corners of her mouth wobbled with the beginning of a sob, so I softened my stance toward her.

She reached for me again, and this time I didn't pull away. I wrapped my arms around her shoulders and pulled her into my embrace.

"Georgia, where were you? You couldn't have stayed on this boat during a hurricane as strong as Boris," I said.

"I didn't. I stayed in the lighthouse, and I left the next morning." She released herself from my grip. "Mr. Harper is a friend. I've known him for a long time, and he knew I needed a place to stay. So, I've been here since then."

I settled back into the familiar comfort of having her close.

Georgia wasn't gone anymore. She was here, in front of me, and all I could think about was how angry I was.

We paused, Mat's name pending in the quiet cabin.

"You know about him?" I said.

Her composure shriveled against the wall. "Actually, Sam, I'd rather not."

My body stiffened with suppressed anger, so I circled the small room and focused on what she was telling me rather what she was hiding. "Okay, I'm sorry for asking. Just tell me if you're okay." I moved close to her again, stopping only inches from her lips.

"Sam, I'm fine. You can see for yourself." Georgia twirled around, giving me the chance to inspect her before she continued. "So, you caught me, huh?" Her face changed, and she flashed me a brilliant smile, but one that was intended to change the subject. It worked. Georgia slid her fingers up my neck to my hairline and tipped my head down to face her. "I wasn't asking you to, you know. I didn't know I was going to come here."

I nodded, not ready to kiss her but to hear her keep explaining.

"Sam, I was going to come find you soon, I swear. But how'd you do it? How did you track me down?"

It almost hurt to be this relieved. Almost too good to be true. "Persistence."

Georgia lifted a brow, impressed, but she didn't press me on the logistics. "I should've come to you sooner." Guilt was sprinkled through each word she said.

"Don't worry about that now. But what next? Where will you go?"

"Maybe it's time I head home. I wonder if they even missed me?"

"Wouldn't know." I didn't want to admit the truth, but as usual, I couldn't hide my emotions from my face. Georgia could see right through me.

"There's something else you need to know, Georgia. It's about what led me to find you."

I felt Georgia's body flinch, and I tightened my hold on her, but she wriggled free.

"You're going to have to let me prove that you're alive. It won't take you long, but there are some questions that you have to answer at the police department."

Georgia backed away from me, then darted up the tight stairwell to the deck. I ran after her and found her caught in Logan's arms as she reached the railing. The sun burned through my shirt once more, reminding me that I was wrong about this moment, which I'd thought would feel like heaven. Still, I was in hell.

"Georgia, wait," he said.

"Let me go, Logan," she yelled, squinting under the bright sunlight. "What are you doing here?"

I touched her on the arm, and Logan let her go. The heat beat down on us, as angry as Georgia.

"What kinds of questions? Why would the police be trying to find me?" Her eyes narrowed, and her gaze shifted back and forth between Logan and me.

"No, no, Georgia, you've got it all wrong," I said, holding out my hands to make sure to catch her if she ran again. "I told you. I've been searching for you since I got back to Ophelia after the storm hit. I was getting desperate; I felt like I was out of options. Logan convinced me that we should go to the police. He was just trying to help me find you."

She started to back away again, but the railing trapped her in front of Logan and me. "What have you done, Sam? What made you think you could go to the police?"

"Georgia, listen to me. I went there to find you. You haven't been seen or heard from in days, and people were worried about you. It wasn't just me. The officer that I spoke with helped me find you, that's it. And, in return, he just asked that I bring you by the station so he can see for himself that you're okay. He just wants to be sure you're alive; it's nothing more than that. He promised he wouldn't take things any further."

Now, she'd never have to know about the potential missing person report or the fact that I had requested the police track her phone.

"Tell me the truth, Sam."

"He is," Logan said. "That's all that happened. It's no big deal."

"Georgia, you know I will," I said. "I'm on your side here."

"Does he think I had something to do with Mat going missing?" This frantic version of Georgia scared me, but just as I deserved answers, she deserved the truth.

"I don't know."

"But you think he does, don't you? You both think that." She pressed her back against the railing and watched for me or Logan to deny it.

Logan said, "The only thing he told us was that the timing of your disappearance and Mat's is weird."

"That's all," I added.

"Well, I'm not going," Georgia said, her voice packed with defiance. "No way I'm talking to the cops about Mat, or where I've been, or anything else. I haven't done anything wrong, so they have no right to force me to answer any questions."

"Georgia, I'm begging you. Just come with me. I promise, everything will be okay. You haven't done anything wrong; you don't know anything about Mat or where he is. Just tell them that. Woods. Palmer Woods. He's really nice."

She remained unchanged, which I took as a good sign. Perhaps it was true that she had nothing to do with Mat's sudden disappearance. So she shouldn't have had anything to hide from the police.

"Besides, if you don't come with me, the police are planning to file a missing person report on you, and that will mean probably involving your mother, which I know you don't want."

Georgia glared at me with fire in her eyes, and my veins ran ice cold. This was the end of us. We'd never recover.

She crumpled and collapsed on the boat's deck, but she couldn't hide the disgust on her face, and I doubted she was even trying to. I offered her my hand, but she shoved it away and stood again. Bracing her back against the railing, she exhaled in defeat.

"Okay," she said. "Okay, fine. I'll go."

I sent Logan to get the Bronco, determined not to give Georgia another chance to bolt, then I climbed off the sailboat and waited for her on the dock so she could tell the old man goodbye.

Logan pulled up and rolled down the passenger's window.

"Did you call Woods?" I said.

"Yeah, he said to head straight there."

Georgia climbed off the boat, and I escorted her by her elbow to the car.

We dove into the back seat together, and Logan drove out of the marina's lot, pointing the car toward the station.

When we arrived, Logan parked by the door and lifted the front seat to help us out. Georgia made her way out of the back seat and stood beside me, but I asked her for a moment with Logan before we continued.

I walked around the car to the driver's side, and Logan handed me back Palmer's card and the keys to the Bronco.

"I'll just head home from here. You two will probably want some alone time when you're finished with Woods."

"No sweat," I said, denying that what he said was true. "He said this would only take a few minutes, then I'll take you home. I owe you for all your help."

Georgia remained silent on the other side of the car.

"Sam, dude, it's all good. My house is like, five seconds away. I'll just walk. The police department gives me the creeps anyway, so I'm not into sticking around if I don't have to." Logan gave me a pat on the back and turned toward home. "It's been good, my friend," he said. "Really freaking good."

"Thanks, Logan. For everything."

"Let me know what goes on," he said.

The color had finally returned to his cheeks, and he looked relieved to be at the end of his road in our story. But for some reason, I felt like he wasn't.

He jogged away, and I met Georgia by the station doors.

The receptionist wasn't there, so I invited myself into Woods's office and waited for him to arrive. We sat in the two chairs in front of his desk.

"Was it because of Mat?" I said in a low volume. "Is he the reason you went away like that?"

She tucked a curl behind her ear. "Yeah. I just needed some time, that's all."

"I understand that, Georgia, but you can't just drop off the face of the earth. People are going to start talking." I thought about Sonya and the concern she had shown for Georgia. "Are you going back to work?"

"If they'll take me back."

"Where will you tell them you've been? They'll want to know."

Her eyes shifted away from me again. She hadn't told me everything.

"Maybe I'll tell them I left the island for a little while. I don't know. I'll think of something."

Why hadn't she said anything at all about Mat? About him being gone? Wasn't she worried?

I thought about the things she had already told me. She needed time? Couldn't go home? Had no place to go after the storm? It all made sense, but there was something missing. Georgia's demeanor stayed cold; I wouldn't be able to pull anything from her right now. I slumped down in my chair, certain that I was still missing a key detail. Whatever it was kept me from feeling close to her. There was an abysmal distance between us, and it was growing by the second.

Woods entered the door to his office. "Welcome back." He looked from me to Georgia in an effort to examine her condition. "You're Ms. Gabehart?"

"Yes." I noted a bit of an edge to her voice. She reached out to shake his outstretched hand but then yanked it back as if it had been loaded with hot coals. At least she was cooperating.

"All right, we'll just jump straight in, shall we?" Woods took a seat at his desk and put on some wire-framed readers before turning on his computer. He meant business, and Georgia had no choice but to be ready for him.

"It seems rather coincidental that you vanished the same time Mat Corbin did. How well would you say you knew him?"

"Mr. Corbin and I were friends. He had a lot of friends. And a lot of girlfriends. Just ask anyone."

Mr. Corbin? Georgia was better at this game than I thought she would be.

"But you and he were in a relationship, is that right? That's what was implied." He motioned to me, and I looked down.

"As I told you, officer, Mr. Corbin had a lot of girlfriends." She was good, but Woods wasn't moving.

"Can you tell me the last time you saw him?" he said.

She didn't miss a beat. "I saw him earlier that day before I evacuated. He was fine. He had been drinking. But he was just a little buzzed."

"No one has seen Mat or heard from him since before the storm, and I find it a bit odd that you, as a friend of his, one that is romantically involved with him in some way, not only didn't report him missing, but actually turned up missing yourself. Can you explain why you don't seem concerned with your boyfriend's disappearance, Ms. Gabehart?"

"As you can see, I'm not missing. In fact, I was never missing. I've been staying with a friend, and I've been there ever since the storm blew through. I've been at the marina the whole time. You're welcome to confirm that with my friend." She shot a dagger in my direction. "And as for my involvement with Mat, we hang out sometimes, that's it. It's not anything more serious than that. I have no idea where he is now." I believed her when she said it. I wondered if Woods did too.

He nodded, buying her story. "Great," said Woods. "Now, your friend here explained to me that he was having trouble finding you, and, well, he filled you in on the missing person report, didn't he?"

Georgia shifted in her seat and sat on her hands, shrinking into herself.

"Okay, well, all I have to do is ask you a few more questions confirming you're unharmed. We'll be just another minute, then we'll get you out of here."

I tried to keep my eye on Georgia to gauge her body language, trying to interpret her actions for hidden meaning. The first time we had been here, she had been cool and had stayed calm. Now, though, she was uneasy and anxious. I blamed it on how confusing the past few days had been for her. That was all. It had to be.

Woods began, "You are here of your own accord, safe and unharmed, correct?"

"Yes."

"And you left your home of your own accord and cut off all communication without being coerced by anyone else. Is that also correct?"

"Yes."

"And you were found at the marina in the location where we tracked your phone, I'm assuming?"

"Right." Another dagger. I still hadn't mentioned anything about tracking her phone.

"Can you tell me why you left and cut off communication?"

Georgia looked down and bit her lip. "Just like everyone else, I evacuated before the storm hit. I was with my friend on his boat, and I've been there ever since. I've already told you this. Is it a crime to want to go off the grid for a while? I didn't want to talk to anyone, okay? I didn't realize there was anything wrong with that."

She took a deep breath and continued, "I just didn't come back for a day or two. That's all. There's nothing more than that. God. I didn't know it would be this big of a deal. I'm sorry I didn't call anyone." Composing herself, she added, "I apologize to you, and I've already apologized to Sam and Logan, and I'm sorry to anyone else who was worried about me. I'm fine." She fell deeper into her seat. "That's all."

Woods must not have noticed her sarcasm. But I did. I played her words over in my mind. *I evacuated before the storm.* That wasn't true. I had found her standing on the beach as Boris started to make landfall. I had driven her to the lighthouse myself, where she had told me she would stay to ride out the storm. Had Georgia been lying then? Because she was lying to Woods about where she stayed, how long she had been there, and the extent of her involvement with Mat.

"Well, going back to Mat's disappearance," Woods said, "we're investigating it. His house wasn't harmed during the storm, so he should've been just fine. His car is there, and the engine isn't flooded or anything of that nature. And you're supposedly the last person he was with before he vanished. Can you tell me anything you think might be able to aid in this case?"

I peeked over at Georgia, but she kept her focus on Woods. "No. But he was buzzed that day. I think it's absolutely possible that he wandered into the storm."

"You believe he died outside in the storm?"

Exactly what I'd assumed, I thought. *Because Georgia wouldn't hurt him back. Would she?*

"I wouldn't doubt it," she said. "That's what the news is saying, isn't it?"

But what were you doing on the beach that morning?

Woods shut off his computer, and I gathered he was satisfied that Georgia's answers had been good enough. She gulped with relief. But nothing felt different for me.

"You're good to go, then, Ms. Gabehart, and thanks for your cooperation."

We stood to leave, but Woods reeled us back in.

"Oh, we'll need to speak with you again, though. I'm not saying you've done anything wrong." He stood and leaned over his desk in one slow motion. "I'm just saying you might be valuable to this investigation right now."

We got back in the car, and the air was so hot, stagnant, and humid that I couldn't breathe, but it was the heat of what was still unknown that constrained me.

"Georgia."

She was acting normal, so normal, which heightened my anxiety even more.

"What was up with you in there? You seemed so tense. You weren't that way last time we were in there."

Her seatbelt clicked into place. "It's just been a hard week." *That's all.* "I'm okay now, Sam. I promise."

Promise.

Georgia put her hand across my arm, and I leaned over and kissed her like I had wanted to since the moment I left her at the lighthouse. In that moment, everything was perfect again.

I drove the Bronco to her house and turned off the engine. Neither of us made an effort to get out of the car, so I used the moment to ask her for the explanation that I was still chasing. It was her timeline that didn't make sense. I had seen her, held her, kissed her while the storm raged around us. She had been at the lighthouse with me, not with the old man on his boat as she had told Woods.

"Talk to me, Georgia."

"Anything," she whispered.

"You didn't go to the marina and get on a sailboat in the middle of a hurricane, did you? Because that man evacuated just like the rest of the island did. The day after I left you in the lighthouse, he would've been long gone. Just be honest with me. Tell me the truth about what happened at the lighthouse. Did something happen with Mat that you're not telling me?"

She moved her hands off my arm and stared down at her lap. "Sam, I never went to Mat's that night."

I didn't believe her.

"Georgia, you can trust me. I love you. Please be honest with me. What happened between you and Mat? You first told me that you were planning on staying with him during the hurricane, then I found you, definitely not with him, wandering the beach by yourself. Now you're telling that cop that you evacuated before the storm hit, which you and I both know isn't the truth. So what gives, Georgia? Just tell me."

She placed her hand on my face and stroked the skin under my eye. "I did ride out the storm in the lighthouse. The brunt of it anyway. Things changed. I was planning on staying at Mat's place during the storm. But he had other plans, and I didn't want to stay. I was on the beach by myself to think. That's when you found me. You know what the lighthouse means to me. I wanted to go there because it's where I feel safe. But after you left, I just couldn't stay there. I changed my mind, okay? I didn't want to be alone."

That much I could understand.

She went on, "When the storm ended, I went to stay with Mr. Harper on his boat once he got back to Ophelia, which was the next day."

The same question I'd already asked started to come out of my mouth again: *Why did you go into hiding, though?*

But she interrupted my thoughts and said, "Thank you for finding me. So much."

"Why did you lie to Woods, then? About evacuating? You told him you left."

"It would've made me look bad to admit I stayed on the island at the same time Mat disappeared."

"But you did. You and Mat were the only two people on the island, Georgia."

"I told you Mat had other plans."

"And you had to do some thinking on the beach, yeah," I said. "So you went to the shore while Mat was at home, buzzed? He wasn't there, and I know he hadn't been there for a while."

"You're on my case now too? I'm not lying to you. He was drunk, and I didn't want to hang around, okay, Sam? The less the cops know about that, the better."

The truth was the only thing I did was find someone who didn't want to be found. But maybe she sensed how badly I had wanted to find her. Maybe she was grateful that someone had made the effort.

"Georgia," I said, tugging at the hem of my shirt, "I'm sorry. I'm so sorry."

"Just so you know, Sam," she said, "I was mad when you found me on the beach, but please know now that I was also really grateful you'd come back for me. I never thought anyone would come for me, ever. I hope you believe me."

While I wanted to grip her fingers tighter with mine and tell her I loved her again, all I could muster was a frail smile because I wasn't sure I could believe a single word she said. All I was sure of was that I wanted to be with the girl I met at the cabana club.

"Hey, can I maybe—and this might be a bad time to ask you this—but can I maybe take you out one night? Just us. Some time when we maybe don't have to think about all this. Feel free to say no. Don't feel like you have to say yes. I'll take you somewhere off the island. If you want to, I mean." My chest throbbed up and down with a heartbeat

I hadn't felt since she left me lying on that bed in the lighthouse. I kind of didn't want that feeling to go away, so maybe if she'd agree to date me, we'd be back on the same page, forgetting this entire mess.

"A date?"

"If you want it to be." I shifted in my seat, anticipating her rejection. "A date. Or just, you know, time off from all this stuff."

She flipped her hair over her shoulder, a familiar sight, which left my favorite single curl springing free beside her eye. "Sure. Next week?"

"Um, yeah, that works," I said. "I can pick you up at your house."

"Perfect. I'll give you my number."

She laughed, knowing I didn't need it since I'd tracked her phone. But then she grabbed my hand, and we kissed goodbye. She noticed I didn't laugh with her; she eyed me before she got out of the car. The moment I drove away, the fullness I'd felt in our kiss flushed away, and the new emptiness in my gut told me this wasn't over.

She's a liar, whispered through my head. And I trusted that voice more than I trusted anything else right now.

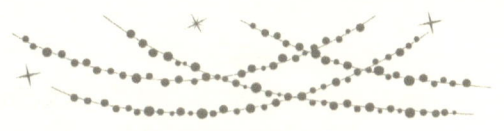

Chapter 23

After I dropped her off, I drove straight to the diner to tell Sonya that I'd located Georgia and she was safe. A glimmer of true joy swept across her face. Then she said, "That was fast."

Sonya told me Georgia was still needed at the diner, that they had kept her on staff and her hours open in case she returned. I was glad to share the good news and even happier to realize that I had earned some kind of approval from Sonya.

I made my way home after that and sat down to a late dinner with my parents. The conversation was centered around everything that had happened and where I had been all day. They congratulated me on my success in finding her, but I left out the details about going to the police and the cop becoming suspicious of both Georgia and me. Mom and Dad were over the moon for me when I told them I was taking Georgia on a date. I wished they'd tone it down a bit; they just didn't understand the weight of my day. Of Georgia.

"Finally. So when do I get to meet her?" said Mom.

"Uh—"

"You have to bring her over, Sammie." She giggled.

"Yeah."

"So call her and have her over for dinner some night soon."

"Maybe you can meet her, okay? Just don't make a big deal of it."

"Come on, Sammie. We really want to get to know her," Dad said.

"We'll see," I said.

***

I ate my breakfast at Joe's for the next few days, sitting in Georgia's section just to see her. We hadn't spoken of Mat, and I forced myself to understand that she needed a few days to relax after her ordeal and get settled back into her routine, so I gave her plenty of space. She had only reached out to me once by phone. For the next three days that I didn't see her, she consumed my thoughts, my mind, my attention. When I thought it had been long enough, I brought up our date again and agreed that I'd pick her up tomorrow night for dinner. I broke it to her that my parents wanted to drop by the diner and meet her, but she was glad. Excited, even, and I wondered if she had ever met Mat's family. If he had one.

Mom and Dad were more than happy to go to Joe's for breakfast after I told them that Georgia would be there to wait on us. When we walked in, Sonya greeted us.

"Let me guess whose section you want to sit in." I let out a nervous laugh, then she walked us through the diner and to our table.

Mom whispered, "Do you know her too?"

"You could say that."

Georgia wore her curls tied back into a ponytail again, her blue uniform crisp and clean. She breezed up to me and gave me a swift peck on my cheek.

"Hi, Sam. Welcome to Joe's," she said to my parents.

Before Mom could say anything to embarrass me, I introduced her to Georgia. "Mom, this is Georgia. Dad, I think you two have already met."

"Right. Hello, Georgia. It's great to see you again."

"So, so nice to meet you," Mom said. "I've heard so much about you. It's nice to finally put a face with the name. Our Sammie has been keeping you all to himself."

My face reddened, and Georgia tried to hide her grin.

"I'm happy to meet you too. I'm sorry we couldn't have met sooner." Georgia glanced at me and smiled.

After she took our order and walked away, Mom said, "Sammie, hon, she is so pretty. I can't believe you didn't introduce her sooner."

Dad had decided to leave his fisherman's hat at home, though it had taken some convincing from both Mom and me. But now he didn't seem to be missing it, which I was grateful for.

He turned to Mom. "I told you she seems like a sweet girl."

They looked across the booth at me, expecting a response. "Yep. She's one of a kind," I said.

Georgia brought me my special order of waffles with ice cream and handed both Mom and Dad the house specialty omelets. Each time Georgia came around, they spoke to her, trying to get her engaged in conversation, but she was either busy or nervous, because she kept the conversation with my parents confined to small talk. Maybe she was dreading the inevitable questions about Mat Corbin, but they didn't bring him up in front of her. For someone with such depth, Georgia stayed shallow this morning, superficial.

Day by day, I was getting better at deflecting my parents' questions about Mat. But they still asked me about him every chance they could.

"Is she still upset about Mat's disappearance?" Mom asked me when she knew Georgia was out of earshot.

A flurry of a hundred possible answers dizzied my head, but I settled on keeping it simple. "She doesn't miss him. I think it's easier for her now."

Mom grabbed my wrist from her spot across the table and gave it a little jiggle. "She's lucky to have such a good one now."

When Georgia finished her shift at the diner, she called me on our house phone. "Hi, Sam," she said when I picked up.

"Georgia, hi."

"I was just calling to find out where we're going tonight. Unless it's a surprise," she purred, urging me to spill.

I stood no chance when it came to Georgia. It scared me how much I wanted her, despite how frigid, how angry, she'd made me in the past few days. "It's not a surprise, but I don't have to tell you."

"Tell me," she said.

Sometimes, she seeped into my skin and warmed my bones. Georgia had an effect on my entire body, one that reached both inside and out.

I lay spread across my bed, with my legs dangling off the edge. "Since you want to know so badly, I'm taking you to a seafood restaurant off the island."

"Sounds dreamy. And the dress code?"

"Do you own a dress?"

"Yes."

"Then, by all means," I said, picturing her long legs in something flowy and pink.

All day and night, the picture of her in that dress wouldn't go away in my mind, but I mostly saw her neck. Her bruise-free neck with a string of artificial pearls and her small curls twisting through the white beads.

Still a tiger with lion hair. A hailstorm that rained jewels.

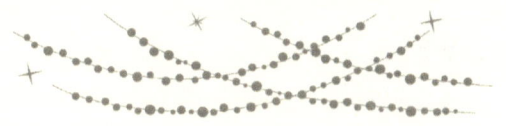

Chapter 24

At six o'clock, I pulled into Georgia's driveway, sweaty as ever. Before I was able to knock on the front door, she ran out to greet me, slamming the door behind her.

Her dress was sunshine yellow. It stopped me in my tracks. Georgia was stunning, always. I hadn't expected anything less.

Caution.

A tiny cream-colored purse hung from her arm, and her curls bounced free, looping around her face. She wore no pearls around her bruise-free neck. My simple Polo shirt paled in comparison to her outfit.

Because it was appropriate, and because it was the absolute truth, I told her she was beautiful. She smiled and tapped her finger on the tip of my nose, which made my insides flutter.

"You clean up pretty well yourself," she said, staring up at me.

The addition of mascara made her eyelashes dance around her emerald irises. We looked natural, normal, when Georgia and I took each other's hands and I led her to the car, then opened the door for her and helped her inside.

This isn't hard at all, I kept thinking. In fact, it all came rather easily.

I started the car. "Hungry?"

"Starving." She sat with her legs crossed and kept slipping one sandal on and off. Her toenails were painted orange, same as her fingernails. She started to play with the radio. "Like music?"

"Of course. Who doesn't?"

"Only boring people." She laughed, but Mat came to my mind in an instant.

Thinking of him put a negative twist on my thoughts, then Georgia started humming to a song that was playing on the oldies station, and every ounce of my pessimism flew away.

We rolled down the windows, and her hair played in the wind all the way to the bridge. The road I needed to turn onto to get to the restaurant I had selected for our date was blocked with heavy caution tape. Two yellow signs stated that entry was off limits, and construction cones on each side of the road flashed orange warning lights.

Caution.

Danger ahead.

Just another repercussion of Boris. Another slice of Ophelia washed away.

"That's the only way I know of to get to the restaurant from the island," I said. "It's just down the road."

"Hold on, let me see if they're even open. If the road is washed out this close, they might be closed." She took her phone from her purse and called the restaurant, which had a voicemail that said they were closed this week due to repairs from flooding, thanks to the hurricane.

"What do we do now?" Georgia didn't show any indication of concern.

"Improvise, I guess."

We turned back and rode over the bridge to Ophelia and stopped at Piggly Wiggly. I told Georgia I wanted her to stay in the car; with my initial plan ruined, I wanted to surprise her with my dinner selection instead of taking her to a restaurant on Ophelia. She'd probably been to all these a hundred times with Mat. That is, if he took her on dates.

I ran in, grabbed a small loaf of bread, pre-sliced tomatoes, pre-sliced mozzarella cheese, a little serving of basil, and a couple of glass-bottled Cokes. My footsteps echoed through the aisles because the store was so quiet, then Logan waved me toward his checkout counter when he saw me.

"Whoa, in a rush?" he said.

"Taking Georgia on a date to the beach. She's out in the car." My words toppled over one another into a sloppy mess.

"Good for you, man. How's she doing? You guys hitting it off?"

"Oh, yeah, we're great. I know she likes me now."

"Cool, man. Really cool."

He gave me the total, and I swiped my card.

"What happened the other day with her at the police department?" he said.

"It was no big deal." I cleared my throat, trying not to let my suspicions about Georgia arise once more. "Like Woods said, he just wanted her to answer a few questions. Then he let us leave."

Logan handed me my plastic bag. "Good luck out there, dude. Have a good date." I was already halfway out the door before I could answer.

"Oh, what's in *here?*" Georgia said once I was back in the car, rummaging through the bag, but I pulled it away and tucked it out of her reach.

"Hey, no peeking," I said, content to have her hand linger on top of my own.

The sun was setting on the south side of Ophelia when we parked in the lot at beach entrance nine, a quieter one. There were only a few other people out tonight, only residents since vacationers had slowed down for the rest of hurricane season. We wandered until we found a nice dry spot to sit on in the sand. I thought about mentioning that her dress might get sandy, but she didn't seem to mind. Stunning as she was in her dress, Georgia was meant for sand and sea and wet hair and jean shorts.

Our shoes were off as soon as we sat down, and I cuffed my pants at the ankle to get a reprieve from the heat. Making our dinner, I said, "It's nothing fancy. It's actually pretty simple, so I hope you like this sandwich. My aunt used to make it for me when I was a kid in West Virginia. Tomato and mozzarella and basil, she said, was the closest thing she could combine to make an Italian meal."

She took the first bite and grinned at me. "I love it."

"Sorry we didn't get to go to that nice place on the mainland," I said.

"Either way, we would've ended up right here. This is where we began, after all. This is where we'll stay."

And I thought for a second, *Of course we will. We'll end up in the sea.*

She took another bite off the edge of her sandwich. "Do you miss West Virginia?"

No one had ever asked me that. Not even my parents. I did miss my old friends and the life I had left behind, but Ophelia was new, exciting, adventurous. Ophelia had Georgia Gabehart. I was content to be wherever she was.

"I like it here better." Without meaning to, I looked right at her.

Her dark eyelashes fluttered as she let me inside her daydream. "I wish I could go north." Then she looked toward the ocean, and the moment was broken.

"West Virginia's not that great. The winters are too cold." *Come back to me,* I tried telling her eyes with mine.

"No—farther than that. I would go all the way to the border of Canada if I could. Might not even stop there."

"What's so great about north?" I asked.

"It's just. . . far away from here. The winters might be too cold, but I'm tired of Ophelia summers."

"I'm not. The things here are growing on me."

"You'll get sick of them. Nothing on Ophelia stays beautiful for too long."

"You do," I said without hesitating.

She aimed her grim down at the sand between us.

She had already told me her plans to get off Ophelia someday. Would she ever come back? We had only discussed it once, when she had said she wanted to go somewhere far away from Ophelia. That the island was too close. To what? Since Mat was still gone, what was it that was still making her feel that way? What was it that she needed to get away from? Because I knew it wasn't the hot summers she hated most.

I tensed up again but tried to ease my confusion by looking into her face right beside me. "That's interesting," I lied. "You wanting to go so far."

"Yeah." She said it to herself, filled with detachment. "You're excited to start college, I bet."

The sudden change of subject snapped me back into the present, but my concentration lay elsewhere.

"Kind of. It's just right around the corner, isn't it?"

"What do you want to study in college?"

I'd had an entire eighteen years to choose my path, yet I was stuck on this gritty beach on Ophelia, answerless. "I'm too young to decide what I want to do for the rest of my life, you know?"

"Agreed," she said. "I'm sure you'll figure it out."

"So will you." *Just make me part of it.*

We finished our meal and rolled over to face each other, propped up on our elbows. When the wind blew, her curls fell, tickling my neck, but I didn't mind.

"I'll race you to the ocean," she said.

The tide was out, but I knew I could beat her even if she got a head start.

"Racing doesn't seem fair. My legs are much longer," I teased.

She sprinted to the sea, anyway, kicking sand behind her with every stride.

And she was hypnotizing. I could have stood there and watched her run all the way to the Keys, but I chased her, catching up to her in the ankle-deep water, and scooped her into a hug. Her arms wrapped around me, and her lips pressed against mine, and I held her there while she was still mine to hold.

***

Georgia and I wandered to the lighthouse at sundown, arm-in-arm, high on each other and dizzy from the evening heat. Once inside, we kissed our way into the bedroom just as we had before the hurricane. I picked her up in another hug, and she wrapped her legs around my hips, causing her dress to inch up her thighs. I pressed her to the nearest wall, and her sandals fell from her feet, slapping the floor as I kissed her lips.

It was dark, and I kept my eyes open so I could see her, see her *be* with me, to watch her learn to trust me. I was in love with feeling how comfortable she was with me this time, with kissing her in total freedom. I was in love with *her*.

No force could pry us apart, nothing could make us stop. Everything around me disappeared. The only noises in the house were the noises that escaped from our lips in fractured rhythms of air leaving our bodies. I combed my fingers through one of her long curls and felt it separate in two, then I cupped the back of her neck, her head, her hair again. But catching a momentary flashback of her flinching the last time I swept my hands over her bruise made me slow my pace.

We came up for air, too close to focus on each other.

I paused, inhaling every scent that belonged to her, moving back in for a moment to sneak a kiss on her lower lip, grasping it with my own and then releasing it with a gentle bite.

She rubbed her thumb down my face and traced my mouth, just a light tickle across my skin.

I kissed her again.

My hands slid up her legs when she released them from around my waist. Standing in front of me, her dress caught on my belt, so I wiggled it free, but I didn't let her lips go. Our kiss deepened, and we moved faster again. She pawed her way up my neck, smoothed my hair, then tugged at the collar of my Polo and slipped it over my head. I stretched back to where the zipper of her dress was and my hand hovered there, letting my finger trace the line all the way down.

"Wait," she said. This time, I wasn't afraid of her hesitation. "Wait."

"Georgia." I kissed her again.

"I'm not afraid of this. Of you."

"Me either."

"But I want things to stay the way they are right now," she whispered. "Everything, just like this." She set a small kiss on my Adam's apple.

"You want me to stop?" I said.

"I don't want to rush this. We can wait, you know. I just—it's so soon."

Our lips brushed together, meeting in a soft kiss to show her that I understood. I would wait as long as she needed me to.

"I know."

She rested her forehead on the bottom of my chin, and I lowered my head onto hers, and we strolled to the edge of the bed. I lay down, and pulled her down beside me, holding her, laughing, kissing. As much as I wanted—hungered—to keep going, we lay there.

And just like that, it was perfect. The moment didn't need to go anywhere. It needed to stay just the way it was, with us wrapped around each other, tied together in a knot.

I searched her eyes for something. Something that would tell me she loved me because I wanted to tell her how much I adored her, but the selfish part of my heart longed to hear her say it back. And I still wasn't certain she would.

But in her eyes, what I saw wasn't love. Rather, it was an unforgiving expanse of time between the moment I left her in this lighthouse during the storm and the second I found her on that old man's sailboat. That gap—it stared at me, then it kissed me as if whispering, *You'll never know what truly happened.*

"Georgia—"

A noise erupted from the living room, and we sat up. Georgia straightened her dress, and I put my finger to my lips, asking her for silence as I got to my feet and picked up my shirt from the floor. The panic on her face sharpened her once-soft features—a look I recognized from the police department, so I mouthed to her, "It's okay."

Sliding my arms through the arm holes in my shirt, I stopped in the doorway at the sound of feet clumping through the next room.

"Sam?" a voice shouted. I pulled my shirt on, realizing the initial noise was a skateboard falling through the open window.

"Logan?" I said.

He ran closer and met me in the hallway, his hair wet and stuck to his forehead. Between breaths, he said, "Sam, where have you been? You said you were going on a date at the beach with Georgia."

Bending over his knees, he coughed.

I put my hand on his shoulder. "Are you okay? Dude, what's going on?"

Beside me, Georgia walked up, timid. Her dress draped around her body, no longer joyful and flowing but flat, as if Logan had stolen the life right from it. From her.

"It's the police," he said. "They came to my work and asked if I knew where you guys were. It was Woods. Palmer Woods."

Georgia grabbed my hand, tugging me close to her.

"Logan, what's going on?" I asked again. "Are you sure?"

He nodded, catching his breath. "Yeah. I looked everywhere for you. They want to speak to Georgia."

She pulled on my sleeve, shaking her head, and whispered to me, "No, Sam. I didn't do anything wrong."

Then Logan added, "Now."

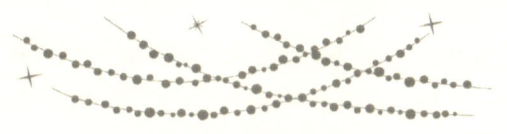

Chapter 25

Woods was taken aback when I walked Georgia into his office, though all he said after a brief hesitation was, "Hello again, Sam." Then, to Georgia, "Please sit."

She and I took the chairs in front of his desk, and Woods held up a finger to keep us quiet while he used his desk phone to call in another officer by the name of Kessler. When he hung up the phone, I said, "Officer Woods, what's going on? Why have we been called here?"

"It's Palmer," he reminded me. "And I just needed Ms. Gabehart tonight, but I'm glad you're joining us, Sam. I hope I didn't pull you away from anything important; you two are all dressed up."

Automatically, I looked down at my Polo, and Georgia glanced at her dress. She crossed her legs, but neither of us thanked him for the compliment.

"I don't want you kids to worry. But we got a little startled when we couldn't find you, Georgia. Thought you'd run off again." Woods chuckled, then he tapped his knuckles on his desk in a playful little knock, knock, knock. "That wouldn't have been good."

Trying to crack a smile to appease him, all I could do was try to summon the professionalism that Logan had displayed the last time he was here with me. I wished Georgia would've allowed him to come in with us, but she was too private about the matter, which Logan had responded to with a stolen glance at me.

"I'm sorry," I said. "We were out."

Woods sighed. Perhaps we were the beginning of his interesting night shift. "It's fine. I found that friend of yours, Logan, at the grocery store and had him track you down for us." His grin fell away. "Small island."

Georgia readjusted in her seat just as another stiff man in uniform walked through the door.

"Officer Kessler, this is Sam and Ms. Gabehart," Woods said. "Ms. Georgia Gabehart."

Kessler simply nodded at the two of us and shut the door behind him. He stepped behind Woods's chair and crossed his arms over his thin torso.

"Like I said," Woods continued, "I didn't have you two in here for a good scare; we've just got some questions for you." He looked at Georgia. "Are you comfortable with that?"

She managed a weak, "Yes."

"All right, good."

Kessler handed him a file I hadn't seen him walk in with, and Woods slid out a few pieces of paper from it.

"We've been doing some research on Mat—on his medical history—and didn't come across anything extremely out of the ordinary. But we found that he was diagnosed with bipolar disorder and schizophrenia when he was a young teenager. Were you aware of this?"

Georgia's chin tilted up, and she closed her eyes for a split second before answering, "No. I was not."

"You said you were his friend. Yes?"

"I did. I was."

"And you didn't know this?"

"I suppose it wasn't something he liked to flaunt."

Her irritation started to pick at the edges of her words, so I raised my hand a couple inches as if in school and said, "Is this helping you locate Mat? I mean, are we helping right now?"

Woods and Kessler shot me hard eyes and ignored my questions.

"Ms. Gabehart, when Mat was reported missing, we went to his house first and foremost to maybe get a handle on where he could be or to see if anything there might lead us to where he could've gone."

Kessler cut in, "His car was there, his television was on. There was hardly any damage done to his property, let alone his house, so if he had been inside, we can't assume he went missing in the storm. Heck, there wasn't even any flooding besides on his porch."

"What we also discovered was alcohol," Woods said. His eyes darted to me. "Lots of alcohol. Do you know what that means, Ms. Gabehart? Sam?"

With a reluctant peek at each other, she and I shook our heads. A silent lie.

"The side effects of mixing his medications with alcohol can be—"

"Dangerous," Kessler said.

And Woods finished, "For you. Or, like you said, for all of his 'girlfriends.'" He made air quotes around *girlfriends,* and Georgia's curls curtained her face as she looked down at her lap.

"Are you following, Ms. Gabehart? Georgia?"

"Yes, I am," she said, staying hidden under her mane.

"If you're still comfortable, Ms. Gabehart, I'd like to ask you a few more questions. Is that all right?"

Once again, she nodded. I closed my hands together to keep from interrupting the interrogation or from fidgeting too much.

"Okay," Woods said. He signaled for Kessler to open the folder so he could slide the papers back inside, then Woods straightened in his chair. "Did Matthew Corbin ever harm you in any way?"

That struck a chord and drew Georgia's irritation to a visible level.

Kessler said, "Was there any abuse going on? Physically? Emotionally?"

Georgia twisted her hair around her wrist and tossed it behind her shoulders, grabbing the armrests of the chair. "Why are you asking me these questions? What does this have to do with anything?"

"Georgia—" I said.

"What does this have to do with finding Mat?"

Kessler lay the file on the desk beside Woods's elbow and said, "We just have to check everything off our list before moving forward."

Woods agreed. "Before we presume him dead, we've got to ask you these questions."

Georgia slumped back in her chair, and I reached for her but yanked my hand back. *Not now. Not here.*

"Ask away," she said.

Woods sighed, clicking something on his computer. "Ms. Gabe-hart, if you'd rather speak to a woman about these things, that'd be—"

"No. What do you want to ask me?"

Staring at his screen, he said, "Did Mat Corbin abuse you sexually? Or do you know of anyone who might have had sex with him against her will?"

I started sweating as I recalled the night I'd snuck to Mat's house and heard Georgia begging for him to. . . *stop.*

Georgia jumped to her feet, the yellow silk of her dress draping around her knees with a subtle wave. "These questions are degrading, and they're implicating that I'm guilty of something I didn't do. Just because he was gone at the same time I was doesn't mean I had anything to do with it."

"Ms. Gabehart, you were supposedly the last person to see him alive, and after discovering what he could've been capable of after mixing alcohol with his medication...well..."

"Well, what?" she said.

Woods leaned back in his chair and held the pen with his thick fingertips beneath his chin. "Well, that's a motive. If he ever hurt you, that is."

The beginning of Georgia's angry defense was about to burst wide open, but Woods stopped her.

I hated myself for thinking that the cops were on to something. The same thing I'd been on to since I found Georgia wandering on the beach at entrance seventeen.

A motive.

"Which leads me to my next set of questions."

This time, I allowed myself to take Georgia's hand and try to calm her down. She wrapped her fingers around mine.

"It's okay," I told her.

This isn't okay. In fact, I wanted to hear more about the digging the police had done. It was far denser than any investigating I could've done on my own, and, this way, I wouldn't feel guilty about going behind Georgia's back and trying to decide whether I believed her or believed all the signs that pointed to the fact that she might have had a hand in Mat's disappearance.

She took a seat, and I sat on the edge of my chair.

"These questions are for both of you," Woods said. "Sam, like I said, I'm glad you're here. We needed to speak with you also."

The only thing I did was find someone who didn't want to be found, I recalled. I hadn't done anything wrong. Maybe this would be about the sailboat.

They have no proof.

Maybe they knew I drove back to the island to save Georgia, which would put me on Ophelia at the time Mat went missing.

Tell them you came back because you forgot your...laptop. Yes, your laptop.

My mouth went dry. "What do you mean?"

Georgia peered at me, clueless, almost as if I'd been hiding something from *her* the entire time.

Woods clicked around on his computer screen, and the white light sparkled on the cuffs hooked to Kessler's belt.

"At the beginning of summer, you and Ms. Gabehart were found by Officer Belcher breaking into the old lighthouse."

He and Kessler looked at me. Did they expect me to deny it? Agree with them?

"Yeah?" I said.

"Is there a romantic relationship between you and Ms. Gabehart?"

My heart pounded in my ears, then in my face, once more flushing me red. All the panic that had once engulfed Georgia was transferred to me, and my leg started to bob up and down.

"You two look like you've been on a date," Woods said.

I folded my collar and grazed the sweat on my neck. "You could say that."

"Well, a lot of people have seen Ms. Gabehart and Mat Corbin together, and there's suspicion now that there's some romantic involvement between the two of you. That's…"

He paused, taking in our reactions, analyzing why I might have wanted to kill Mat.

"That's something to look into. Yet another motive."

Georgia stomped her sandaled foot on the floor and rose again, ready to leave.

"This is pathetic," she shouted. "I told you I evacuated for the storm like everyone else. Somebody had to be the last person to see Mat alive, and just because it was me doesn't make me a suspect in his disappearance."

"The dots just don't connect," Woods said.

"So you're trying to make me confess that I killed him? Why, because you think he abused me? Because I might be seeing someone else now?"

She pounded her fist on the desk. Kessler stepped back, and Woods's eyes blinked as he startled.

"I had nothing to do with his disappearance, and no matter how much you beg for a confession from me, you won't get one. Not from me or from Sam. Take a look, Officer." She held her palms out over the desktop. "I don't see any blood on my hands."

Then she stormed out.

***

Despite the police being suspicious of me, I knew I was innocent, and they had nothing to go on.

But Georgia.

She hadn't called me after our date like she told me she was going to. And despite her frustration with the police, I couldn't share her anger because I'd been wondering the same things they had.

Why had she and Mat disappeared at the same time, from the same place, in the same storm, but only one of them came back?

It was murder, I kept hearing in the back of my mind. But my heart said, *If it was murder, then it was justified.*

The next morning, I rode Ole Red through town to get to the diner so I could check on Georgia. On the sidewalk that would lead me to Joe's Pancakes, a patrol car pulled out of a side road behind me. By default, I slowed down, waiting for it to ride past me.

I turned my head and saw the car a few yards behind my bike, tailing me. The silhouette in the windshield belonged to Woods, but I pretended not to notice and clicked Red up to seventh gear.

Matching my pace, he kept up with me; I could still see him in my peripheral vision.

The diner was just ahead, but I wouldn't put Georgia through another interrogation. What did Woods want with me? Would he follow me into the diner?

I sped past Joe's Pancakes, making a point of not looking inside, and took a sharp turn into the parking lot of the gas station where Mat used to work. Woods glided in behind me, but I popped Red up to his highest gear and circled the building, coming out behind Woods and darting in the other direction.

I wasn't going to the diner. And I wasn't speaking to Woods. Not until my head was clearer. I couldn't answer the cops' questions right now; I was afraid I was more on their side than Georgia's.

So I biked to Georgia's house. Mat's house had given me a handful of answers in the previous few weeks. Maybe Georgia's would give me evidence of her innocence. Of *my* innocence. Of something that would prove me wrong.

Her little brother, Jeffery, was playing outside when I wheeled up, and his mom was coming out the front door just as I placed Red against the porch.

"Hi," I said to her.

"Hey. I remember you." She gave me a yellow smile again. Her eyes were darker green than her daughter's, fogged over by years of cigarette smoke.

"Yeah, um, can I come inside for a minute? Georgia is at work and asked me to pick something up for her. From her room."

With her hand on the doorknob, she checked me out from head to toe, then swung the door back open.

"Of course. Take whatever you need, dear. She's probably forgotten her apron again."

"Thanks," I said, jogging up the stairs and through the door.

The house was dark inside, and the blinds were closed. Only streaks of yellow shinned through to the carpeted floor, so I turned on a light switch that lit up the narrow hallway.

Down the corridor, I came to three doorways. The first was her brother's room. The second was hers. No photographs hung on the walls, no baby pictures of her or of Jeffery, and no moments with Mat.

Georgia's bedroom smelled like her, like cherry Chapstick and coconut shampoo. Her belongings scattered all around me made me feel like I was violating her in some way. Because I was. I absolutely was violating her—her privacy. She hadn't asked me to come here, and I hadn't told her. But here I was, scouting her dark room for secrets.

I opened a little jewelry box beneath her wall mirror, but nothing in there gave me the answers I was seeking. Her stacks of high school textbooks didn't have any secret notes inside them, and her chest of drawers didn't hide anything except clothes. Neither did her closet of shirts and jackets nor the pockets of her jeans. I checked the gaps between her tables and the wall for a weapon that she could've tossed back there, and when I found nothing, I checked under her bed.

Piles of clothes and some of Jeffery's toy trucks lay in the dusty darkness, but I still stretched my arm under there to feel for a knife. A blade of some sort that was crusty with Mat's blood. Or the cold barrel of a gun. A rope. A rock.

No, no, no, she wouldn't have those. She didn't kill him.

I lay flat on the floor and stretched my hand farther back under her bed, and my fist knocked on something wooden. Feeling around all corners of it, I grabbed a box and dragged it to me.

A bare, untreated rectangle of wood sat before me, the lid closed.

I stood and set the box on her bed, then checked the hallway to make sure her mom was still outside before I dug through the box Georgia kept tucked away in the shadows.

Standing over the box, I rubbed my thumb over the lid. No dust. The silence swelled around me, emphasized as I opened the lid and a minor squeal came from the hinges.

Inside was just a rag. An old cloth. But the weight of the box had been too heavy, too unequally distributed on either side.

I picked up the cloth. Underneath, I saw a black hunk of steel that I realized was part of a handgun lying before me.

My breath caught, the start of a hyperventilation episode, but I calmed myself and took a step back. Clutching my chest, closing my eyes, trying to breathe—*in through the nose, out through the mouth*—I took a steady inhale. An audible sound escaped me when I looked down at the gun again, but I picked it up by the cloth and held it in my loose grip. I'd never held a gun. It was heavy. And my gut told me it had shot a bullet at Mat and taken his life.

The barrel hung down toward my feet, making me nervous, so I placed the gun back in the box, unable to tell whether it was loaded or whether the safety was on.

"Oh my God," I whispered.

The front door creaked open, and Jeffery's little steps pattered through the living room. His mom's scruffy voice said, "Keep the TV down, J. We've got company."

She called to me, "Hey, kid, you find what you're lookin' for?"

"Um," I shouted back. "Yes. I did."

I heard plates clattering in the kitchen sink and the water faucet turn on. She must've been cleaning the dishes.

Would I leave the gun here?

No, I couldn't. The police would eventually search her place if they saw through any one of her lies. Could I take it? I couldn't bring it to my room; they could search mine too if I started to show any signs of suspicion. Any more than I already was, that is.

The cold gun on Georgia's bed was not hers. It couldn't be. She wasn't old enough to buy a gun. If it had been her mother's, Georgia wouldn't have put it under her bed. This had to have belonged to someone else. Mat, maybe. A stranger. Stolen for protection.

Had I just touched the thing that killed Mat?

It can't be true.

Georgia's mom shut off the water and mumbled to Jeffery, "Stay here."

With frantic hands, I shut the lid to the box and tossed a shirt over it, turning around just in time to find her mom standing in the doorway.

"Was it her apron?" She dried her hands with a dishrag, staring right at me.

"What?"

"Her apron? Is that what you came to get?" she asked.

"Oh. Oh." I held up the first piece of fabric I found on her bed. "No, just her jacket. You know how cold she gets."

Her mom huffed out a scratchy laugh and left.

I dropped the jacket and took the gun with a firmer grip this time. The box would have to stay there, along with the cloth. If I were going to make the evidence of Mat's murder disappear, the only thing that needed to disappear was the gun.

Tucking the pistol in my waistband, I tore some notebook paper from Georgia's stack of textbooks and grabbed the nearest pen.

I left my note for her on top of the cloth in the otherwise empty box and hid it back in its quiet place under her bed.

I picked up Georgia's jacket and walked out of her room. Her mom was sitting on the sofa with her back toward me, and Jeffery was on the floor in front of the television.

The steel on my waist pressed into my flesh, too bulky to fully cover with my shirt, so I let my arm drop to mask it. I rushed past the sofa and made it to the front door before Georgia's mom turned around.

"Thank you," I said to her, opening the door.

"Yeah, dear," she coughed out.

At the bottom of the porch stairs, I hung Georgia's jacket on the newel post and repositioned the gun into a tighter spot in my waistband, then hopped on my bike, leaving the jacket, and went straight to the Chinese restaurant on Main Street. I couldn't walk into Piggly Wiggly with this thing on my hip, so I prayed Logan would be at his dad's place. Where else would I go? Who else would understand that I had to dispose of a gun so Georgia wouldn't go down for murder?

Duct tape. That's what I needed. I needed that to sink the gun on a rock in a swamp, in a marshy swamp, so no one would ever find it, so it'd never wash up on any shores. It'd just stay there with the alligators until the end of time.

I took backroads that stayed parallel to Main the entire way there, only passing a handful of other cyclists and families of golf carts. Keeping my head down, I flew past them all and raced across Main Street to another side road that led me to the back entrance of the Chinese restaurant.

Of the dozens of scenarios I played in my brain, I hadn't come up with a way to defend Georgia to the police. Not if they kept getting more suspicious of her. Of me.

I made sure the gun was tight against my side once more, then propped Red against the back of the narrow building. From out here, the noises of the kitchen banged against the wall, so I banged back on the door, and a Chinese man popped his head out.

"What?" he said. "What are you doing back here?"

I pulled at the hem of my shirt so the gun wouldn't make a suspicious bulge, but the man eyed me anyway.

"Can I see Logan? Is he here?"

"Of course he's here. This is his work when he's not at the supermarket."

"Well, can you get him for me? I'm in a bit of a rush—"

The door slammed closed, and I heard a muffled shout for Logan, who responded in Chinese. A moment later, he came out in a long, white apron, and shut the door behind him.

His black hair was pulled back halfway in a little bun. "Sam, what's going on?"

I pulled him by his black shirt sleeve to a corner between two dumpsters. Here, under cover, I was confident enough to stop trying to hide the lump in my waistband.

"What's happening?" Logan said. A strand of hair fell down his cheek, but he made no effort to put it back in place; his focus was on my hurried breathing, my paranoia. "Is this about Georgia?"

"Logan, I need your help. I—I couldn't go home."

"Sam, what's going on?" His dark skin went pale as he reached to put his hand on my shoulder, and I backed away.

"It's Georgia," I said, lowering my voice to a whisper. "I think the police are right. I think...I think she killed him."

Just saying the words spread a chill across my back and up my neck.

Logan looked back at the door of the restaurant and dragged me deeper into the corner. "What are you talking about?"

"I came here because I need tape. Duct tape."

"What?" Logan stopped, moving an inch away from me. "Sam, what's—"

"Listen, I just need some tape. Or rope, or something."

"Why? Do you need it or does Georgia?"

"Would it make a difference either way?"

He sucked in a shuddering breath and took another step back. "What are you going to do with tape or rope, Sam?"

"Please," I said. "Please just get me some tape, Logan. I don't wanna make a purchase at the hardware store, okay?"

"I don't—"

"Are you my friend?"

He offered a slight nod.

"Then trust me."

Sweat rolled into my eyes, but I ignored the sting and held Logan's wary stare.

"If Mat is already dead," he whispered, "because Georgia killed him, then why do you need these things, and why can't you tell me?"

I trembled at the thought of dumping such fresh information on Logan, so I had to tell him again, "If you're my friend, then you'll trust me."

Logan glared at me, then he walked out of the dark corner and back inside the restaurant. A minute later, he returned empty-handed.

Before I could ask where the tape was, he pulled a roll of gray duct tape from the pocket in his stained apron.

"Here." He handed it over, and I put the roll on my wrist like a bracelet. "Now, tell me what's going on. How do you know Georgia killed him? Did you have anything to do—"

Then his black eyes made their way to the bump in my waistband. Resisting the urge to yank my shirt down farther, I simply picked at the hem, making sure the handle of the pistol wasn't visible.

"It's nothing," I said. "That's nothing."

"Oh my gosh."

"No, Logan, it's not what you think it is. I had nothing to do with it."

He backed into the dumpster with an echoing thud, waiting for me to explain. When I remained speechless, he started to turn away, but I grabbed his forearm and came face-to-face with him.

"You want Georgia to be safe, right?"

"Yeah."

"Then you'll just have to trust me."

He looked down at the gun again.

"And you'll have to forget you ever saw me here."

Giving his arm a conclusive squeeze, I pulled my shirt over the pistol handle and ran back to Red, leaving Logan between the dumpsters and pedaling to the swamp at the dead end of Sea Dragon Lane.

Near the edge of the island at beach entrance five, the beach was just behind the mossy oaks, but it was a quiet Tuesday morning, and no one made it to the shore before noon.

I dropped Red in the gravel and followed the edge of the swamp into the woods a bit. The still water was covered by a film of green muck, with not even the slightest indication of a rippling wave. This was where the alligators were rumored to have lived. Our realtor had told us during our move that we needed to stay away from the swamps; the alligators gathered there, and all it took was a good chomp on your arm to take it right off.

I kicked the sticky leaves and mud in search of a rock, something heavy enough to sink to the bottom of the swamp and stay there, never to rise again.

A few feet away from the water, I finally kicked a stone. Getting on my knees, I lay the gun beside me in the mud and dug my fingers around a stone that was bigger than three of my hands. I pried it up from the mud, which sucked it into the ground.

The rock gave way, and I pulled it from Ophelia's tight hold. Around my wrist, the roll of tape fell into my hand. I wiped the dirt from the stone and positioned the gun on top of it, then tore off a strip of tape and placed it over the trigger, just beneath the barrel. Then I wrapped another strip around the handle. Two more over the barrel. The last ribbon of tape screeched off the roll, loud and final, covering the last bit of black steel exposed on top of the gray rock.

I stood and picked up the stone. It would sink all the way down.

Lugging it to the edge of the swamp, the extra weight made my sneaker dip deeper into the mud, so I backed away from the edge and hurled the stone—the gun, the weapon, the thing that killed Mat—into the water.

The green film cracked open, widening in the aftermath of the rock slapping the surface, waving out to the bank on which I stood. I waited for the water to settle, for the last bit of green to stop sputtering against the draping palm tree branches, for the murder weapon to land on the bottom of the swamp.

As the sloshing came to a subtle end, I cleaned my face with my T-shirt. Georgia's secret—the evidence of her guilt—was buried in a grave of alligators. The murder had been a justified attempt at self-defense, I believed, but that wasn't what the authorities could understand. Not with all the lies. Not with all their opposing beliefs.

And now, there was another trace of evidence disposed of. Another way to prove Georgia's false innocence.

Another secret drowned in Ophelia's waters.

CHAPTER 26

The diner was full during the lunch rush, but I spotted Georgia the instant I breezed through the front doors. She was behind the milkshake bar in her blue uniform, her hair golden. Then I saw Officers Kessler and Woods on the other side of the counter.

From the register, I watched Georgia stand motionless in front of them, tense, angry like she had been before.

I had ridden here to confront her—not about the gun but about my suspicions. About the police's spot-on theories. With the cops here, I should have left. But no, I needed answers. Correct answers. I wanted her to know that I knew, and then we could have kept that secret together. Forever. Mostly, it was closure I needed.

So I pushed forward. She saw me coming and started wiping down the counter with a cloth that looked too familiar.

"Hey," I said. "What's going on?"

It could've been my imagination, but I saw Woods grin at me.

"We were just leaving," he said, waving Kessler along. They stalked past me and out of the diner.

Georgia and I watched them exit.

She said, "They're just looking for an excuse to arrest me, but they have nothing. Only coincidences."

I wondered if they'd checked her for signs of abuse, but, by now, her bruises would've healed, and they'd have found no evidence on her skin.

"I hated Mat, but I didn't murder him."

"I know," I lied. Then I walked around the counter and met her by the soda machine. "Listen, I just dropped by to chat for a minute."

She paused. "All right. I've got a few tables, so can I meet you at a booth?"

"I need to talk to you now, Georgia."

A faint grimace twisted her face, and she fired a look of disbelief at me.

"Listen," I said, "if you want me to trust everything you've said, you have to tell me everything."

After tucking her cloth under the counter, she leaned her weight on the counter and closed her eyes. "You too, Sam? Really?"

"Tell me why you were on the beach during the storm. Tell me why you left the lighthouse. Why you promised I'd find you there afterward."

She pushed me out of her way and walked away, but I followed and stopped her at the end of the bar.

"Tell me why you weren't with Mat like you swore you'd be. Tell me why you didn't tell me you were staying on that old man's sailboat after the storm. Tell me everything, Georgia." I gathered her small hands in mine and pulled them to my chest. "I want to be on your side, but I have to know your secrets. All the monsters under your bed—you have to tell me about them. All of them."

Even I could hear how desperate I sounded, and she heard it too, because she led me out of the dining room, through the kitchen, and into the freezer. The chill of the frosty air lowered my heart rate, slowing my thoughts.

"I told you everything you need to know," she snapped. "What is this really about?"

"I know you did. But tell me everything I want to know. The things you're afraid to tell me, say them anyway."

She spun away from me and ran her fingers through her hair. "I don't know what you want from me. I've told you everything, and I don't want to keep talking about this. The police are on my case, Mat is finally gone, and now, when I should feel free from the hell he put me through, you're attacking me too?"

She turned back around, facing me again. I expected to see tears, but her anguish hurt me more.

"Georgia, you can trust me. I'll believe what you say is the truth, but just let me ask you again why you were out on the beach, because I know you weren't out there thinking like you said you were. Nobody would do that."

"I don't have to prove myself to you. For God's sake, Sam, do I look like a murderer?"

"Of course not. I just want you to know you can tell me anything. I'll keep your secrets. I kept Mat's, didn't I?"

She closed her eyes and angled her body away from me. "Get out of here. I can't be with you right now."

"What? Georgia."

"Sam, I can't. Not if you don't trust me."

"I told you I would trust you if you'd just tell me why—" *Why there was a gun under your bed.*

"Tell you what? That I killed Mat? Well, I've got news for you, Sam—I didn't, no matter what you believe." She walked past me, ditching me in the freezer. "I have to get back to work."

"I'm just trying to help you, Georgia."

"Well, stop trying to save me all the time, Sam. I don't need rescuing."

***

Logan came out of the back door of the restaurant on my fourth knock. Instead of going back to the dumpster, we stayed there by the closed door.

"Is everything okay?" he said.

"Yeah. Well, better, at least." I unbuttoned my shorts pocket and gave him back the roll of tape. He investigated its thickness for how much I'd used, which wasn't a lot. I could see his relief loosen the tendons in his neck.

He came closer to me and whispered, "Please tell me why you had a gun. And please tell me you didn't use it."

"No, no, I didn't. That's not a concern anymore. I came here to ask you for a favor. Another one."

He didn't budge, and I was certain he wouldn't commit.

"We can help Georgia. Okay? I've done my part, but you can help her, too. Just go to the police and tell them that you remembered seeing Mat wandering in the storm while you were evacuating. They would have to assume he died in the storm, and Georgia would be off the hook. It would work. It'd—"

"Sam, wait. Stop." Logan held up his hand and then dropped both arms at his sides, exhausted, ready to give up. "I don't think so. Listen, I don't know what's going on with you, but you're sounding insane today, dude."

"Logan, please, you can help her."

"No, I can't. The only person who can help is Georgia herself, I think. And I don't want to lie to the cops, bro. You know what kind of trouble you could get in for that?"

Yes. "They'd never be able to prove that you were lying."

"It's not about that. Dude, I'm doing this thing where I'm trying to, like, improve my flaws or whatever, so I can't lie to the cops. And I definitely don't want anything to do with a handgun."

I could only listen to the thoughts running through my frantic mind. *I'm so close. We're almost clean. She's nearly free.*

My heartbeat moved to my throat. If anyone could have understood, I thought it'd be Logan. He'd have been the one who put the nail in the coffin, tidied up the mess. His statement to the police could've changed everything. It would have. I knew it would have.

"I'm sorry," he said. He then gave me a single nod and went back inside the restaurant.

That was that. I'd done everything I could to cover Georgia's tracks. To force her innocence. To keep her mysteries unsolved.

But were we broken up? Had she broken up with me at the diner? Were we even in a relationship to break off?

Maybe I hadn't processed what she'd said until this moment, but she had said it. *Right?*

Maybe not. She was angry and confused. Yet I was panicked and desperate.

I'd just sunk what could've only been the murder weapon.

I'd just been tailed by the police.

The night before, I'd been questioned by Woods about my involvement with Georgia, with Mat, with everything.

On my ride home, I came to a halt and leaned against a tree, my vision prickling with black dots.

My God, I thought. I was just as much a liar as Georgia and Mat. *What have I done?*

***

My parents tried dragging me out for dinner, but I insisted they go without me because, as I'd told them, Georgia was going to stop by to maybe watch a movie with me or something. Dad nudged Mom and gave me a little smirk, telling me they'd make sure to stay out for a while.

I hadn't spoken to Georgia since I was at the diner, and I didn't have any plans to call her either, but I didn't have the energy to hang out with my parents tonight.

As soon as I pushed Mom and Dad out the door, I ran up to my bedroom and paced from my window to my closet. Window, closet. Window, closet.

Georgia's purple ring sat beside the lamp on my nightstand. I hadn't picked it up in days—I was so distracted by my nerves before our date that I'd forgotten she even gave it to me. She'd said that I must promise to not tell her secret.

I supposed I had kept one and spilled another.

The ring slid down my middle finger, and I held it there in my clutched fist. It made an indentation in my palm, and I watched as my skin filled it in before I put the ring back down.

Downstairs, I made a microwave dinner but didn't eat it, and I poured a glass of milk but didn't drink it. I turned on the TV but didn't watch it, and I thought about calling Logan's dad's restaurant but couldn't bring myself to dial the number. What would I have said anyway?

Sorry about trying to make you lie to the police, having you aid in hiding the murder weapon, and for telling you not to ask me any questions about it.

In a single day, I'd lost Georgia's trust and Logan's respect. Probably. All evening, I planted myself near windows so I'd be able to see any approaching police cars. Whether the cops knew Georgia had a gun or not, I thought they would never assume I had it, and, if they did, I could easily lie about it. They didn't have any proof that I'd gotten rid of the gun. They didn't know Georgia and I were supposedly a couple. If she even wanted that anymore.

I turned off the television, checked for a car in the driveway, and then went upstairs. Halfway up, the doorbell rang. Freezing in place, I let silence follow the *ding-dong*, tricking the visitor into thinking no one was home. After all, the Bronco was gone, but my bike was lying on the porch stairs.

Despite the urge to run away from the source of danger, I tiptoed to the nearest window and didn't see a car outside. But the black tip of a skateboard rolled beneath the window on the porch, and I pressed my face against the glass to see down the porch and find Logan waiting by the door.

I swung the door open.

"Logan," I said. "Hey."

He put his hands in his pockets, his brows furrowed in concern. "Hey. Can we talk?"

I hadn't rehearsed how I'd break it to him about what happened with the gun, where it was, or why I had it. No matter how much I wanted to keep it between me and that swamp, I invited Logan inside, and we went up to my bedroom.

Though I told him my parents were out for the evening, he still closed my door behind him, then dove straight in.

"Okay, we gotta talk about what the heck you were doing with a gun today. I mean, a gun, Sam? You had a gun?"

"All right, let me explain. I couldn't leave a paper trail at the hardware store, so I had to borrow those things from you. Plus, I kind of wanted to tell you everything, but I didn't. I don't know." I scraped my fingers through my hair as my internal temperature felt like it was rising.

"Yeah, you wanted—what—tape? For a gun? What was that about?" He threw his hands up, starting to pace as I had been doing before.

"Just sit down. You're making me nervous."

"Nervous? That's what's making you nervous?"

I motioned to my bed, and he sat with a reluctant slump.

"Okay," I began. "The other day with Woods at the station got a little…real."

"What do you mean?"

"I mean, he had some good points. Everything he said about Georgia and Mat going missing together and stuff all made a lot of sense. I'm pretty sure they think she killed him, and they think I had some part in it because we're dating. Or we were. I don't know."

"Wait." Logan gripped the edge of my mattress. "Do you actually think she murdered him? With that gun?"

"Well, that's the thing." I went to my dresser and grabbed her ring, holding it up for Logan to see. "A while back, Georgia got drunk and gave me this, making me promise to never tell anyone about Mat. He does things to her, you know."

He closed his eyes and nodded. "I figured. Never put it past him. But I've known Georgia since I've lived here. Everyone knows her. She's the diner girl; she'd never kill someone."

Setting the ring back down, I said, "But I went into Georgia's room today, and I found a gun in a box under her bed. Obviously, I didn't help kill Mat, but she might have actually done it, Logan."

He slouched under the heaviness of this information, his unfocused gaze landing on me.

"I couldn't leave the gun there," I said. "Could you imagine what would happen if the police found it? She'd go to prison for murder."

His cheeks puffed out with a sigh as he folded a loose wave back into his bun. "She would," he admitted.

"So I took it and taped it to a big rock and sank it in the swamp at the end of Sea Dragon Lane."

I was talking too fast, so I tried slowing down when I said, "The police were right about her. It was a homicide, Logan. Not another Boris fatality."

Bending over his knees, Logan rubbed his face with his hands. No matter the weight of this, I had to provide him with closure. If I hadn't, he would've asked for years about what happened with Georgia. And this had to end as soon as possible. The quicker we had closure, the quicker this would end.

My muscles clenched and unclenched with anxiety, which made its way into my shaky voice.

"They'll never know now, though, because the weapon is gone, and they haven't got any evidence."

Without warning, Logan jumped to his feet and came to me in one quick stride. He pointed a finger at me, his pinched features flattening into an expression of anxious anticipation.

"Did you make absolute certain that the gun went to the bottom? Sam, if they find that gun, then—"

"Then what? It couldn't have been hers. She's not old enough to buy a gun. Plus, she had it hidden. It wasn't hers."

"Did you confront her?" His nostrils flared open with each hot exhale that blew straight at me.

"Not exactly. She just kept saying she didn't kill him. But, Logan—" I stepped closer, feeling the need to whisper, to keep this as quiet as possible—"it was a choice I had to make. She was either going down for murder the moment the cops found that gun, or I could get it out of there and make her look as innocent as possible."

Logan reeled back a foot. "Sam, you can never tell anyone what you did. What she did. This has to stay locked up forever."

I nodded.

"And, between you and me," he said, meeting my low tone, "she was getting too hurt by him for too long."

"So," I said, "you think it was justified?"

He didn't have to say it. We knew. Everyone would be able to understand except the authorities. Logan had every reason to get out of here and never commit to being responsible for Georgia's secret, but here he was, my gracious new friend, standing before me, telling me he knew she'd had to do whatever it was she had done. Though Logan was new to me, and I was new to him, and I'd had no reason to trust him in the first place, he and I would forever stay linked by Georgia's God forsaken secret, and we'd earned each other's trust through it.

Adrenaline coursed through me and dissipated with a nod of Logan's head. "It's finished now. At least, it should be," he said.

"What am I supposed to do, knowing she did what she did?"

Logan shrugged. "Either stay with her and pretend you don't know or leave and never revisit this mess again. Your choice."

Stay was my immediate desire. But there was a certain amount of freedom in the idea of leaving.

Logan plopped back down on the bed, and I walked to the window. Georgia's ring—I felt it looking at me, making its presence known and demanding our respect, forcing us to keep the promise it symbolized.

Like the first day I met Georgia, I glared outside at the white sky, the white sun, and even inside at the white walls surrounding me. They did nothing but disappoint.

Logan tapped his finger on the bed, a light pat, pat, pat.

At the diner, Georgia had asked me not to rescue her, and I couldn't anymore. The rescuing was finished.

As I opened my mouth to tell Logan about Georgia's potential breakup with me, the doorbell rang once more. Logan's eyes darted to me at once, but I assumed the person behind the front door was Georgia. I started to run out of my room, and Logan called, "Sam."

"Don't worry."

I didn't realize how much I'd been craving Georgia's apology all day, then I felt dumb for having been worried that she wouldn't come by and tell me she was sorry for what she'd said, that she was just in a bad mood, pissed because the police had just questioned her again.

Logan jogged behind me down the stairs, waiting on the last step as I swung the front door open, about to rush into Georgia's arms.

But Officer Kessler stood before me, dressed in uniform. By accident, I looked straight to the gun on his hip before I pulled my attention back up to his stern face.

"Mr. Carter." He nodded to me. "Good evening."

I let my hand fall from the door handle, unable to make small talk.

"I'm here tonight to chauffeur you to the police department. Woods would like to have a word with you."

"What?" I said it before his statement even resonated with me.

Kessler sidestepped me and tilted his chin toward Logan on the stairs. "You've got company. Is anyone else home?"

"No, sir," I said, glancing down at the handgun again.

"You should know that Woods will think it's peculiar that Logan is here with you."

"Wait," Logan said. I heard him walk off the steps and come to a stop behind me. "What do I have to do with anything?"

The weapons and cuffs on Kessler's belt clunked together while he shifted his weight from one leg to the other. "There are some conspiracy theories about you two."

"What about Georgia?" I asked, grabbing the door handle again to brace myself.

"We just need to talk to you tonight, Mr. Carter. And Logan, since he's here."

I turned around to Logan, who was already looking at me. He hadn't done anything wrong, yet I could see exactly what he was thinking:

They think we're guilty too.

CHAPTER 27

E ach time I entered Officer Woods's office, it seemed smaller. Darker. With less chance of survival.

Kessler sat in the corner behind Woods's desk, flipping through another file. Meanwhile, Logan kept looking at me, the bun on his head falling into chaotic strands. I wished I'd brought Georgia's ring for luck, for a reminder, for anything, but I left it on my table, where it would stay until I knew Georgia and I would be okay again.

"You two," Woods said.

"What's going on?" I asked.

Logan shuffled in his seat and crossed his legs, some subliminal way of telling me to calm down.

Woods held up a finger to shush me while he clicked around on his computer, and Kessler handed him a file.

"All right," he said. "Just had to get some files straight." He locked his hands together on the desk and pinched his lips into a white line. "I'm just going to jump right in, boys. Now, I don't want you two getting nervous or anything, but you have to understand that you are both persons of interest in an investigation."

"Wait, both?" Logan said, uncrossing his legs. "Why am I—"

"Please," Woods cut in, "let me explain and ask you a few questions."

My core tightened, but despite that, I sat back, playing off my nerves, and Logan hunkered down into his seat again.

"Logan, I'd like to start with you."

He perked up, flushing white.

"Were you aware that Matthew Corbin and Georgia Gabehart were supposedly in a romantic relationship when you began helping Sam, here, track down Georgia after the storm? We've had some people around the island confirm they were a couple."

Blinking, Logan looked to the base of Woods's desk, wavering between a confession and denial.

My arm slipped off the chair, but no one noticed, both Woods and Kessler focused on Logan.

"No," he said. "I didn't know anything. I was just helping."

"So were you aware that Sam and Georgia had previously been caught trespassing at the abandoned lighthouse at the beginning of summer?"

"No. Dude, like I said, I was just helping out. Sam told me Georgia didn't show up after the storm, and I got worried."

Kessler closed a folder on his lap and jumped into the interrogation. "Did you know Georgia before you met Sam?"

"Yeah, of course. I've lived on Ophelia my whole life; she and I went to school together." A hint of annoyance underscored his answer, but I couldn't blame him.

"But you didn't know she was in a relationship with Mat?"

"No," Logan huffed.

Woods's shoes knocked around under the table in a chaotic rearrangement of his feet, which probably meant he was annoyed too. "So you and Sam became friends at the beginning of summer, around the time you"—he pointed to me—"made friends with Georgia?"

I stuttered, trying to agree, but Logan interrupted and said, "Yeah, that sounds right."

"Can I—" I started.

"Hold on. I can't help but notice that there seems to be a connection between the two of you." Woods looked from me to Logan. "And the three of you started to hang around each other at the same time? Logan, were you aware of Mat's drinking problem?"

Without hesitation, he said, "Yeah, dude, everyone is. He's a freaking drunk. Everyone knows that."

"Were you aware he was on medication that treats bipolar disorder and schizophrenia?"

Logan tilted his head toward me and resisted what I could sense was a call for guidance. He chose to lie—the right decision.

"No, I didn't know until now. But, okay, you do realize all I did was help find Georgia, right?"

"Listen," I said, "I knew Georgia and Mat were hanging out some when we became friends, but that was it. Logan doesn't know any more than I do."

Woods shook his head. "You're getting worked up, all right? You boys just need to calm down."

"Well, he didn't do anything wrong," I said. "Neither did I." But I couldn't trust that he bought my lie.

"I'm just doing my job, kid. We have to consider every possibility before presuming Corbin dead. And there are just too many suspicions about his disappearance—too many red flags—to come to a simple conclusion." Biting his bottom lip and letting out an exaggerated sigh, he turned to Kessler, who only responded with another long breath.

"What red flags do Logan and I raise together?" I said.

Woods looked skeptical, his stare boring into me. I tried looking away, and dipped back into my pool of lies for defense.

"We didn't do anything," I repeated.

"Remember when we discussed motives to murder Mat Corbin? When we talked to Georgia about Mat's abuse and alcoholism? How that could've been, in Georgia's eyes, reasonable cause to kill him?"

That combination of words took me back to my state of panic, to begging Logan for help, to the gun.

Motive. Georgia. Abuse. Reasonable cause to kill him.

"Uh," I said, "yes."

He sucked the breath right out of me, that Palmer Woods. I'd thought he had been on our side, but he was stabbing a knife right into my back. Then again, I was spitting lies like razors right at him.

"This is pathetic," I muttered.

"If there were any such romantic relationship between you and Georgia, then we could assume you and Logan—and Georgia—" he added as an afterthought, "worked together to get rid of Mat. Whether that was Logan helping a friend, as he would say, or setting Georgia free from her abusive boyfriend, or you, Sam, removing Mat from the picture. The storm would've been an opportunity to cover up a murder. You just have to understand where we're coming from."

As if Woods could tell I was about to get up and walk out, he said, "People do crazy things for love. Crimes of passion are more common than you'd think."

His conjectures landed on my shoulders, each one heavier than the last, and I started to break under them, unable to hold myself up anymore. My silence made me look guilty of murder, but I couldn't say anything to convince him otherwise. Even I didn't know exactly what happened. The details Georgia wouldn't give me were only assumptions in my mind, but to Woods, they were evidence that all led to one of us killing Mat. If only he knew what she'd gone through. If only he knew that she had needed a gun to protect herself and end her pain once and for all. But Georgia had her own truth, and I had mine, and Woods had his, and that would be the one to win.

In a clinking of his necklaces and swish of his loose pants, Logan stood and threw his arms out.

"This is insanity. You want to know what happened after the hurricane? I ran into Sam, and he was concerned that our friend hadn't come home. So we got together and came to you, Woods, for help, and we found her, and you seemed cool with it, but then suddenly we're suspects in a murder investigation?"

"Persons of interest," Kessler said.

"It doesn't matter. Some drunk went missing in a deadly storm, and you think we had something to do with it only because his girlfriend might like Sam and because she evacuated without leaving a map of where she was going. You must be really bored to come up with an entire murder mystery just from that."

My white-knuckled fists unclenched when Logan finally stepped back and lowered his voice. Perhaps he'd made the perfect point. Without knowledge of the gun's existence or the fact that Georgia had been wandering on the beach, Logan and I should've been off the hook.

"Yes," Woods said, "but also because he could've been physically or emotionally abusing her."

"Can I leave?" Logan said. "Do you need anything else from me?"

From the chair behind Woods, Kessler started to say something, but Woods broke in.

"Yes," he said through tight teeth. "You can leave. We'll contact you when we have more questions."

Logan turned around and contemplated me for a moment, and I began pushing myself out of the chair to follow him out when Woods said, "Sam, I need another minute with you."

I let myself collapse back down, and Logan hesitated in the doorway. I gave him a nod—*you can leave me here*—and the confidence on his face told me in response: *You were right; they'll never catch you or Georgia. They'll never solve this puzzle.*

He walked out, but I knew he'd be waiting for me when I got out of here. Woods angled his computer screen away from me, the light from it no longer illuminating him or Kessler, and his office seemed to shrink into an even smaller cube, but I sat on the edge of my seat, sure of myself, sure that I had all the pieces of the puzzle hidden. Drowned.

"Sam, can you give me the details of your evacuation?" he said.

The heartbeat came back into my throat like it had done earlier today, but I swallowed it. "I left with my family the day before Boris hit. We stayed at a hotel a few hours north."

"And who went with you?"

"My parents."

"What time did you leave?"

"Around four in the afternoon," I said.

Kessler leaned up and asked, "When was the last time you saw Georgia before you left?"

The night before when we were kissing in the lighthouse. "I saw her at the diner a few days earlier. She was working."

Woods took over again. "When was the last time you saw Mat, if you saw him at all?"

In his house, doing unspeakable things to Georgia. "I've never met him. Only heard of him around the island."

"All right." He didn't waver, and neither did I. "You and Georgia are close, yeah?"

I'm in love with her. "Somewhat. We're friends."

"Nothing more?" he said.

I don't know. "Nothing more."

"So did she ever come to you for help? Did you notice any bruises on her? Mention anything about Mat?"

Promise, Sam. "I don't know if he abused her," I said. "All I know is that he drinks, and now I know he was mixing alcohol and his medication. Which makes me wonder why you're suspicious of me. Why aren't you searching for Mat?"

Kessler snapped, "We are."

"We'll deal with him once we find him," Woods said. "If we find him. Which is why you're here. We just need answers from the people who knew Georgia and Mat so we can determine exactly what happened."

"No," I said. "You aren't using me to help find him. You're trying to determine who killed him, as if all three of us are murderers. So you can sit here all night and ask me what happened during that storm, but I'll deny having anything to do with either of their disappearances. Even if Georgia or anyone else killed Mat, there's no way to prove it."

Woods crossed his arms and got comfortable in his chair, reclining, while Kessler lay his chin in his hand, waiting.

"This investigation is based purely on circumstantial evidence, so if the coincidence of Georgia and Mat going missing at the same time is what's keeping you guys going, you've run out of fuel. Any physical evidence you might've had washed away with Boris. And," I said, "you're assuming Mat is dead."

Before I realized what I was doing, I had already stood and pointed a finger at Woods.

"You don't know anything. He could be off in bed with some girl down the coast. You don't know. I don't know. But if he's dead, he deserved it, and if he's abandoned Ophelia, then all the better for Georgia. You can keep combing this island for clues, but, in the end, you're just going to have a handful of perfectly sensible facts we've given you, and that's going to have to be enough, because what we've told you is a flawless story. Georgia left. She came back. Somewhere in between, Mat disappeared. No one will ever know what happened, but until you find any evidence against me or her or Logan, you have no reason to call us back in here."

I turned to leave.

"You're done," I said. "And I'm done here too."

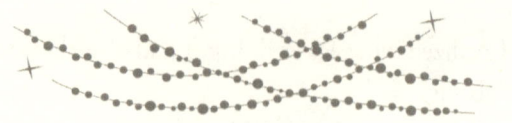

CHAPTER 28

For two weeks, the police seemed to be everywhere I went. Ole Red and I would make our way down Main, and they'd be parked by the sidewalk. I'd go to Piggly Wiggly, and they'd be there buying coffee, eyeing me in Logan's checkout aisle. I'd step into the diner, and the bell on the door would ring, and they'd turn around at the milkshake bar.

They'd watch Georgia greet me once Sonya handed me a menu, then we'd run away before they had another chance to investigate the web of lies we had trapped them in.

Three nights after Logan and I were interrogated by Woods and Kessler, Georgia called me for the first time in days to tell me they'd let her off the hook and that they'd check in with her if they had any more questions. They'd told her the investigation had slowed down, which was good, though I wanted it to close and be stacked on a shelf to grow cold with all the other cases.

But Georgia didn't want to talk about the investigation. She wanted to forget. Forget about Mat, the storm, the police. And I wanted to forget about the sounds I'd heard as Mat threw her onto his mattress. I wanted to forget about the alcohol, the drugs, the gun.

The gun.

Every morning, I woke up with the grip of the gun still imprinted on my palm. The slide of the barrel was still cold on my skin. The roll of tape still hung on my forearm. Logan's warning still hovered over me at night.

I went to sleep in my bed and woke up under a swamp, lost under the green film above, sinking to the bed of alligators below. And then I'd wake up. Empty-handed. Dry.

So Georgia forgot, and I couldn't wash the secrets off my flesh, even though summer was coming to a close and a colder season was on its way to end the previous one for good. The days moved at a slow pace while I waited for Georgia to get off work. We did normal things together, and we didn't talk about Mat. Those were the best days, the ones we filled with bike rides around the island, picnics on the beach, swimming in the ocean. I bored her with my bicycle trivia, and she challenged me to learn to surf, though I wasn't getting the hang of it, even after a few afternoons of practicing. Every single evening, we stood in each other's arms at the top of the lighthouse to watch the sky turn pink and orange, and I loved her more at the end of every single day. And I kind of hated that I loved her.

I hadn't told her again that I was in love with her, and she hadn't said it to me either. I wasn't sure what was holding me back, and even though I felt the words, I couldn't get them past the tip of my tongue.

For the first four weeks following Hurricane Boris, there was no sign of Matthew Corbin. While he had been a nightly news feature immediately following his disappearance, reports about him had begun to dwindle, and he wasn't such a big story anymore. I figured that was partially because people just didn't like the guy, but I knew Mat was dead.

Since Georgia had never answered my questions about the night I'd found her on the beach, I buried them away with secrets of my own, and they'd never resurface again.

I kept searching the internet for Mat and news related to his disappearance. I even searched for random John Doe cases around the state of Florida, making note of any that occurred just after Boris. Georgia never found out what I was doing, and I wasn't planning on sharing with her what I had found. Eventually, all leads ran dry, and there was nothing new about him on the internet or local news channels.

The final mention of Mat's name came just a few days after my last surfing lesson, and to anyone who didn't know him or care about him, it would have provided closure.

"Twenty-one-year-old Ophelia resident Matthew Corbin is still missing. Police have recently discovered that he was addicted to alcohol, was on bipolar medication, and is believed to have wandered into the storm. Police have been investigating his disappearance during the weeks following Hurricane Boris. It's looking more and more like Matthew Corbin was a potential victim of Hurricane Boris, but certainly, hope remains."

Once the news channel reported that they were hopeful for Mat's return, the news never mentioned his name again.

***

When Mat had been gone for almost six weeks, the City of Ophelia placed a headstone in the island graveyard in memory of all the victims of Hurricane Boris, including Mat, though he hadn't technically been presumed dead. Either way, he was the only island resident who disappeared in the storm and never came back. By the way Georgia told me, I sensed it was Sonya who informed her of the news because she'd said, "A friend thought she should let me know. To prepare me that the city wanted to honor him in some way."

Georgia and I both knew Mat didn't deserve a memorial of any kind, even if it was only his name plastered on a tombstone with eleven other names, but she wanted me to take her there. She wanted to say a spiteful goodbye. She wanted to stand over his name and see for herself that he was never coming back.

I was pleased to see that there were flowers on the cement plank, and none on Mat's name. Georgia was pleased too. We liked that his body wasn't under the stone, and we liked that his name was the only one that wasn't adorned with ornaments that said he'd be missed.

The headstone with three rows of names lay in the soft ground, peppered with oak leaves and strings of moss. The tips of Georgia's sandals stopped at the base of her ex-boyfriend's name, right there on the bottom right corner, and I waited behind her with my hands in my pockets. Looking down at his headstone could only anger her, and I wanted to smooth down her sharp edges, but I was afraid I'd get cut in the process.

A breeze filtered through the trees above, and Georgia's hair lifted and floated and fell. She didn't move, but she sniffled and wiped her cheek.

"Are you okay?"

"I'm fine."

I grazed my fingers across hers, and she snatched them away.

"I said I'm fine."

Then she growled something too low for me to hear.

Her fists were balled up, and she kicked dirt over the headstone, recoiling back and kicking again, so hard her sandal flew off. With her bare feet, she propelled soil over Mat's name, scowling over and over, "I'm glad you're dead. I'm glad."

She bent into the cloud of dust and grabbed her shoe, picking up a mass of leaves and sticks along with it. Then she threw it all on the dirty rock and beat it. Once. Twice. Fifteen times before I dove into the mess and dragged her into my lap. A sob came hurling out of her, but she pushed against my chest, and I found that her face was dry, only red with a frustration I'd never understand.

"I'm fine," she said. "I'm fine."

We both stood, and I wiped myself off, but Georgia left the remnants of the earth on her.

"I know you are," I said. Side by side, we looked down at the muddied headstone, her shoe still on top of it. I picked it up, and she balanced herself against me while she put it back on her foot.

Behind us, a pair of voices muttered across the shaded graveyard. Two girls walked toward us, but I turned my back to them. I didn't think they would be on their way to pay respects to Mat. I didn't think anyone would. After all, he was the only Ophelia resident who was assumed dead.

Georgia didn't notice them until they were standing right beside us. She and I moved out of their way, but Georgia gave them a confused tilt of her head. Backing away, she looked at the girls from their flip-flops to their ponytails, as if they were trespassing on Georgia's property.

The girl with brunette hair ignored our presence and said, "He just…just went missing."

It was bound to happen on such a small island.

Ophelia was no good at keeping secrets.

The girl's long brown hair reached her hips, which sparked something in my memory.

"It doesn't make any sense that he's just gone. Vanished. I didn't even know he drank. Who knew he had all that stuff wrong with him? Mat never said anything about that to me."

I glanced at Georgia. Her head was down. She was hiding behind her hair, but her heavy breathing told me she was ready to pounce. I hunched my shoulders and stayed still, not wanting to call attention to myself so I could keep listening.

The other girl leaned in and said, "I know it's hard for you, but he was a jerk to everyone. You know, he was probably cheating on you. He had that kind of reputation. That's why everyone warned you about him. Mat was no good for you."

When the girl twisted her thick brown hair around her wrist, I recalled where I had seen her. Her face belonged to the girl who was making out with Mat in the back seat of his car in the Piggly Wiggly parking lot.

"Georgia, we can go if—"

She held up a finger, eyes still hidden behind her curls. She wanted to hear this.

"Maybe I could I have helped him. Talked him down from the ledge? Maybe he would've opened up to me if I'd just tried talking to him?"

"There was nothing you could've done," her friend said. "He didn't even care enough to tell you."

"Telling him goodbye would have made this whole thing easier. The last time I saw him, we had a fight about why he never wanted to see me. Like, why he never put forth any effort."

"You shouldn't have been the only one trying to make things work. He was probably with some other girl. I hate that I'm not supporting you, and I know this is hard for you, but you had to know it was going to end sometime, and, well, maybe this was the only way."

"But why would he hurt me the way he did?"

That was when Georgia lurched at the brunette and drew her close by the girl's small arms. Her friend screamed and backed away when she saw me coming right behind Georgia. The girls both shriveled in fear, screaming as Georgia yanked down the collar of the brunette's T-shirt and exposed her collarbone.

"He hurt you?" she yelled at her. "He hurt you? I don't see any bruises on you."

I stepped behind Georgia and pulled her arms back, holding them away from the other girl. She fought against me, thrashing to be released, while the brunette's friend cried for Georgia to leave them alone. She screeched at us to leave, claiming she did nothing wrong, but all Georgia could do was heave herself at the brunette. I restrained her, wrapping an arm around her waist, but she got loose for a moment too long and pushed the girl to the ground.

"He didn't hurt you," she screamed. "You have no idea what hurt is until you've gone through what he put me through."

I grabbed Georgia and lifted her feet off the ground.

"Mat Corbin deserved everything he got."

The other girls fell silent.

"You meant nothing to him," Georgia shouted as I dragged her away, tearing at me to let her go. "He got what he deserved."

Each loud word was infused with her pain.

Our escape was chaotic, and Georgia was almost impossible to manage, but I got her to the parking lot and didn't put her down until we made it to the car.

Hot, steamy tears streamed down Georgia's cheeks and ran onto my neck. I kept my hold on her, fearing what else she might do.

"Calm down," I said. "Georgia, just calm down. What was that?"

"Mat lied to me from the beginning." She was still shouting. That fire inside of her was still burning. She flailed underneath my grip and demanded she be released. "He was a liar and a cheater, and he finally snapped, taking everything out on me. After that, he just—just wouldn't let me go."

"What do you mean?" I held her by the arm to contain the wild animal inside of her.

"Mat was too controlling to let me go. I tried to leave, but he got so angry at me. It was better for everyone if I stayed."

Nothing but broken-down, rusty arguments came to mind, though I wanted to say something to comfort her. I couldn't put up a fight, though. Not right now.

"Sometimes he wouldn't even let me—" she started. "He threatened to—"

I skimmed my hands down her arms, unable—or maybe unwilling—to hear her finish. "Mat can't hurt you now, Georgia."

She buried her head in the nook between my neck and shoulder. "It's over now."

"There's something else I need to tell you."

This is it.

I led her over to the Bronco's passenger door and motioned her to stay quiet until we were inside. Stuck in the dark cab of the car, we stared out the windshield in a terrifying silence.

"People get away with these things all the time," she said. "And I still can. I know I can, but you deserve to know the truth."

The truth? My instincts told me to expect more lies, but I craved her honesty. I needed it to go on.

She spoke in a low voice, watching me the whole time, but I sat immobile, glued to my seat, eyes locked in a blurry, black vision.

"It's about that day you came and found me."

I braced for impact, for the punch I'd been expecting to plow into my gut.

"Wait," I said. I needed everything to be clear; I needed all my questions answered before she continued. "Okay, that day I came and found you on the beach, what were you doing?"

A shaky breath tumbled out of her.

"When I went to your house," I said, "no one was there. No one was at Mat's house either. I thought he was home, but no one answered the door. Where were you, Georgia? Where was Mat? What happened that caused you to leave his house?"

She waited before she answered. Truth takes more time than a lie.

"Mat was at the house. He was there before you came back to Ophelia. But I got out of there and wanted to go to the lighthouse to ride out the storm, and then he called me because he was on the beach, drunk, having a stupid hurricane party alone at the cabana club." Her voice shifted to a whisper, her nostrils flaring. "That's what this is about."

My car keys fell into my lap, slipping from my fingers, which had lost all feeling.

"So he called me," she said. "Told me I needed to come join him. I thought I would be helping him. I wanted to pick him up and bring him home, and that was my plan. I was going to get him back to safety and then get off the island, like you wanted me to. And I decided that I was going to leave him once and for all when the hurricane was over."

"Why didn't you drive his car to the beach?" I said. But the question begging to escape me was, *Did you want to leave him for me? Or leave him because you came to your senses?* Part of me hoped it was the latter. I couldn't have her depend on me. She never did and never will, and she needed to put herself before me. I just wondered what prompted her to finally make a break for it.

"Mat had the keys with him," she said.

This new bit of information put miles between us. I didn't know the person who was sitting right beside me. Georgia had strayed, and she was too far away from me, and I couldn't stretch far enough to bring her back.

"Go on," I said.

"I found him passed out drunk."

She laid the whole wretched story out in front of me. I wanted every detail, and Georgia gave them to me. She explained everything, every minor detail, every major sentiment, from the beginning, middle, and end. The police wouldn't have been able to figure it out. Nobody would have.

"I was such an idiot; I should have just stayed at the house. But I thought I could save him. I didn't think I had the heart to let him drown in the storm. It was the right thing to do, you know? To go get him? So I went to the beach to look for him, and I found him. He was unconscious in a pool of water on the floor of the cabana. I had no idea how long he had been there. I couldn't move. I could only stand over him and think how disgusting he looked. I wanted to spit on him. I wanted to hurt him while he couldn't hurt me. But I had to be better than he was. If I could just get him home, I thought, I could have saved him and then left him forever.

"And then I caught sight of the newest bruise on my wrist, and I couldn't stop thinking about all the times he had dragged me to his bedroom. All the times he had hit me. He rarely used to hit my face because, well, people would see that, wouldn't they? Every single time he'd had too much to drink or hadn't taken his medication, he took it out on me. It was my chance. I could hurt him while he was down, and maybe, for once, he would know how it felt. I looked out to the ocean, Sam, so hungry for some kind of disaster."

I couldn't tell what she meant by that.

"The tide was coming in, and the storm was getting stronger. The whole time, the water kept coming closer and closer to where Mat was lying." She looked at me, her eyes earnest. I think she was waiting on me to fill in the blanks for myself, but I wouldn't do it. I deserved to hear every last ounce of truth.

"I left him there. Right there on the floor like the scum he was. I left him there at the cabana at boardwalk twenty, and I ran away, and

I never looked back. Not until you showed up on the beach, that is, at entrance seventeen."

Georgia's confession came out dripping with bile from where she'd kept it hidden for all those weeks. Mat's fate had been determined before I found Georgia wandering the beach. Everything was finished—done, completed—before the eye of the storm even hit the island.

"And I let the hurricane have him."

We broke into a disjointed stillness, and my body locked down, numb. I watched everything I thought I knew about Georgia fall away, just like when she was gone and I couldn't feel her. I couldn't see her. I couldn't know her.

Ophelia, known for drowning. And all these drownings, they didn't go down in clear waters. These were muddy deaths. They were all dirty.

Each of Georgia's emotions, all the revenge-filled thickness in her throat, came out of her like vomit. Her lips were still moving, but I didn't hear her words. She moved toward me, snapping me out of my momentary trance, but I jerked away from her.

"Now," she said, "I finally know where he is. I know what he's doing and who he's with. I wish I had known who he was before it was too late. But now when people ask, I'll know he's sleeping with the fish."

My parched mouth was closing up, but water wasn't what I needed. I needed Georgia. The Georgia from the beginning of summer, not this girl I barely recognized. This was why she had been on the beach that day, why she had been nervous at the police department, why she hadn't answered the phone or given me a straight answer about anything. Why, on the surface, things between us seemed fine, but underneath she had been lying to me ever since she came back. Everything unraveled right before me.

Georgia had let Mat die. She hadn't killed him, but she hadn't saved him either. That should have made me feel better, but still, I couldn't pin why it all felt worse somehow.

"Oh my God, Georgia," I choked out. "Why didn't you tell me?"

She looked at something off in the distance, and I couldn't quite follow her gaze. Whatever it was, it stood miles away from me, and I felt like she did too.

"Why didn't you just break up with him before that?"

Her answer was simple. "Because he knew where I lived, and I never had the guts."

"If you thought Mat hadn't survived, why did you still disappear like that?"

"It was best for me to be out of the picture while Mat was big news." She stiffened. "Do you think I killed him? I could've tried to drag him off the beach. Could've tried to rouse him or call for help or *something*." Another pause. "But I didn't."

"Why would you go save him, Georgia? After everything he did, why did you go to the cabana in the first place?"

"I couldn't leave him there in the storm. And then…" She gulped and closed her eyes. "And then, suddenly, I could."

"Georgia," was all I could say. Even that was difficult.

"I was going to come back out of hiding the next day. But you found me first. I'm still scared. He held a gun to my head, Sam. That night he died, we were in his house, and I tried to leave, but he put a gun in my face and told me I had to stay."

That gun—it wasn't hers. It was Mat's. And she hadn't shot him with it.

"Somehow, I got the gun and threatened him with it, aiming at him until I could get out of there."

If she went looking for it under her bed, she'd see that it was gone. That I took it. I wasn't ready for that this soon.

She seemed so frail, and I wanted to wrap her in my arms to comfort her, but I couldn't. Not yet. *I can move past this, right?*

"I didn't shoot him. I couldn't. I had every reason to, but I didn't. That's when I escaped and tried to go to the lighthouse to hide out during the storm, but I stopped at my house first and ditched the gun. Then he called me, and I didn't think I wanted him dead, because if

I wanted him dead, I could've just shot him. So I went to the beach, and I left Mat there, and you found me, and ugh—"

"Everything is okay. No one knows," I said. But I couldn't even feel myself talking. I could feel only the vibration of those false words—*everything is okay*—slipping off my tongue.

"Thank you for caring so much about me." She sounded finished with me, thanking me for everything and leaving again after the closure of coming clean to me. Then she kissed me. I didn't kiss her back, at least not at first. I thought I could handle her truth, especially since she didn't use the gun, but. . .

But.

But she still let him die.

This truth was tangible, right in front of me, and my assumption about the gun, the cold-blooded murder, hardly left my imagination. The real story, though it was less severe than the one I'd fabricated, was somehow worse.

I thought. . .

I thought that if she hadn't shot Mat, she wouldn't have had anything to do with his death.

"I'm not who you think I am, Sam."

There could never be a balance between this love and that trauma. Any judgments I had, I erased. She left me no choice but to understand why she wanted to do it. Why she had to.

I thought of saying something that would confirm us still being *us* after her confession, but the brokenness of what had happened with Mat might've been getting ready to shatter me too.

"Do you see, Sam? I'm sorry for this. But—but do you understand?"

Since Mat had disappeared, I'd been convincing myself that his death was justified, but the picture of it—the image of his body being swept out to sea, of his gun aimed at Georgia, of her running down the beach in the storm—it was an entirely new skeleton that I had to stuff in my closet. That I had to sink in a swamp.

"I'm not guilty, Sam," she said. "I'm just not innocent."

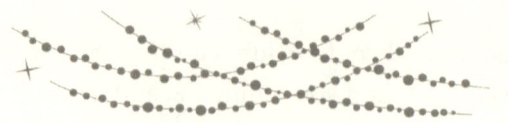

CHAPTER 29

Although nothing was supposed to change between us, something did. A fault line had appeared, and we stood on opposite sides of the void, the distance between us growing wider, deeper.

She scared me sometimes. She unsettled me. She kept me running, always. No matter what, deep in the cloudy recesses of my mind, I was afraid that one day I wouldn't be able to catch her again. She was detaching from Ophelia and from me. My grasp on her seemed so loose. Georgia was sand dripping from my palm; I could only keep it in place for so long before it slipped through my fingers and fell away. She wanted freedom, and being in a relationship with me wouldn't free her, but I couldn't force myself to let her go.

A few days after her confession in the car, I told Georgia I was going to Joe's Pancakes so she could serve me waffles and ice cream. How could I have acted as though nothing had happened? I'd known and accepted that she killed Mat, but hearing from her own mouth that she had let him die—it stuck with me. It clung to me just like the gun, and I woke up and went to bed with it every day.

Nothing about me and Georgia felt real anymore. We hadn't spent much time together since she admitted the truth. That could have been blamed on her increased hours at the diner or my preparations to attend college in the fall, but perhaps it was because we hadn't found much else to say to each other. I tiptoed around both of our secrets, and she avoided talking about the previous few weeks. My classes started in three weeks, and I wasn't sure how often I would see Georgia after that. I wanted to be there for her anytime she needed me. Anytime she felt scared. But she hadn't beckoned me once, and that told me everything I needed to know.

Ole Red took me to Logan's restaurant, and I banged on the back door. His dad opened it and then shouted for Logan, who stepped out, wiping sweat from his brow.

By the dumpster, I explained the truth. I explained what had happened at the cabana. I told him why Georgia had had the gun. Why she had left. Where she had gone. Why she hadn't come back. He learned it all, and he didn't respond with questions about Georgia but with one for me instead.

"Are you all right? You don't look all right. You're not acting yourself."

"I am. Yes, I am."

"But, Sam, are you and Georgia going to survive this?"

We were too new and fragile to weather this storm. "I'm not sure."

Before I started wondering whether I was actually all right, I left.

When I saw Georgia, it was usually at the diner. Some days, she greeted me with a kiss on my cheek. But instead of feeling fluttery excitement, I felt relief that I'd gotten another kiss at all.

One morning I got there, and she seemed happier than I had seen her in a while. "Hey, there," she said, bright as sunshine. "I guess you'll take a Coke and Georgia's Favorite this morning."

"Oh, they renamed it, I see." Times like these reassured me.

After I had eaten, she sat down with me and started telling me about how Joe was thinking of changing the menu design, when a break in the conversation led to silence.

"I told Logan everything," I blurted.

Her smile drooped. "Okay." She took in a slow breath. "Okay. That's fine."

"It's just that he helped me with so much, and he knew a lot already, so I thought he should know. He asked me," I lied.

"I said it's okay, Sam. You were right to tell him." The way she pulled her hands into her lap and looked down made me reach out to them under the table.

"I'm sorry. I shouldn't have. It wasn't my business to tell." Guilt cramped my chest, but it did in hers too, I thought. She hated herself. I could see it in her sudden lack of confidence. She didn't strut across the island anymore; she was a recluse until she had to move from one place to the other.

"So, um," she said.

"What?"

"Sam, I—"

Someone yelled from the back, interrupting her before she could say anything else. "Georgia, stop with the slacking."

She shot out of my booth and smoothed down her apron.

"What is it?" I said, nauseated, wishing I hadn't eaten anything.

"I'll have to tell you later."

"Call you tonight?" I said.

"Yeah, of course. Bye." She blew me a kiss, and it came to me on a bitter, thin breeze. With that, she was gone.

***

Though I was planning on calling her, Georgia called the house phone as soon as her shift was over. I leapt for the phone and took it up to my room, putting off my parents' weekly vintage movie night. On any other evening, I would have been excited to hear from her, but the fact that she called me—that she was the one reaching out for once—terrified me.

I answered the phone.

"Sam?"

"Yeah, hey, Georgia. Is everything okay?" I'd been asking that question too much this summer.

The background was quiet, then a breeze crackled through the line. That's when I heard the ocean waves, and I knew exactly where she was standing.

"Can you and Logan meet me at beach entrance seventeen?" Where I had found her moments after she'd left Mat's body to rot in the storm. The abandoned entrance. The one least traveled. "I need you guys to come out here. Alone. Don't bring anybody else."

"Wait, is this what you were trying to tell me at the diner today?"

"Well, not exactly. But this is still important. So can you meet me? You and Logan?"

My eyes went straight to the ring on my nightstand, so I walked over and picked it up. Slid it down my pinkie. Let it fall into my pocket.

Too scared to question anything and knowing I wouldn't get an answer if I did, I said, "I'll be right there."

Logan answered just before voicemail picked up, and he agreed to meet me at entrance seventeen. He didn't need an explanation; the second I mentioned Georgia's name, he settled into a brief, wordless daze.

"I'll be there in ten," he said.

My parents were snuggled together on the couch, so my absence would only mean more blankets for them. Mom let me jog out the door with no more than a "Where ya off to, Sammie?"

"Georgia's," I spat off the top of my head. "She just wants some company."

"You two have fun."

Dad laughed. "But not too much fun."

I left them giggling on the sofa, bolted out the door, and steered Red down the dark road in the opposite direction of Shell Way.

Logan stood at the boardwalk access when I arrived, so I dropped my bike at his feet and started walking down entrance seventeen.

"You waited for me."

"What the heck are we doing out here?" he said in a harsh whisper. Our shoes made loud steps on the planks of wood, which would warn Georgia of our presence, so I slowed down and lightened my step. I needed time to decide how I would handle whatever she was going to tell us. But my nerves weren't as unsettled as I thought they should have been. I'd become numb. Georgia, at one time, had made me feel every sensation all at once and then, all at once, she had sedated me with a single snap of her fingers. A single sentence.

I left him there.

"I don't know," I said to Logan.

"Her sleeves are filled with tricks. Twists and turns. We were wrong. Can you believe that? The whole time we thought—"

"I know. Whatever we thought we knew…" I couldn't finish.

Right there on the floor like the scum he was.

We walked onto the powdery sand and slipped out of our flip-flops at the #17 sign. When I looked up, I found Georgia's silhouette at the edge of the shore. The waves crashed around her ankles, but she remained still. A flame in all that water. Her back was to us, but she knew we were coming up behind her. She knew. She knew everything. Because she was the artist, and I was the brush, and she'd turn our meeting into whatever she wanted it to be. Georgia was the one in control. I had no choice but to succumb to the power she'd had over me since the beginning. She had hypnotized me the moment I saw her walking into the cabana.

Logan and I stopped a meter away from her, but she faced the sea, and I thought I saw part of her soul swimming away from us and out into the ocean's oblivion. Perhaps that was where she belonged. In a sea devoid of people. A place she could escape to and rule over and hide forever. A place I'd never belong.

"Georgia."

With a definitive nod to the black ocean, she turned around. She didn't hug me. She barely looked at me, but if she had, I wouldn't have been able to tell.

"I'm glad you both came."

Logan sent a secret glare my way, but I pinned my focus on Georgia.

"I had to see you two."

"Should we be concerned?" Logan said.

"Let me just say this." Georgia's curls fell around her face when she looked down at a glass bottle in her hand. She spun it in gentle turns, indicating it was empty of liquid. "I'm ashamed. Logan, I'm ashamed you know what I did, and I'm eternally grateful for your willingness to keep me…safe. I didn't mean for any of this to happen."

"Georgia," I said, "you don't have to apologize."

"Yes, Sam, I do. I put you through hell for something I did, and I made you lie. I made you wonder. I probably made you wish you'd never met me."

"I could never."

"Please," she said, "let me say this."

I backed a few inches away from her. That was what she wanted from me—space.

"I'll never assume respect from either of you. Not after what I did. How could I, after all, if I don't have respect for myself? You didn't deserve to be responsible for keeping my wrongdoings to yourself. You'll have to carry this burden forever, just like I will, and I hate myself for being the reason for that."

Logan tucked a wave of hair behind his ear. "We did what we wanted. You didn't make us do anything."

"Yeah, Georgia," I said. "We chose to be on your side."

"But I'm guilty of everything the police asked me about, and I was a liar, and I ran away from my problems instead of confronting them. And then, when I came back, you were both forced into pleading my innocence. You were dragged into an investigation that I started, and I'm sorry. I'm sorry you have to live with everything I made you do."

"Georgia," Logan said, "I know we aren't really close, but I know you, and I know the girl I went to school with all my life, and I know you wouldn't have hurt someone if it wasn't necessary. If it wasn't to save yourself."

She let him keep talking.

"I know Mat too," he said, "from around the island, and anyone would deserve better than him. You shouldn't be in trouble for that."

"We know you had to do what you did," I said. "Look at what Mat did to you."

"Which is why I'm going to force you to do one more thing." She held the glass bottle in front of me and Logan. He brushed his finger down its neck, grabbing the base to inspect the faded Cola logo before releasing it to Georgia again.

"What happens on the beach stays on the beach," she said. "You've kept my secret for this long. I'm asking you to keep it until you die."

She let the bottle hang by her side while she grabbed a necklace that I hadn't noticed she was wearing. It was a choker necklace, made of twine that held a little white seashell. Gripping the shell, Georgia yanked it from her neck.

"I made this when I was a kid. The week I moved to Ophelia."

Holding the bottle and the shell necklace level with each other, she dropped the necklace into the mouth of the bottle, and the shell clinked against the glass.

"This symbolizes that I'm never going to tell anyone what happened on this island. It stays right here in this bottle, and when we're done here, I'm going to throw it into the ocean, and we'll never speak about it again, or see it again, or think about it again. All right?"

Yes, I told myself. But I'd never stop thinking about it. Like she said, it'd be with me till I die.

Her ring unbalanced me in my pocket, heavy all the sudden. I took it out and held it to the moonlight. The purple stars on it winked at me one last time, then I dropped it into the bottle. It landed with a final clink beside her seashell.

"Promise," I said.

Her green eyes stole up those purple stars and sparkled with the memory of the night she gave it to me. I imagined the stars taking a bow in tribute to the fight we had put up and won, and then they fell away like tears that she had cried.

Logan reached under his hair and tilted his head to the side. Then he exposed a diamond stud that flickered in the night.

"My earring. I wear it everywhere."

"You swear that this stays between the three of us?" Georgia said.

He took the neck of the bottle once more, and they both held on to it while he let the diamond roll from his fingertips to join our objects of promises.

"Absolutely."

Georgia nodded at him and sighed down at the bottle, then took a cap out of her jean shorts pocket and screwed it on.

"What happens on Ophelia—"

"Stays on Ophelia," I finished.

Giving me the slightest hint of a smile, Georgia handed me the bottle. "Please."

My warm skin grazed her cold hand as I seized the bottle. Logan and Georgia parted before me, and I stepped toward the waves. The bottle chimed with our seashell, ring, diamond. With our forgiveness. With our resolution.

It sang with our quiet song of release.

I raised the symphony of freedom high above my head and swung it back, so breakable in my strong grip. Then I launched it out to sea with that piece of Georgia's soul, and yet another secret sank in Ophelia's ocean.

The three of us stood at the shoreline, the blood no longer on our hands, and we breathed. I breathed because, finally, I had resurfaced from the swamp.

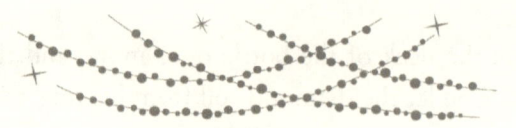

Chapter 30

That thing she'd wanted to tell me at the diner two days ago, before she was called away—maybe it was nothing. She could have just wanted to tell me that the diner was taking the waffles and ice cream combo off the menu. It was possible that she had decided to get another job. Maybe she was going to take up fishing. Whatever. The only thing that mattered was finding out what she had to say.

Earlier today, I had stopped at the diner for a to-go milkshake for my dad, and Sonya had caught me by the sleeve and pulled me to the side on my way out the door. She had never touched me before, but, this afternoon, she kept her moist hand wrapped around my forearm.

The alarm in her whisper made me worry that the police had come back to search for Georgia or me, but she instead told me, "Be careful playing with knives, kid. You might very well get cut. You take care of her because she's a good one. And remember,"—Sonya jerked me closer—"she was brilliant enough to get rid of her last problem. She'd be just brilliant enough to get by with it again."

I yanked my sleeve away and backed toward the door. "You—you know?"

"I know everything, Sam. So you be good to her. She's a daughter to me."

Though I had already known that to some extent, I still couldn't respond with an answer that would satisfy Sonya. No one was good enough for Georgia.

The only thing I could do was nod. Then Sonya spun around and walked away, and I ran out of the diner.

My fingers trembled as I dialed Georgia's number at 9:48 that night.

"Hey, Sam."

"Georgia?" I said.

"Hi," she said again, and I heard her plop down on her bed.

"How was work?" My small talk came out tight and forced.

"Work was great. One of my favorite customers came in today."

It took me a second to realize that she meant me, so I lay back against my pillows and tried relaxing. "Well, I hope he didn't get you in trouble for talking to him."

"He didn't. But I like this guy—he always orders my favorite."

"That's the only reason you like him?"

"One reason among many."

We bantered on like that for several minutes, and I found myself basking in the beauty of her voice again, of everything she'd ever said to me, and I let myself get lost in that illusion. The ice was well broken then, so I decided to come right out and ask, "What was that thing you wanted to tell me the other day at the diner? You were called away, but you seemed like there was something you wanted to talk about."

She was quiet for a moment. "Oh, it was nothing."

"Oh," I said. "That's fine." Relief and disappointment warred within me, tugging me in both directions, but I didn't know which way to fall.

"I would love to see you tomorrow, but I have to work in the afternoon," she said.

"Okay, let's get together in the morning. Where do you want to go?"

"Let's take a bike ride." She was too quiet, too quick to answer. Whatever she had wanted to discuss with me earlier was still present on her mind. "I've enjoyed that a lot lately." Her voice was barely a whisper now, but I was afraid to push her any further.

Georgia didn't enjoy bike rides as much as I did, though I allowed myself to at least respect her effort at pretending. But something else lurked just beneath her motive—another secret, one more lie, another plan for an escape.

***

The next morning, I met Georgia at the end of her drive for that bike ride she wanted, but after an hour of idle conversation, I pedaled Ole Red in front of her, heading toward the beach. I hoped that if we took a break from riding, we would have another chance to talk because, even though she was right behind me, Georgia was a million miles away.

We parked our bikes at the end of the boardwalk and sat close to the dunes. Georgia collected a handful of sand and sprinkled it through her fingers, allowing it to rain over my toes.

"You know, Susan B. Anthony called bicycles freedom machines," I said just to break the silence.

"Hmmm," she mumbled, but she wasn't really listening. I could tell she didn't know who Susan B. Anthony was. She knew about freedom, though, and she gazed out over the ocean, and I wished for just a moment that we could swim away together. Or that I could send a slice of my soul out there to meet hers.

Her face was inches from mine, and even though she wasn't looking at me, she still had the ability to reach the depths of my heart and wrap it around her finger. I expected her to say something funny or at the very least laugh at my nerdy obsession with bike history, but she did neither.

"This has been a really good day," she said, but she was still far away.

Concern pulsed through me. "It was a good ride."

"I wish it could have lasted longer."

"Let's do it again tomorrow," I said. "Next time, I can bring lunch."

Georgia finally turned to look at me. "We can't."

An abrupt, recognizable ache began to spread across my body. "Why? What's wrong?"

"Sam." She pushed the powdery sand beneath her fingers, forming it into the shape of a volcano. "I wanted to tell you this sooner, but

I just found out a few days ago. I haven't had much time, and it was just never the right time to tell you. Telling you over the phone just didn't feel right."

The bad feeling I'd been having all week—that cold, obscure ghost that had been haunting me—slapped me in the face.

"What is it, Georgia?" My heart plummeted to the ground, and my stomach turned to concrete that set harder each time Georgia tossed me around her scary carnival ride.

She paused and bit her lip, turning it white. "I have to get out of here. This is my chance to leave Ophelia." Slouching down beside me, she placed her hand over mine. "I can finally go north."

Something choked me—something that had probably been there all along but came alive only now to make me sick. "Why? When?"

"I have to go," she said.

The beach was quiet. It was such a beautiful day to ruin.

"Some of my high school friends from last year are taking a trip to Michigan, and they're going to drop me off in Grand Rapids. This is my ticket away, Sam. I have to go."

"What?"

"Listen, please."

"What will you do? Where will you live or eat or work?"

"Sam, I've saved every dime I've ever made from the diner. I'll get another waitressing job, and I'll find my own apartment or something. I can't stay, Sam. You know I can't stay here."

"How will you get around once you get there? Grand Rapids isn't Ophelia. I mean—"

She gave my hand a hard squeeze. "Maybe I'll get a bike. I'm sorry, I should've told you sooner—"

"Well, what about your little brother?" I was grasping for anything to anchor her to Ophelia or to me, trying to say anything that would make her want to stay. But there was nothing on the island that gave her reason to stay.

"He'll be okay without me," she said. "It's going to be all right."

"What about us?"

"Sam, you made this summer unforgettable. We both did. But that's not enough now. I wanted to tell you sooner, I did, but I couldn't hurt you like that. It was never right between us. I was never right for you."

"But—" But what? She had made her decision, and she had spent the past few weeks letting me go. "Georgia, that's not true. You are right for me. I can be good for you too."

"You *were* good for me Sam, but I can finally do what I've always wanted to do. It's not all about that, though. Since Mat, I just can't stay here. Not after what happened."

"Georgia, you can still stay here. Nobody will ever find out about what happened."

"It's more than that. Bad memories are all over this place, and I just can't do it anymore. Please understand, Sam. It's everywhere I go. He's there. He's in the big thundering clouds, and he's at the gas station, and he's all over me. I look in the mirror, Sam, and I see him. I come out to this beach, and I see what I did to him and what he did to me, and I know that the tide came and got him—these very waters came and swallowed him up—and I know no one will ever know, but I will. I do. And so do you."

I pressed my nose to hers, closing my eyes and grabbing her face. "Don't say those things, Georgia."

"When I'm here, I'm still with him. It doesn't matter whether Mat is dead or alive, he's never really gone."

"He is, Georgia. Mat can't hurt you anymore."

She nudged my face away from hers.

"Just don't…please stay." It was the only thing left for me to say.

Tears rolled down her cheeks.

"I can't. I can't stay here anymore. I feel trapped on Ophelia. I'm too afraid here. Moving on here on the island just isn't possible. I've wanted this for a long time, and you know that. Now I can. Sam, it's the best choice for me. For us. You have school and your parents. I need a fresh start, and so do you. I can't ask you to protect me forever; I won't do that to you. I've done enough to you. I know it's terrible timing, and hurting you is the last thing I ever wanted to do. If I had known this was going to happen—"

My heartbeat thumped behind my eyelids, but I couldn't cry in front of her. I couldn't cry at all; I had been expecting this for days.

"Georgia, do you have to go? I thought you were fine again, and we—*we*—were fine again. I mean, the bottle—we forgot all about the bad stuff, right? I'm willing to make it work. I thought you were too."

And then it hit me, breaking my back and crushing me under its mass—Georgia was being more honest with me now than she had ever been. Her words tumbled over and over in my mind. I had been nothing more than just the passing crush of a dying summer. A small grain of sand, which she would lose the second she stepped into a city.

She turned and half stood, resting on her knees and pulling me into the same position. I wanted to crumble into her, but that was no longer possible. Neither of us was stable enough to hold the other up, and we hadn't been for a long time.

"Forgive me, Sam. I never wanted to hurt you."

I said nothing.

"You've helped me. You made me better when I wasn't okay. If you hadn't been there, I don't know what I would've done. No one else has ever cared for me the way you did. The way you do. You made me a better person, and I know I didn't seem like I appreciated it much, but I did. I still do. I'm so sorry."

Every inch of me resisted gravitating toward her, but if I had permitted it, I'd only be fighting a losing battle.

"I wish I could make you stay," I said.

"If anyone could, it'd be you. But don't ask me to stay. Please."

"When do you leave?" I hadn't yet shed a tear, but my surroundings were under water.

Georgia shuddered. "I head out next Saturday at seven in the morning."

The magnetic pull that I was resisting released me, and I sat there all by myself. Shattered. "But that's so soon. What about—"

Georgia stood, and I followed. Always following her, it seemed. "Sam, I love you. I do. And I'm sorry I never told you until now."

She kissed my numb lips, but I couldn't find a way to return her kiss.

"This is just something I need to do," she whispered.

Georgia loved me, but it wasn't enough to make her want to stay. The possibility of something bigger waited for her somewhere other than on Ophelia.

Nothing I could do would keep her here.

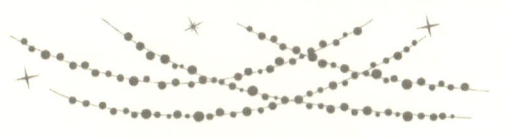

Chapter 31

I slept.

And when I awoke, I begged her to stay. Every day, I asked her to stay, despite her asking me not to.

She hadn't asked me to come with her once. She didn't want me. So I went to bed early every night and woke up late, coping, I thought, by minimizing the sting of her leaving while I was unconscious.

If I'd spent our last days together, I would've ruined them by arguing that I wanted her to stay. I was only human, trying to pursue something my flesh wanted and knew it couldn't keep.

But I was being selfish. She couldn't stay here. Not after what she'd done.

I'd have to remain on the island without her, imprisoned here in a cell built of lies and secrets and seashells and diamonds and rings.

This was our ending.

Chapter 32

I learned from Google what the Alfred, Lord Tennyson quote truly meant. Parents say one thing, teenagers assume another, but Tennyson meant for his line to be about something else entirely.

Most people think the quote is about a wife, or a husband, or possibly a crush, or even a long-lost lover. Because it's better to have loved and lost than never to have loved at all, right? That's what they say, but it's taken out of context. Tennyson wrote that line for his best friend when he died. And the thing is, Tennyson said so many other beautiful things in that same poem, "In Memoriam." But that quote is the only one that people seem to remember. It's the one that every human being can relate to. The poem was in memory of a man he never kissed, never held, never saved. They weren't gay. Tennyson just loved him and would rather have lived in the pain of losing his best friend than live in the pain of never having experienced him.

After that famous line, Tennyson *does* mention the part after losing. The problem is no one bothers to read past it.

Because living beyond the loss demands an energy that love steals away. It comes in like a storm and turns everything over.

Over.

It was a single word that could draw me into a dark pit with enough power behind it to destroy me, and I was the only person who could wrench myself out of it. Only I could save myself.

Once Georgia was free from Mat, it should've been over. That was all she ever wanted. But I was losing everything. Georgia had made her decision to move away from Ophelia long before I came along. And I understood the appeal of not wanting to be here and turn out like her mother, I did understand her desire to seek a greater life, but that didn't take the hurt away. I should have predicted it, expected it under any circumstances.

At the end of the day, I settled on the agonizing realization that putting her happiness ahead of my own was more important. Her future would be overshadowed by her past and limited by her regrets if she stayed. She wanted new possibilities and the freedom to start over someplace new.

I was in my room flipping through a magazine and waiting for Georgia to call me the night before I was supposed to meet her on the beach, but she never did, and I didn't call her either.

That word *over* shuffled through my mind on repeat. Every memory of our relationship replayed again and again.

But I knew she wouldn't be here forever. Things that good didn't last.

One night, when we were lying on the beach, a shooting star had streaked across the sky, bright and falling heavily, vanishing before it reached the ocean. Georgia had told me to make a wish, and I had wanted so much to know what she was wishing when she closed her eyes. With mine open and on her, I had wished that I could make her happy.

And here it was, the almighty wish granted right in front of me, lingering in the night, sweeping in and shaking me awake every time I dozed off. I made her happy, she'd said. I helped her more than I knew, she'd said. I cared for her more than anyone. *I made her better,* she'd told me.

It isn't fair for people to fall in love. There should be rules against loving without the promise of a happy ending, and we should be punished for breaking them, for crossing yellow caution tape, for diving into a tide that's known for drowning people.

The truth also kept shaking me awake every time my eyes closed because, in the dark behind my eyelids, I pictured the entire crime all over again, as if Georgia and I were still sitting in the Bronco outside of the cemetery.

It was the perfect scheme. The perfect crime.

Georgia knew his body would never be found.

The old man Georgia had stayed with on the sailboat had come forward and told police that Georgia had been with him the entire time. Her alibi was trustworthy. Solid.

Last week, Sonya had told me that, when police had come in to question her, she stated that Georgia and Mat had never been in a relationship, despite what some residents told them, which eliminated my motive to kill Mat. If Sonya knew everything, then she knew about the gun. And I wondered whether she had encouraged Georgia to keep the gun right there under her bed or had urged her to plant it back in Mat's house.

It didn't matter—his weapon would never reemerge. Georgia had gotten away with her perfect crime.

There was no counting down the hours to sunrise like I had done so many times before. Tonight, it was simply six o'clock in the morning and time to go.

As the sun peeked out from behind the ocean, Georgia appeared beside me and gave me a kiss on my cheek. I scooped her up in my arms and let myself memorize her and the feeling of her arms wrapped around my neck and the way her head felt as it rested on my chest. These moments—I committed them to memory. I'd keep them forever.

She grasped my hands in hers. "Hey, Sam."

"Georgia," I said, fighting against the lump in my throat.

"I know, I know," she whispered. "I'm sorry."

"You don't have to apologize."

"Yes, I do, because goodbye hurts. I know I'm hurting you, and that is the last thing I ever wanted to do."

Neither of us could deny that.

"So you've already told everyone else goodbye, I guess?"

I couldn't look anywhere but the ground; her face made this harder.

"Not many people to tell goodbye."

An immense sadness blanketed our conversation and forced me to look at her. "You're still leaving at seven?"

"Whenever I'm finished. . ." She couldn't go on. *Whenever I'm finished telling you goodbye. Whenever this is over.*

"Do you know what you're going to do when you get there?"

A grin broke through her tight lips, and a hint of anger bit at me because she was happy, and she was leaving me here as broken as she had been when I found her on the beach.

"I'll figure something out."

"Please stay safe, Georgia. Don't get hurt, okay?"

"I promise I won't. I won't get hurt anymore."

It was quiet while we stood there in the dim morning sun, our toes fumbling in the sand.

"I wish I could've saved you. Is it too late for you to decide to stay?"

"Yeah. It's too late. And you did, Sam. You did save me. There's nothing I can say to tell you how grateful I am that you were there."

"Will you ever come back? Your family is here." I regretted asking such a dumb question.

"They're a reason not to come back."

"Can we call each other? I'm going to get a phone as soon as you leave, and we'll call each other, and we'll text. Whatever you want to do."

Georgia shifted her attention toward the ground. "We'll see what happens. You know, once I get there."

She saw how desperate I was to hold on to something that was already gone, and she couldn't encourage it anymore, so I stopped asking questions. Plus, pity was the last thing I wanted from her.

"Thank you." She brought my face up with her fingertips and met my eyes. "Thank you for saving me."

We moved toward each other at the same time, and I pressed my lips to her forehead and left her with a wet kiss, while her lips brushed softly against my cheek. She knew I loved her, so I didn't say it again.

She knew. For the first time, I was comfortable with the idea of just having loved her before losing her.

"We'll see each other, okay?" she said.

"Okay."

She took two steps back and stood there in front of me for the last time. She was put together. Healed. Happy.

"You'll never stop meaning the world to me," I told her.

"Sam." She said my name as though she'd known it for years. The tiniest of smiles accompanied it. "You'll forget about me in time."

Other people might have forgotten Georgia, and Ophelia still went on without her, and the world would keep turning even in her absence. But, on the beach that morning, I was certain I would never forget her.

"No," I said. "I won't."

Georgia Gabehart nodded because she believed me. Then she backed away and gave me a low wave goodbye. The wind caught her curls, and it blew them into a majestic wave. For the first time, I didn't follow her. I could only watch her walk away, going forward with the wind. Time could never force me to forget something so beautiful. Maybe she would be even more beautiful in a big city, if that was possible. Maybe I would visit her, maybe in the summer, after school, or maybe I would never see her again, even if I wanted to.

***

But she knew I wanted to.

Because when she got to her new home in Michigan, she was going to unpack her suitcases, and, among her belongings, there would be a little wooden box, an unforgettable detail she could never have left under her bed. She would pull out the box, which seemed lighter than she remembered. And she would open it only to find an old cloth and a folded note that was crinkled and torn around the edges.

She would pick it up while was I was sitting in a Fay University classroom wondering whether she had found my letter, and she would read the only words I ever wrote to her.

Georgia,

It doesn't matter what you did or how you did it. I love you, and I hope you can love yourself that much someday. Don't worry about the gun—I've taken care of it, so I hope that by the time you find all this out, the police will have forgotten all about you, and you'll have the happy ending you deserve. And I hope it's with me. No matter what has happened by the next time you open this box, just know that I still love you, and I'll never stop finding you when you're lost, and I'll never stop solving your mysteries or chasing you when you're running.

Love isn't the reason we have tragedy, Georgia. It's tragic when we run away from love. So run to me, always. I'll catch you before you hit the waves, and I won't let you drown.

The End

Acknowledgments

I wrote this book during the summer of 2017, a summer of love and heartbreak, of people leaving and coming back. Those few months were very emotional for me for a lot of reasons, but I won't bore you all with the details. Instead, I want my readers to know that I wrote this book for them. These painful words from Sam's heart bled through the miserable heat of '17.

So I raise my glass to the teenagers who think they're in love, to the ones whose friendships shattered like glass, who don't understand anything in their life or family or thoughts, and who just want to get a steady footing on whatever ground they're treading.

The thing about Young Adult Literature is that it represents teenagers at their best and worst, and it shows their beauty and their ugliness, but mostly it shows the resolution of their struggles. These characters aren't ideal, and that's the point. Understand? You're exactly who you're supposed to be.

I also raise my glass and give a loud "Cheers!" to countless people who aided in the creation of this book, but I'll name the ones who mean the very most.

When a senior a high school tells her parents that she wants to be a writer, normally a parent would say, "What a joke! That's not a career." But my parents never questioned my decision to pursue such an uncertain calling. They encouraged me when I was discouraged, pushed me when I slowed down, and read every word I ever wrote.

Dad, you worked with me through every writer's block from which I suffered, and you thought out every little detail with me.

Mom, you instilled in me that I could conquer everything in life, and you never wished me luck because you said I had skill.

For these things, Mom and Dad, I am a very grateful daughter. Here's a message I should have pasted to my college graduation cap: "THANKS MOM AND DAD" and the rest of my entire family. (You don't realize it, but you all had a hand in this book.)

Grandma, you're so very loved by me. Thank you for being so eager to read this book and celebrate it with me. I hope you keep it right there tucked between Grandpa's old, tattered novels.

To all the hard workers at IngramElliott Publishing and every editor who sharpened the words in this book—thank you for your faith in me. Thank you for your enthusiasm about my writing. Thank you for caring for a story that I hold so closely to my heart, and thank you for being the lovelies who chose to share it with the world. I couldn't be more grateful for all of you at IE.

To my very best friends who I leaned on and who gave me every ounce of support when I needed it during the publication of this book, you have meant the world to me. All of you—Bethany Nelson, Citlaly Arevalo, Austin Joyce, Levi Morales, Adrian McGee, Beccy Braun, Lauren White, and Cassidy Lappin—deserve your very own underlined and italicized thank you. I love you endlessly.

To all my English professors at North Greenville University, I give a huge thank you, but to Dr. Cheryl Collier and Dr. Becky Thompson: I have you two to thank for my knowing anything at all about writing. Though I picked up this craft at a young age, you both shaped my writing into what it is today. I think you believed more than I did that I'd be here right now. A simple thank you isn't enough.

Deno Trakas: You were one of the first people to read this book, so thank you for suffering through the very rough draft that I handed you as a teenager, and thank you for helping me mold this story into the one that I get to share with the world. Our friendship means so very much to me. Can you believe it's been nine years? In that short time, your honesty and encouragement has brought me much joy, and I always smile when I see an email in my inbox that says "Just checking in."

A big, warm, sweet "I appreciate you and your love and support and friendship" to all my ladies who were in the English Department at NGU with me: Logan Boldog, Charissa Garcia, Jada Barr, Hannah McCall, and all my other dears. Truly, you girls rule. Thank you for believing in my words when we were in all those writing classes together, and thank you for supporting me on my writing journey from the moment we met.

I owe a very special thanks to my new friends who let me inside the Haig Point Lighthouse on Daufuskie Island (i.e., the lighthouse from this novel). Valorie and Edmund Catalano, and Debbie and Dennis Blondin, thank you, also, for not kicking me off your rental property when you saw me snooping the lighthouse's front porch. Next time I'm on vacation, feel free to pop up unannounced and wander through my rental house. It's the least I could do for being the reason one of my dreams to come true.

Even though I drew much inspiration from the two summers prior to writing this book, I should rightfully thank the summer of 2017 for sticking me between the ocean and the stars. Thanks for making me look at you in the eyes and say, "I'm writing my way out of this."

At last, I can throw up my feet, pour a cup of coffee, and finally say,

Finally.

ABOUT THE AUTHOR

M. M. Cochran is an award-winning fiction writer, who lives in Greenville, South Carolina. With an educational background in English and creative writing, she is currently a journalist for the world's smallest daily newspaper. She has also worked in the agenting and publishing industry. A lover of all things coffee, autumn, and baking, M. M. delights in spending her afternoons in the kitchen creating  goodies for her family, and when she's not scouting for new coffee shops, she can be found listening to a Frank Sinatra vinyl or hanging out with her standard poodle, family, and friends.

IngramElliott Publishing

IngramElliott is an award-winning independent publisher with a mission to bring great stories to light in print and on-screen. We publish stories that will translate well into film, broadcast, and streaming television projects across many popular genres. We look for a great story, unique voice, and the author's ability to build a strong platform. Please review our current submission guidelines for more information.

IE Snaps!
by IngramElliott

Our IE Snaps! imprint features novella-length genre fiction in favorite genres like action, thriller, mystery, romance, and young adult. These titles are designed for a quick read on the go. Visit our website for all of our IngramElliott and IE Snaps! titles and to follow us on social media.

www.ingramelliott.com

www.ingramcontent.com/pod-product-compliance
Lightning Source LLC
Chambersburg PA
CBHW031147190526
45286CB00008B/147